Our common Thread

PRAISE FOR *OUR COMMON THREAD*

"Kahli Scott's beautiful debut is equal parts heartfelt romance and magic-dusted mystery, as one woman works to untangle the ties that bind her to one man across every possible universe. *Our Common Thread* is a warm, thoughtful exploration of the turns our lives might have taken, the people we might have been, and all the ordinary miracles that make a life."

—Ellen O'Clover, author of The Heartbreak Hotel

"*Our Common Thread* is a love story for anyone who has ever wondered if they're in the right timeline. Kahli Scott's debut brims with chemistry and is as sweet as Casey River's signature apple pie ice cream."

—Thea Weiss, author of The Second Chance Cinema

"*Our Common Thread* is a must-read for anyone who never stopped hoping that magic can be found in unexpected places. Scott weaves together a tale of romance and self-discovery that will have readers racing to see how all the strands fit together. The perfect blend of *Sliding Doors* and *The Lion, the Witch and the Wardrobe*, this story is sure to enchant and linger long after the final page is turned."

—Stacy Sivinski, author of The Crescent Moon Tearoom

"*Our Common Thread* will have you climbing through every wardrobe just like Mattie (with two T's) on her magical journey of self-discovery. In her debut, Kahli Scott brings to life a delightful cast of characters and a swoony romance with confidence and wit. I couldn't put it down!"

—Amy E. Reichert, author of The Kindred Spirits Supper Club and
Once Upon a December

Our Common Thread

A Novel

Kahli Scott

Little a

Published by Little A, Seattle

www.apub.com

Amazon, the Amazon logo, and Little A are trademarks of Amazon.com, Inc., or its affiliates.

EU product safety contact:
Amazon Media EU S. à r.l.
38, avenue John F. Kennedy, L-1855 Luxembourg
amazonpublishing-gpsr@amazon.com

ISBN-13: 9781662538179 (hardcover)
ISBN-13: 9781662538186 (paperback)
ISBN-13: 9781662538162 (digital)

Cover design and illustration by Philip Pascuzzo

Printed in the United States of America
First edition

For Bruce, who was found in a wardrobe

I: THE MYSTERY

ONE

"What if," says the director, "this all happens differently?"

There's a shuffling of scripts and call sheets. I see creased brows and hear badly stifled sighs, but none of us should be surprised. Our director has a reputation for doing this. It's not the first time she's suggested a sudden change to the script or schedule, forcing the rest of us into overtime to make it all work.

"How differently?" asks one of the producers in a tight voice.

"Well, this is a love story, right?" says the director. "Love stories are normally about fate. What if, at the Christmas party, Raquel rips her green dress? She takes it to the tailor when she arrives in her hometown, and that's where she meets Grant instead—rather than through mutual friends."

I feel myself wince as soon as the director says the words "rips her green dress." The emerald dress that Raquel—our main character—wears in the Christmas party scene is gorgeous and custom made and expensive, and I should know because I've spent hours working on it.

"Think about it," the director continues. "The rip will be a metaphor for Raquel's life unraveling. It's a literal and figurative breaking point. But when she goes to get it fixed—when she meets Grant—that's the beginning of it all being stitched together again. That's fateful. That's a love story."

The actress playing Raquel—Kandace Connolly—is nodding thoughtfully, while one of our producers is starting to bite her nails down to the quick.

"We don't have a tailor," the producer says.

I'm standing by the window of our production office, not important enough to have a seat at the table where we're holding our production meeting. But my position does give me a good view of the cobblestoned Main Street of Casey River, which we've transformed into our film set for the next few weeks.

Casey River is a small town over an hour away from any major city, with a population of approximately nine thousand people. Surrounded by pine forest and with a glittering river running through it, the town is charming even when it hasn't been turned into the set of a Christmas romance. But like always, our art department has done a great job at dialing up the whimsy.

There's a dusting of artificial snow over the cobblestones. Christmas wreaths and golden bells hang from the lampposts, and warm twinkle lights are wrapped around almost every surface possible. Each of the shop windows has been carefully dressed with festive merchandise, and signs written in a vintage font spell out their names—we have a bakery, a bookstore, a coffee shop, a bar, and a florist. But the producer's right; there's no tailor.

"Art department can handle that, easy," says the director flippantly. "And wardrobe can help. Where's Deidre?"

I snap to attention at the sound of my boss's name.

"She sent me this morning instead," I say.

The director swivels around in her chair to face me, squinting through her glasses.

"Deidre's working on that change to Grant's Christmas party costume we decided on yesterday," I continue. "But it sounds like I'm telling her to scrap that, make some duplicates of Raquel's green dress to account for the rip, and sort out clothes for a tailor."

The director nods, satisfied. "Thanks, Mattie," she says. "You're on it."

I try not to look too pleased that she's remembered my name and focus instead on actually getting on it. Even if I'm dreading telling Deidre—our costume designer and my formidable boss—that the last two hours of her morning have been wasted and that we need to make extra versions of Raquel's beautiful green dress just to put a rip in it.

But as a wardrobe assistant, that's why I'm here. That's why we're all here, in Casey River, for the next five weeks. We're here to listen to whatever the director tells us to do to get this movie made.

Magic Season is a festive romantic comedy about a jaded journalist—Raquel—who, after making a severe career misstep at her work Christmas party, gets drawn back to her hometown for the holidays. There's a sick aunt involved who helps her see the real meaning of Christmas, and, of course, two warring love interests who represent her shiny new life and the comforts of her old hometown, which she has to choose between.

The movie will go straight onto a streaming platform in December, along with every other festive romantic comedy the industry is churning out this year. People will watch it with mugs of eggnog and hot cocoa, find it charming or corny—or both—and largely forget it once it's over. But, honestly, the way the director muses and the way the producers stress, you'd think we were making the next awards-season front-runner.

Magic Season is the kind of movie I used to like. In fact, I used to be pretty nondiscriminatory about the movies I liked. Mystery, fantasy, romance—I'd devour it all, so long as it provided a window into another world. I just enjoyed being entertained, swept away to other places, caught up in other people's stories. It's why I got into the industry in the first place.

As I head off to find Deidre, I try to retrieve that feeling of wide-eyed wonder and creative potential. It's only week one of this shoot, after all—way too early for me to be feeling disenchanted already. That normally comes closer to wrap, when the twelve-hour days have finally caught up with me. But even now, my head is feeling swollen with call times and cast lists and fitting schedules, and it's difficult to find any remnants of myself among the demands of other people. It's like I'm drowning in an ill-fitting outfit that's wearing me, rather than the other way around.

Our production office is actually a cute bed-and-breakfast off Main Street that we've taken over for the film. We've slapped whiteboards over floral wallpaper and hauled desks into the doily-draped dining room. The atmosphere in the office is the exact opposite of the cozy, relaxed ambience you'd normally expect in a small-town bed-and-breakfast, especially given the latest script change. Our art department is in a frenzy, tasked with designing interiors and exteriors for a tailor in an almost impossible time frame. Our script supervisor is chain-smoking out back, while our travel and accommodation coordinator is trying to figure out if the cast hotel rooms need to be extended.

I find Deidre in the room we've taken over as our wardrobe space. The room smells like citrus laundry detergent and steam from the irons, and it's an organized mess of clothing rails, shoe racks, mood boards, sewing machines, and boxes of accessories. Deidre's standing in the center of it all, looking effortlessly chic today in a black jumpsuit and thick black glasses.

Unlike a lot of people on set, Deidre Dotto—iconic costume designer—never really gets ruffled. She's always cool and calm. Which somehow unnerves me even more. Her emotions show only in her eyes, which manages to make them cut deeper than if she yelled or threw a steam iron across the room.

I think, deep down, that Deidre likes me. Or at least, I don't think she hates me. This is the third production I've worked on now as one of her wardrobe assistants. After the first one, I was pretty sure I wouldn't be asked back. I didn't do anything wrong, but Deidre's demeanor was so icy the whole time, I was sure I hadn't done anything right either.

But then I got the call for the second job with Deidre. And then the third one. And now, I think I see signs that indicate I may have passed a test or broken through a threshold. Sometimes, Deidre will throw out tidbits of industry advice to me, just casual comments flung effortlessly over her shoulder like a shawl as she leaves the room. Or she'll unexpectedly hand me bigger responsibilities, like asking me to attend the morning production meeting in her place. And the other month, she even invited me to an industry party, where her wife, Eleanor, told me, "Deidre speaks very highly of you." I have no idea what Deidre's version of "speaking highly" of someone is. But I'll take whatever validation I can get.

When I tell Deidre about the director's latest script change and the repercussions for the wardrobe department, she doesn't immediately respond. All I see is a flutter of something in her eyes behind her glasses. It's an indecipherable flutter. It might be irritation, might be inspiration. Could be hunger. Could be nothing. Three productions in, and I still can't totally read Deidre Dotto.

"I know, it's frustrating," I continue. "But I was thinking, with the green dress, maybe we don't have to make a full duplicate. Maybe we can just duplicate the skirt, which is the part that rips, and make it a two-piece—"

"It's not frustrating," Deidre interrupts. "It's a challenge. And we like challenges, don't we?"

I don't even have to think about it. If Deidre says we like something, then we like something. We like organic cotton and vintage denim and silk. We like fabrics that don't make too much noise when the actors move, lest the mics pick up the sound. We like contemporary over period. We like dressing the heroine in different earrings throughout the course of the film to symbolize her character growth, even if the audience probably won't ever notice it.

"Yes," I say, nodding like a parrot. "We do like a challenge."

TWO

I don't like a challenge.

I get back to my temporary apartment just before midnight after working overtime to accommodate the director's script changes. The senior crew and cast have hotel rooms or apartments closer to downtown Casey River, whereas those of us on the lower rungs have been put up in short-term rentals or motels on the outskirts of town. My apartment is a short drive away, in the suburbs. Too far out and they'd have to pay us extra for our travel time.

The apartment isn't the best, but it isn't the worst either. It has a homey, lived-in feel to it rather than the stark vacation-house vibe you'd normally expect from a temporary rental. There are plenty of throws and cushions around the place, a variety of mismatched mugs on the shelves, and artwork hanging on the chipped-paint walls that all seems themed around trees. Which makes sense because there's a pine forest right behind the apartment complex. I even have a little balcony that juts out to meet the forest, which I imagine would be a lovely spot to sit and enjoy a cup of coffee in the morning and listen to the birds sing. If only I hadn't developed a terrible habit of waking up way too close to call time.

I used to be a morning person. Back in college, I used to cherish that sacred time when the sun was still rising. I'd go for a run, have a long shower, carefully do my hair and makeup, and select a well-curated outfit that told whatever story I wanted to tell that day. Was I feeling romantic, athletic, classic, bohemian? I'd always loved fashion as a vehicle for storytelling. Until, ironically, I started to get paid for it.

Twenty-eight is way too young to feel this old.

"I like my job," I say out loud to no one as I open the fridge. "This is a dream job."

The apartment, shockingly, doesn't answer back. I pour myself a glass of wine out of a local bottle I bought from a little artisanal grocer the day I arrived in town, and I step outside onto the balcony.

The forest beyond is dark and calm. I can hear running water from somewhere in the near distance—louder than the river, perhaps a waterfall. The weather is mild for a July evening, with the barest hint of a chill. That's why all the snow back there on the cobblestones is artificial—we have to film these movies in the middle of the year so that they're ready in time for Christmas.

As the first few sips of wine hit me, I feel almost relaxed. Casey River is a beautiful place. I get why they chose to film a romantic movie here. As I glance to my left and right at the apartments on either side of me, I wonder what kinds of lives these Casey River residents are living. Do they have storybook small-town existences? Is the woman on the left, with the garden on the balcony, a florist recovering from a broken heart? Are the occupants on the right, with the plain wicker outdoor furniture, harboring some kind of forbidden secret?

I've always been curious about other people's lives. In college, my curiosity made it hard to decide on a major. I started out with a haphazard mix of film, fashion, and journalism classes while I tried to figure out what I wanted to focus on. Originally, I'd imagined going the journalism route. I liked the idea of researching other people's stories, excavating their lives through interviews, crafting the findings into something meaningful.

But then one of my favorite film professors hooked me and some of my classmates up with production runner placements on a local TV show. And when the wardrobe department found out I was good with a sewing machine, I ended up spending most of my days with them.

I have to admit that I got lucky. It can be hard to carve out a living in a freelance industry like film, especially for someone like me who doesn't like hustling and apologizes a lot. But I kept my head down, made some good impressions, got word-of-mouth referrals, and have managed to get enough gigs over the last few years to keep food on the table—even if some weeks back at the start it was little more than ramen noodles spruced up with vegetables from my discount harvest-box subscription.

And now here I am. Working on my third film with a well-respected costume designer who *maybe* doesn't hate having me around. If I stick at it, I could keep working my way up the department ladder. At some point soon, I could even think about stepping into a supervisor role, and if I really committed, I could aim to be a costume designer myself one day.

I have all the makings of a dream life. I should be so grateful.

So why aren't I?

I haven't told anyone this yet, but I'm secretly considering taking a break after this job. I can't help feeling that something's missing. Going to set just doesn't feel exciting anymore. I'm getting tired of the long, inconsistent hours, tired of always working to bring someone else's vision to life, tired of never wanting to *go* to the movies anymore because the thrill is gone.

"This is a dream job," I murmur to no one again.

But this time, I hear something in response.

It came from inside my apartment. And it sounded like a small squeak or whine.

I step back inside and look around. I can't see any movement. There are no doors ajar, no open cupboards creaking.

But then the sound comes again, from the direction of the bedroom.

The bedroom is just off the living room—a small space with an en suite bathroom. I open the door and look around.

I haven't been here for long, but already the room is a mess. There are clothes spilling out of the large wardrobe and thrown over the chair in the corner. You'd think that, given my job, I'd be more careful with my clothes. But I spend so much time organizing and ironing and folding clothes at work, my at-home wardrobe has paid the price. I also didn't make my bed this morning, which my mom taught me to *always* do. It symbolizes your first achievement of the day. If you can't even get that accomplished, you're setting yourself up for failure.

A chill brushes my arm, and I realize that the window in the bathroom is wide open. The curtain is fluttering in the breeze. When I walk over to close the window, I notice movement in the street below.

My heart patters unevenly for a moment.

But it's just a cat. A tabby cat with yellow eyes glowing under the streetlight. It looks up at me, and I look down at it and murmur, "Hello," like a fool. The cat doesn't respond.

I realize that the squeaking sound *could* have been a meow. And it *might* have sounded like it was coming from my bedroom if it had floated up through the window.

I slide the glass down, blocking out the chill. Outside, the cat turns and walks away, uninterested.

I stand waiting for a bit longer, listening. But the apartment remains silent. No more noises. Just me.

Mystery solved.

I crawl into my unmade bed, the rumpled linen a symbol of my lack of achievement. As I start to drift to sleep, I promise myself that I'll make my bed tomorrow. Maybe that simple action will beckon the sparkle into my day that seems to be missing lately. Maybe tomorrow, things will be different.

THREE

We have a new actor arriving this morning. He's playing a supporting role and is due for his fitting, which I've been assigned to prepare for while Deidre takes care of the leads.

The character's name is Mitchell, and he's our heroine Raquel's high school sweetheart. Mitchell's not actually the guy we're meant to be rooting for in the movie—that's Grant, the semiaristocratic millionaire played by former soap opera star Hayden King. Hometown sweetheart Mitchell acts as a foil for Grant, coming into the picture to tempt Raquel with the comfortable, cozy life she *could* have chosen but ultimately turns down.

I can see how the plot of *Magic Season* is trying to subvert the story we've grown used to, where the princess chooses the humble country mouse instead of the prince. But it's funny how *that* type of story subverted the original classic fairy tale, where the princess chooses the prince. We've come full circle, and we're choosing princes again. That's how the industry tries to keep things fresh—it essentially starts eating its own tail.

Mitchell's costumes aren't especially exciting—denim jeans, backward baseball hats, and flannel shirts, most of them in various shades of green and red to match our Christmas palette. We have daytime flannels and nighttime flannels for him, and I check over all our size options meticulously in preparation for our actor arriving.

His name is Austin Farrow, and according to his size card, his measurements are height six one, chest forty-two inches, waist thirty-one inches, arms fifteen inches. Shoe size eleven. All fairly standard for a run-of-the-mill actor. I hadn't heard of Austin Farrow before this gig, but then again, we're not dealing with Hollywood A-listers here. We're making a straight-to-streamer Christmas romance, after all.

Austin's due to arrive for his fitting at 8:30 a.m., and I have everything ready to go at 8:10, when Deidre comes bustling over to me with Henry, our other assistant.

"Matilda," says Deidre.

Deidre has this habit of calling me by my full first name. I kind of hate it. I've been Mattie for so long that Matilda makes me feel like I'm back in school, or in trouble. *Matilda Bridges.* I can just hear my mom's voice in my head, scolding six-year-old me for breaking the zipper of her favorite evening gown that I used to "borrow" to play dress-up.

But if Deidre prefers to call me Matilda, then that's that. I wouldn't dream of correcting her.

"Morning!" I say brightly.

"I know you like shopping," Deidre says, launching right in, like she always does. "So I'm leaving it up to you and Henry to decide. I need one of you to stay here and do the support fittings. And I need one of you to go to the mall in Carrickvale to do returns and buy some new jewelry for Raquel's green dress."

I feel my eyes light up. Deidre's right—I do like shopping. The mall in Carrickvale, a slightly larger town about twenty minutes from Casey River, is hardly full of high-end boutiques, but still. It's shopping. And shopping for jewelry is far more interesting than the regular kind of errand running I usually have to do, like returning items we've decided we're not going to use or stocking up on lint rollers and blister pads.

Next to Deidre, I see that Henry's eyes are also alight. Henry's a nice young guy with a good sense of humor who says lots of things out loud that I only say inside my head. I like Henry, even though I should technically see him as competition. If I ever want to step into a super-visor position, then Henry's a clear rival.

However, I'm missing that competitive streak. If you asked me who should get a job between Henry and me, I'd probably vote for Henry. He dresses better than I do. Neither of us can afford our dream ward-robes on our assistants' paychecks, but while I resort to making and tailoring my own clothes and expertly thrifting, Henry saves and then splurges on high-end pieces that he rotates in a masterful way so that they always seem new.

Both of us obviously want to go shopping. Maybe Deidre wants us to fight for it. Maybe this is one of those unspoken Deidre Dotto tests.

"What kind of new jewelry are we looking for?" I decide to ask first.

"There's more of a focus on the dress now, with the new script change," Deidre explains. "So, we need bolder accessories to match. I'm thinking white gold, perhaps some deep-red gemstones to complement the emerald green. I'll email some photos and sketches for reference. Come and find me once you decide who's going, and I'll give you one of the credit cards."

Deidre turns on her heel then and leaves Henry and me to it.

"You can go if you really want to," I say to Henry.

Henry sighs. "Well, that's no fun," he says. "I thought we could arm wrestle for it."

"Honestly, it's fine."

"You want to go."

I shrug. "It's always nice to get out."

I realize that sounds like I'm a poor house cat who's been trapped inside for days. Henry frowns at me, then reaches into his pocket and pulls out a coin.

"Heads or tails?" he asks.

I roll my eyes.

"Come on," Henry insists.

"Fine. Tails."

"Right, so tails, you go shopping. Heads, I go."

I watch as Henry flicks the coin into the air. He catches it neatly, then flips it over on the top of his hand.

"Ah," he says. "Sorry."

It's heads.

"It's okay," I tell Henry. "You have fun. But also, there are a few extra things we need."

I type out a list to send to Henry, including safety pins, shoe glue, and tape.

"If it makes you feel any better," Henry says to me as I type, "this means you get to hang out with this guy instead."

He reaches over to the table where I've been preparing Mitchell's costumes for Austin Farrow. He swipes up Austin's headshot and shoves it in my face.

I push it away.

"So?" I ask Henry.

"*So.*" Henry brandishes the photo at me again, and I have no choice but to look at it.

Austin Farrow isn't good-looking in the obvious soap-star way that Hayden King is. He has more of a boy-next-door aesthetic, the kind of guy you'd slowly fall for in high school after realizing foolishly late that his baby face has taken on an unexpected symmetry. He has medium-length light-brown hair bordering on dark blond, like honey. Natural tan, modest stubble, light freckles on his cheeks, and a genuine smile. His eyes are a shade of green that makes me think of rivers and country fields.

I push the photo away again.

"Henry," I say. "Be professional."

"I'm *always* professional," Henry argues. "He's not my type anyway. Too clean cut."

"And what makes you think he's my type?"

Henry holds Austin's photo next to my face, as if testing out how we'd look together. I duck away and head over to our clothing racks, shaking my head.

This isn't the first time Henry's tried to play matchmaker for me. We've worked on a few productions together now, and, since I've been single, he likes using crew drinks as an opportunity to point out what guys he thinks I'd look good with. This is all based on aesthetics, rather than personality, of course. Sometimes he goes so far as to drag a potential match over to talk to us, which is always mortifying.

I know Henry means well, but not a single guy he's tried to set me up with has been of interest to me. In fact, I've found it difficult to be interested in anyone for a while.

Ever since Jack.

At this thought, my stomach drops. And my feelings must show on my face, because Henry gives up trying to force Austin's photo on me for a third time. He slides it back onto the table and smiles sympathetically at me.

"Fine," he says. "Keep being classy, then."

"Only you could make being classy sound like a character flaw."

Henry grins. "Is there anything I can get you in Carrickvale to make it up to you?"

"I sent you the list."

"No, I mean, like, any special treats? Something you can't get from crafty?"

Crafty, or craft services, is arguably the most important department on any film production, responsible for providing an endless supply of snacks and sustenance to crew, in between our sit-down meals. Even on a lower-budget feature like *Magic Season*, the crafty selection is decent, but Henry's right; they don't have everything.

"Maybe some of those canned iced coffees?" I say. "Oh, and cinnamon pretzels, if you can find them. And make sure you remember the shoe glue. It's normally—"

"Don't worry; I got this."

Henry leaves, and then it's just me and Austin Farrow's headshot.

I pick it up and look at it again. Over the years, I've learned how to switch into robot mode when it comes to working with actors.

Obviously, our industry is full of incredibly good-looking people. And working in wardrobe adds an extra level of intimacy, because you're tucking shirts into trousers and putting safety pins in all kinds of places. But I've become desensitized to it all. When I look at a lovely pair of green eyes now, normally all I think about is what colors go well with green.

It also helps that my last relationship almost turned me off men for good.

I've tried my best not to think about Jack lately. Whenever I do, my stomach lurches in that terrible way and I start to feel sick, like I do when I've had three coffees in the morning without eating and all the acid is roiling around in my gut with nothing to soak it up.

But now here I am, thinking about him for a second time in one morning.

It's embarrassing. I've been through breakups before, but this one was different. I know everyone says that, but this one was *really* different. Normally, after a breakup, you miss the person you've lost. But this time, I think I miss myself. The person I was before Jack.

I think it's all connected. What happened with Jack and the way I'm feeling about my job and my life and myself. Like I'm not in control of things. Like someone else is always writing the script. And they're not even bothering to make any interesting changes, like our director does.

I don't even realize I'm still holding Austin Farrow's photo, deep in these thoughts, until I hear a voice from behind me.

"I've heard I look better in real life."

FOUR

I drop the headshot back onto the table as if it's suddenly scalding and turn around to find Austin Farrow standing behind me.

He looks both like and unlike his photo. I knew how tall he was, because I've memorized his measurements, but he somehow seems to take up more space in front of me than I expected. His hair is messier than in the headshot, like he's just run his hand through it. And his smile makes his eyes crinkle so much at the corners that I can barely even tell they're green.

"However," Austin continues, as he steps forward. "The person who said that was a director after a screen test, so it wasn't exactly a compliment. Given that my job is to look better on camera than in real life."

His tone is playful, and I'm flustered, so I don't think properly before saying, "I think it's a good photo."

"Oh?" Austin's eyebrows shoot up.

"I mean, it's perfect for what we need," I cover, waving my hands around the headshot. "Neutral, truthful, up-to-date facial hair. That's always a big one."

"So, it's a good thing I didn't grow that goatee, then."

"That would have been hair and makeup's problem."

Austin laughs. "I'm Austin, by the way."

He holds out a hand for me to shake, and I take it.

"I figured that. I'm Mattie. With the wardrobe department."

"I figured *that*." His eyes crinkle further. "You know, that's actually my niece's name."

"Mattie?"

"Yeah. Short for Madeline."

"Ah, so probably Maddie with two *d*'s, right?" I say, as I walk over to the rack of outfits for Mitchell. "That's the more common way of spelling it. Mine's Mattie with two *t*'s."

"Oh! Like, from *True Grit*."

I smile from behind the clothes. "That is a great film," I say. "But her full name is actually Mattalyn, whereas mine's Matilda."

"It's a *great film*," Austin concurs. "Have you read the book?"

"No, I haven't."

"You should, if you're into westerns."

I shuffle through the flannel shirts, still trying to compose myself. It's not the most outrageous thing for an actor to make small talk—they're just people, after all—but mostly, we're advised as crew not to get overly friendly with the cast. Austin's already caught me staring at his headshot. Like I said to Henry, I have to be professional.

"Westerns do have a lot of fun costume opportunities," I say. I pull out three size options for the flannels, then reach for a measuring tape sitting on an overturned box. "Here, do you mind if I take your measurements again in person? Sometimes they've changed."

"Sure. Let's see if my new personal trainer has made any difference."

I step in close to Austin and pull the measuring tape around his body. As the two ends of the tape meet on his chest, I remind myself that this isn't intimate. I've done this a hundred times before, and robot mode has always been easy to engage. Noting the chest measurements, I move down and loop the tape around his hips. I can smell a sweet yet earthy cologne as he shifts his arms. Trying to ignore all this, I check the numbers on the tape and realize I've forgotten the chest measurements already. That's when I make the mistake of looking up again.

Austin's looking down at me, and our eyes lock. I drop the measuring tape, and he catches it in one swift movement.

"Sorry," I say quickly.

"No worries," he replies, handing me back the tape. "My trainer's also got me working on my reflexes."

I smile weakly as I rush through the rest of the measurements, saying them out loud to stop myself from forgetting and to remind us both why we're here.

"Well," I say, once I've finished. "Thank your trainer. Some of your measurements *are* slightly bigger than on your card—mostly around the, uh, shoulders and arms. But that's okay, because we have a few size options for you."

"Hit me," Austin says, rubbing his hands together and looking at the clothes I've pulled for him.

We have a private fitting area constructed in the back of our wardrobe room, so Austin takes his clothes in there and proceeds to try them on and then parade them for me. Some of the pieces already fit him perfectly, but there are a few that we're going to need to tailor. This requires me to pin the material in place to better fit his body, and I use the same tactic of murmuring things out loud to stay focused as I navigate my way around his torso and limbs. I also don't make the mistake of looking up into his eyes again. I stare so fixedly at the flannel and the denim that, by the time we're finished, my vision is swimming with swirls of green and red and blue, and I can barely see straight.

"I think we're done," I say, making my final notes.

Thank God, I add in my head.

Austin emerges from the fitting room in his original clothes, and I see that his white T-shirt is accidentally tucked up on one side, revealing a glimpse of his hipbone. Before I even know what I'm doing, I'm reaching out to tug the shirt back down, even though it's not one of our costumes.

"Sorry," I say, immediately horrified that I've touched his personal clothes. "It's a habit."

Austin gives another of those eye-crinkling smiles.

"Not a problem," he says. "I'm going to meet the director now and should probably be covered up for that."

"Probably," I agree weakly.

Austin pulls out his phone to check the time. Then he looks back at me.

"Hey, have we worked together before?"

I shake my head. "No, I don't think so."

"Are you sure?"

"I'm pretty sure."

Austin frowns. "You just look familiar. Do you live around here?"

"In Casey River? No, I'm just here for work."

"Ah. I actually grew up nearby, so I thought that might be it. Maybe we met at an industry thing, then?"

"Possibly. I have been known to go to industry things on occasion."

"Well, so have I."

I'm almost positive I haven't met Austin Farrow before. I have a feeling he's the kind of person I'd remember. Chances are, he's mistaking me for someone else. I do have a generic "wardrobe girl" look. Light-brown hair that I've pulled up in a claw clip, letting only the bangs escape. Denim-blue eyes, winged liner. My standard crew outfit of an oversize men's corduroy shirt that I've tailored to fit me better, black jeans, and comfortable white sneakers.

My phone starts ringing then, and I look down to see Henry's name on the screen.

"You need to get that?" Austin says.

"Yes, sorry," I say.

"Don't be. I'll see you 'round, Mattie . . . with two *t*'s."

He gives me a final smile before leaving.

I wait a few seconds after Austin's left before I answer Henry's call. I don't want Henry to hear the weakness in my voice and guess that this fitting has been anything other than standard. Because it hasn't been. At least that's what I keep telling myself.

"Okay, so, I need you to cover for me," Henry announces when I pick up.

"What happened?" I ask.

"I *maybe* spent a bit too long shopping, and now I'm stuck in traffic trying to get back," Henry explains. "It's bad—I think there's an accident or something?" I can hear car horns beeping and a distant siren. "We're not even moving."

"There's a back road," I say, remembering this from a trip I made to Carrickvale earlier in our prep period. "Turn right at the gas station, then left at the little school. It's a country road, so it's normally slower, but it's your best bet if the traffic's backed up."

"Oh, thank God," says Henry. "Deidre's already texting me about the jewelry. And I'm supposed to be helping with the background extras in, like, ten minutes."

"I'll do the extras," I say. "And I'll talk to Deidre. I have to run some things past her after Austin's fitting."

"Ooh, how did that go, by the way?"

"It was fine."

There's a pause, and then I hear the sound of Henry slamming his hand on the dashboard in triumph.

"I knew it!" he declares. "He's even better in real life, isn't he?"

"Goodbye, Henry."

"On a scale of one to ten, how would you—"

"Good*bye*, Henry."

I hang up the phone and then turn the headshot of Austin Farrow face down on the table. As if doing so might also make his face fade from my mind.

FIVE

The rest of the day passes without incident. I don't see Austin Farrow again. Henry is back sooner than he thought thanks to my back-road tip, and he only gets a mildly frosty reprimand from Deidre for his tardiness. I've already corralled the extras, so we're back on schedule. And then things get so busy with costume adjustments, running between the set and the office, and trying to keep track of the director and Deidre's requests that the day's over before I know it. And even better, there's been no chance for Henry to interrogate me further about Austin's fitting.

As usual, I'm exhausted by the time I get back to my apartment. I take a hot shower first, to wash off the day, then pour myself a glass of wine. I try to call Margot, my best friend back home, but she doesn't answer. And it's too late to call Mom and Dad—they're never up past nine o'clock.

So, it's just me. I pull up our schedule to run over what's on the agenda for the next few days. We have another week and a half of our first block of filming in town. After that, we head into a nearby state park to do a hiking scene. I'm looking forward to this part of the shoot. It will be nice to be out in the forest, among the trees.

I'm just starting to feel relaxed now as I sip my wine and scroll through social media. The algorithm is showing me the regular posts. Fashion influencers and film reviewers, cute animals, and the latest trend in healthy recipes. Nothing interesting enough for me to pause on.

But then I see a recent post from Loren, who's one of our makeup artists on *Magic Season*. It's a selfie of her and one of our hairstylists in downtown Casey River. My gaze is tugged to the background of the photo, where I can see half of Austin Farrow, standing there in his white T-shirt talking to someone off screen. I kind of hate myself for doing it, but next thing I know, I'm typing Austin's name into the search bar.

He doesn't seem to have any findable social media. So I end up on the industry sites instead, browsing his list of credits. While Austin isn't an A-lister, he seems to be on the rise. He's done a couple of indie projects, the occasional music video, a supporting role on a TV show I've vaguely heard of, and another rom-com. Like he mentioned earlier, his biography confirms that he grew up nearby, out past the pine forests of Casey River in big fields and bright orchard country.

Austin's the same age as me—twenty-eight—and he studied acting at the same drama school as Hayden King, the actor playing Grant. He was briefly linked to the lead singer of a girl band, which is the only time he appears in any gossip headlines. I note—with no emotion that I want to acknowledge—that they've since broken up.

I'm just beginning to question how far I want to go down this Austin Farrow rabbit hole when I hear the squeaking sound again, the same one I heard last night.

My ears prick up. I was right—it does sound like a cat. But this time, it doesn't seem like it's coming from the street. It sounds like it's coming directly from my bedroom.

I place my wine glass on the coffee table and pad over to the room. The sound comes again as I stand in the doorway. It's louder and more urgent now. And as I move into the room, I realize it's coming from the wardrobe.

It's an old-school wooden stand-alone wardrobe, the kind you're more likely to see on a film set than in a real apartment these days. There's a narrow mirror embedded in one of the wardrobe's double doors, and its reflective glass is distorted, making my body look abnormally stretched, like something from a fun house.

The other double door is flung open, revealing how I've been using the bottom of the wardrobe as a pseudo laundry pile. I spot a black bra draped over a pair of shoes, some worn T-shirts, a pair of jeans, and a cute sundress I made that's fallen off its hanger.

I stare at the pile of clothes in the bottom of the wardrobe, contemplating for the first time that they kind of look like a nest. The back of my neck prickles as I run through a list of animals that might make squeaking sounds and be attracted to a warm, cozy clothes nest. Rats and mice, obviously. Squirrels, even—we are near a forest.

This is my punishment for not keeping my room clean and taking better care of my clothes. I'm about to be attacked by a rabid squirrel wearing a pair of my underwear on its head.

"Hello?" I ask.

There's another squeak and a scratching sound coming from the back wall of the wardrobe.

"Oh God," I murmur.

I realize that whatever's making the noise isn't *in* the wardrobe. It's in the wall *behind* the wardrobe.

My relief at realizing there's no animal making a nest in my clothes is short-lived. Because I quickly deduce that if there's an animal of some kind trapped in the wall of my apartment, then that means there might soon be a *dead* animal trapped in the wall of my apartment. And I really don't want to deal with the logistics and bad vibes associated with that. Not to mention the smell.

I move around to the side of the wardrobe, where it meets the wall, to see if there's a hole where an animal might have gotten in. I try to tip the wardrobe forward to look closer, but it's too heavy and barely budges beneath my touch.

I figure if I take out the contents of the wardrobe, that might make it light enough to move. So I work on doing that, digging out clothes and shoes like I'm burrowing a tunnel in a child's sandbox.

It's only once I've removed all the clothes that I find the secret compartment.

I didn't notice it when I first unpacked, but I was in an exhausted daze that night after traveling up from the city.

Now I can see that, in the back of the wardrobe, behind the hangers, there's a large panel of wood that's a different color than the rest. It's about the size of a kitchen cupboard. When I press my hand on the panel, it springs open, revealing a gap that meets the back wall of the room.

And in the back wall, there's another panel the same size.

My heart starts to patter as I hear another squeak. This time, I'm almost positive it's a meow.

I press my hand against the second panel on the back wall.

And like the one in the wardrobe, it springs open at my touch.

SIX

The first movie I worked on as one of Deidre's wardrobe assistants was a children's film, based on a little-known book series about a ragtag group of kids who solve mysteries. It was a fun assignment with a bright and gaudy color palette, and it kind of felt like working in a circus for a couple of months.

Unfortunately for our director, it was almost too much like working in a circus. The kids were hard to control. For a lot of them, this was their first acting gig. Their talent and willingness to follow direction varied, and we had to do *a lot* more takes than we would with older actors.

There was one scene in particular where the kids discovered a secret passageway at their local library. I remember our director really struggled to get authentic reactions out of the young actors for this scene. They just kept being too excited to rush through the revolving bookshelf door—beautifully made by our art department—that they were failing to pause for long enough to demonstrate their disbelief at their discovery.

"You're supposed to be *stunned* to find this secret passageway," the director said. "Surprised. Shocked. In awe."

The kids had been confused by this.

"Okay." The director sighed. "Let's try the Stanislavski method."

"They're kids, Jay," someone pointed out.

"They're *actors*. All right, here's how it works. Imagine you're you, living your own, real life. And you discover a secret passageway in your library. What would be your reaction?"

The kids blinked at each other, even more confused.

"I'd just go in," one of the kids said with a shrug. And the others nodded.

"I'd *run* in," another added.

"I'd run faster!" a third countered.

The director put his head in his hands. Honestly, he probably shouldn't have been working on a children's film.

At the end of the day, we had to get close-ups of the kids' faces looking surprised at something else, rather than the passageway, to edit into the wider footage. It turned out a bit clunky in the final cut, but all I cared about was that the costumes looked great. I was so fresh back then, just like the kids. I remember being so grateful for the opportunity to work my first proper feature film, so in awe of the cheap red carpet we had at our low-key premiere, so nervous about saying the right thing around Deidre. That last part hasn't changed, but the freshness has. Those kids must be almost finished with high school now. And most days, I feel about a hundred years old.

But right now, I'm staring at my own secret passageway. And I feel a thrill creep through me that makes me momentarily feel much younger. If the camera zoomed in on me right now, the astonishment on my face would satisfy even the pickiest director.

It really is like something from a storybook or a mystery film. A secret passageway concealed in the back of my wardrobe.

Only, if this were one of those, then the passageway would lead to a fantasy world or a secret speakeasy. Or maybe even a villain's lair, which it did in that children's movie.

This one, however, doesn't lead to any of those things.

It appears to lead into another wardrobe.

The recess in the back wall of my room has revealed the back of another wardrobe—logically, the one next door. The wardrobe looks nearly identical to mine, with its own concealed panel in the back. And when I pop that one open, I'm staring at a rack of someone else's clothes.

The clothes hanging from the rack have a minimalist, masculine style. There are a couple of T-shirts, several button-up shirts, a leather jacket, and a coat. I can smell crisp laundry detergent and the lingering scent of a piney cologne.

On the floor of the wardrobe is a collection of shoes that matches the simple aesthetic of the clothes. Sneakers, boots, oxfords. Everything looks a little worn and medium quality, but tidy and organized. Not like mine.

"What the hell?" I murmur.

I should shut the door right away. I'm looking into someone else's wardrobe. I'm looking into someone else's apartment.

But that's when I spot a pair of yellow eyes blinking at me from the corner of the wardrobe, just beyond the shoes.

I let out a small yelp.

I was originally looking for an animal, and yet I'm still somehow startled to find one. It's a black-and-white cat with golden eyes that are as round as full moons in the dark. It's sitting in the wardrobe, staring intently at me.

The cat lets out a meow, and I know definitively that this is the sound I've been hearing.

But that doesn't exactly solve the mystery. This cat is obviously stuck in here, which is why it's been meowing. But that doesn't explain why there's a secret passageway connecting my wardrobe to the one next door.

The cat shifts its weight. It's squishing a pair of nice boots, and I kind of want to reach in and shoo it off, to save the boots if nothing else.

But wait. I should reach in and shoo it off. I should reach all the way in and open the wardrobe door and *save the cat*. I know it seems intrusive, but the poor thing's obviously trapped in here. That's why it's been meowing so loudly.

So I tell myself I'm being altruistic, rather than intrusive, as I reach in and press the wardrobe door open. The cat slinks out, and I catch a glimpse of my neighbor's bedroom beyond.

The bed is neatly made with basic navy-and-cream linen. A book lies open on the nightstand, next to a half-full glass of whiskey. A thick leather folio lies on the bed with papers spilling out of it. Leaning up against the wall, beyond the bed, is an empty guitar case.

I have a strange urge to crawl through the gap in the wardrobe and over to the bed to inspect that folio of papers. The cat is sitting in the doorway of the room now, blinking at me, as if inviting me in.

But no. I'm being a creep. If the gender roles were reversed here, I'd think it was incredibly creepy. Imagine some strange guy peering through a secret gap in his wardrobe, looking into my mess of underwear and bras, at the bed where I slept the previous night . . .

Oh my God. What if that's exactly what this is? What if this isn't some intriguing secret passageway but a sinister peephole?

A chill comes over me, and I slam the doors shut.

I think I might hear another meow from the cat, but I can ignore it this time. I rescued it from the entrapment of the wardrobe, so I've done my bit. Now I just need to make sure my wardrobe stays firmly closed for the night. I shove my clothes back in, close the doors, and fasten the handles together with a thin belt so that it can't easily be opened from the inside.

As I stand there staring at the closed doors, my strangely stretched reflection in the mirror looks pale and alarmed.

What possible reason could there be for my wardrobe and the one next door to be linked by a secret passage? Did the apartments used to be connected? Or could it be some kind of fault in the wall? The apartment complex is pretty old, after all.

But no, those hidden doors seem deliberately constructed. They don't seem like an accident.

I go back to my peephole theory, and my heart rate speeds up. Do I need to tell the apartment owners or our production's travel and accommodation coordinator about this? I think I should. I need to do something.

But not tonight. I can't call anyone this late. It will have to wait until morning.

Plus, I reason, I've been here for several nights now, and no one's come through the passageway to harm me yet. I haven't heard any sounds from next door except for the cat meowing. Maybe the occupant has been away—that could be why the cat was trapped.

With all these thoughts tossing around in my head, I try to go to sleep. Though of course, sleep evades me. I lie there listening so hard I realize I'm holding my breath, waiting to see if I can hear any more noise from the wardrobe. Another meow, a door creaking open, a rustle of clothes, a thud of boot steps.

I don't hear anything. But when I finally do drift off to sleep, I dream of it instead.

I dream that someone comes into my room from the wardrobe.

I've had dreams like this before. In them, the shadowy figure approaching me from the corner of the room has always been a menacing figure that makes my bones freeze and an invisible scream catch in my throat. I've read about night terrors and sleep paralysis, and these dreams seem consistent with that. It always seems to happen at times in my life when I'm feeling anxious or out of control.

But this dream, this dream is different. The faceless figure that approaches me from the wardrobe isn't menacing. It isn't shadowy. In fact, it seems awash in a soft, golden light, like sunlight. And I'm not frozen. I can move.

I sit up in bed, propping myself on my elbows, and I feel myself smiling even though I have no idea why.

"Finally," I say.

SEVEN

In the sun-dappled clarity of morning, I've decided.

I'm going to go knock on the door of the apartment next to mine and try to speak to whoever lives there.

Sure, I could just report all this to our travel and accommodation coordinator and let her sort it out for me. That seems like the easier, less confrontational way to go about this, and a big part of me is tempted to go that route.

But another part of me is strangely compelled to do this for myself. I feel like I need to know, firsthand. Who owns that cat? Who owns those boots, and that guitar case, and the folio with the papers? Who might potentially have access to my room as I lie sleeping at night?

My best friend, Margot, is always trying to tell me that things that make you uncomfortable are good for you. That stress in small doses is actually beneficial for our brains. So, I tell myself this is healthy—the way my heart thuds as I stand in the hallway outside my apartment, looking at the brown door in front of me.

I'm in apartment number eight, and the apartment connected by the passageway is number nine. It has a brass 9 on the door that curves down and around like a cat's tail.

I take a deep breath in. Then I knock gently on the door and wait.

My palms are clammy, and my leg is jittering, which is embarrassing. All I'm about to do is have a conversation. A weird conversation, but still . . . I'm not about to leap out of an airplane or make a speech in front of thousands of people.

A few moments pass, but no one comes after my first knock. So I knock again, in case they didn't hear the first time.

When I hear a lock clattering open, my heart rate rises even more.

But it's not the door of number nine that's opening.

It's number ten, on the other side.

The woman who peers out of number ten is an eccentric older woman with a cascade of silver-and-ginger hair and a kind face. She's wearing a long purple dress, dangling silver earrings, and a wooden pendant on a chain around her neck that looks like an amulet to ward off evil.

If I were going to design a costume for a retired art teacher or a modern-day soothsayer, this woman is wearing exactly that.

"Who're you looking for, my dear?" the woman asks.

"Oh," I reply, thrown off a little. "I just wanted to talk to whoever lives here, in number nine."

The woman frowns.

"There's no one in number nine at the moment," she replies. "Hasn't been all summer."

My skin prickles. Because that doesn't make sense. I saw clothes hanging in the wardrobe. I could smell a lingering cologne.

"You mean, it's completely vacant?" I ask, trying to keep my voice steady.

"At the moment, yes. The owner of the apartment complex keeps number nine reserved for family and friends, but the last guest was back in April."

"Are you sure?" I ask.

The woman gives a small, knowing smile. "Oh yes, I always know when I have neighbors."

"All right," I say slowly. "Well, then, do you know how a cat might have gotten in there?"

"A cat? What kind?"

"Like, a black-and-white one? With big yellow eyes."

"Hmm." The woman cocks her head. "The couple at the end of the corridor has a tabby, and I had a beautiful ginger up until Christmas, when he finally moved on to the next world. But I haven't seen a black-and-white cat around recently. Why do you think there's a cat in there?"

"I—" I hesitate, suddenly shy about mentioning the passageway. "I swore I could hear a cat meowing in there last night."

The woman and I both turn to look at number nine again.

"You heard it," the woman said. "But then, how did you know what it looked like?"

I feel myself growing flustered. "I went out onto the balcony to check," I make up hastily. "And that's what I saw through the windows. I think."

"I see." The woman nods, and I have a feeling she knows there's something I'm not telling her. But if she does, she must decide to humor me. "Well, there are a few other neighborhood cats that hang around on this street. Maybe one of them jumped up and got in somehow. I can ask the cleaners to check next time they're in there."

"Sure," I say. "That sounds like a good idea."

"I'm Florence, by the way." The woman extends a paper-thin bejeweled hand, and I shake it tentatively.

"Mattie," I reply.

"And you're with the film crew, aren't you?"

I force a smile. "Yeah, I am. How did you know?"

"Oh, it's a small town. What's the movie about? Anything exciting?"

"It's a Christmas romance," I say. "I mean, I technically signed an NDA that tells me not to talk about it, but it's pretty obvious when you walk down Main Street."

"A romance, you say," Florence replies. "It's been a while since I watched a good romance. I'm more into mysteries these days."

Mysteries sound about right. My head is swimming, trying to reconcile the new knowledge that no one lives in number nine with what I saw last night. I contemplate Florence, who's still smiling warmly at me as she plays with the wooden pendant hanging around her neck. Maybe I should tell her about the passageway. She seems like the kind of person who knows things.

But my phone starts buzzing then with a message from Deidre, and I realize I've been standing here talking for longer than I expected.

"I've got to run, sorry," I say to Florence.

"Of course," Florence says. "You have a romance to make."

When I'm outside in the street, in the fresh air, I turn and look up at the apartments behind me. The lights of number nine are off. I glance quickly at the row of mailboxes by the gate. There are some papers peeking out of the dark slot to number nine, but they all look like political pamphlets and other circulars. Nothing of interest.

As I drive into town, I tell myself I need to leave all this behind me in the apartment and focus on the day ahead. There's likely nothing to worry about. If Florence is right and no one's staying in number nine, then I don't need to be concerned about anyone using the secret door to watch me sleeping. And the theory about the cat somehow getting into the apartment from the street seems plausible. Maybe I should just leave it at that.

Only, I can't leave it at that. I feel unsettled all day, like there's something I'm missing. I'm distracted as I help dress Kandace Connolly as Raquel for the nighttime scene we're filming later at a bar in town. I use the wrong belt to start, crumple one of her freshly steamed blouses, and then can't get it to tuck into her jeans properly, pinching her a few times in the process. Kandace is lovely about it all, as she always is, but still. I don't like making mistakes.

Thank God Austin Farrow hasn't started filming his scenes yet, because I definitely don't need anything else to muddle my brain today. Deidre has obviously noticed that I'm off kilter, because she sends me away to deal with the background extras in the afternoon instead of the leads or supporting cast, like I normally do. Which is clearly a relegation. Yesterday, Henry was in the doghouse for being late back from Carrickvale, and now it's my turn. I need to get my head back in the game.

We've told our background extras to wear their own clothes for this bar scene, which we normally do for contemporary films with a budget like this. But I still need to go check them over to make sure they fit the brief we gave. The extras are milling about in one of the event tents we've set up in the town square, mostly all wearing typical clothes you'd wear to a small-town bar. T-shirts and plaid, jeans and khakis, and casual summer dresses. There's one guy in a full suit who looks out of place, so I instruct him to take off his jacket and untuck his shirt. Then there are two women wearing the same dress, so I make one of them change into her backup outfit instead.

As the day starts to darken around us, we head to the bar. We're using a real bar for these scenes, rather than building a set, which comes with its challenges. The art department has been in there all day redressing the interior to make it suit the bright, hyperreal aesthetic of the film. More string lights glisten in the windows and candy-cane-striped tablecloths bedeck the bar tables, just in case the audience forgets this is a Christmas movie. They've also rearranged the furniture to fit in all the camera and lighting gear.

With minimal room left inside the bar, we have a video village set up on the street outside, which is the area where we can watch live feeds of the filming without getting in the way. I cast my eyes carefully over the background extras through the monitors. They're scattered in booths and tables and at the bar counter. My eyes fall on one of the women who was wearing the duplicate dress. She's changed into a blue dress now and is nursing a fake glass of wine. The guy sitting opposite her is holding a glass of whiskey. They've been positioned to look like they're on a date.

It's only then that the mild unsettled feeling I've been having all day cinches around me, like a scarf tightening around my neck. And I suddenly realize what I missed about what I saw in the apartment next door and my conversation with Florence this morning.

Florence said this morning that number nine has been unoccupied since April—that's at least three months ago. But as I cast my mind back to the bedroom I glimpsed beyond the wardrobe door last night, I think about what I saw.

A neatly made bed. An empty guitar case. A leather folio. A book.

All things that reasonably might have been left in an unoccupied apartment for three months.

But there, on the nightstand, was something that seemed much more recent.

A half-finished glass of whiskey.

EIGHT

"Hmm," says Margot. "What if it's a squatter?"

Margot, my closest friend of the last few years, is back home in the city, looking at me through my phone screen. I can see the bright lights of neighboring apartments through the window behind her and hear a siren wailing on the street below. I can imagine that, if I were in the city, I might be thinking about squatters too.

But here, in the safe, quiet charm of Casey River, I'm not buying Margot's squatter theory. Casey River just doesn't seem like the type of town to have squatters. Its resident population seems to consist mostly of retirees and bed-and-breakfast owners. Plus, it's a tight-knit community. People would notice newcomers to town.

I explain this to Margot over the phone, but she doesn't seem convinced.

"You've brought a whole troupe of strangers to town," she points out. "They might just think that he—or she or they; remember, we can't assume gender just based on clothes in the wardrobe—is part of the film crew."

"I just wasn't getting squatter vibes from the room," I say. "It seemed too . . . neat."

"That's a bit judgmental. Squatters can be neat."

"I guess so."

"Or it could be something else. Something obvious. Maybe your witchy neighbor lady was wrong and there is a guest staying there after all."

"Did I call Florence witchy?"

"You didn't use those exact words, but she sounds witchy as hell."

"True, which makes it even less likely that she would have missed something like this. She seems like she *knows* things."

"So, why didn't you ask her about the passageway?"

I chew on my lip. "I thought about that. But I wanted to talk to you first, to hear how crazy it sounds to say out loud."

"Oh, it sounds crazy in all the best ways. I've always dreamed of finding a secret passageway somewhere. I ripped out the floorboards in my childhood bedroom once because I thought they sounded hollow, but all that led to was Mom using my allowance to get them fixed."

"Okay, yes, secret passageways seem very cool in theory. But let's just say there is a squatter or an unexpected guest on the other side, right? That means that whoever it is has access to my bedroom. I think I need to tell our travel and accommodation coordinator about it—she's the one who booked the place for me."

"That seems like a sensible thing to do."

There's a pause. Normally when Margot says something is the sensible thing to do, she's not implying it's the right thing to do.

"What?" I sigh.

"Well, it's just, if you report it, someone will probably just come and board the passageway up, right?"

"Yeah. And then I can stop worrying about it."

"But then the mystery won't be solved."

"We don't even know if this is a mystery!"

"If we don't know the answer to something, then it's a mystery by default. And honestly, why did you even call me if we're not trying to solve a mystery? I need some excitement in my life."

This isn't true. Margot's life is nonstop excitement. She's one of those outdoor fanatics, the kind that's always got some semipsychotic trail run or mountain bike adventure planned that sounds like a fast track to the hospital's emergency department. Margot thinks that any camping trip where you're not sleeping in a bivouac sack on the side of a mountain is basically glamping.

To be honest, we didn't exactly click right away when I first met her in college. I found her kind of frightening. But over the years, we've realized we balance each other out. Her fire sign and my earth sign meld to create something warm and comforting for both of us.

Plus, Margot was good for me through the whole Jack thing. She's always been skilled at asking the right questions, even when they scare me.

Which is exactly what she does right now.

"Have you thought about going in there?" Margot asks.

"Going in where?"

"All the way through the passageway. Into the room."

"Um, no. Because that's trespassing."

"Technically not. Technically you're just walking through a door in your room."

"And what if there *is* a squatter? What do you think their reaction will be to seeing a strange woman suddenly appear in their bedroom?"

"Just because they're a squatter doesn't mean they're dangerous. Remember, we're trying not to judge here. Besides, they're the one squatting in someone else's apartment. *They* should be scared of *you*."

"Yeah, because we both know I'm terrifying."

I laugh nervously as I take a gulp of my wine. I've probably had too much. I can tell I've had too much, because even though I'm trying to dismiss Margot's typically ludicrous idea, a small part of me—a very small part—is considering it. Considering that maybe, deep down, that's why I called Margot. Because I knew she'd push me to the edge.

"You can stay on the phone with me," Margot urges. "When you go through. So I'll be here in case anything goes wrong."

"You're not even here! You're a hundred miles away."

"I'll have the local police station number on standby."

"You're making this sound so appealing."

"I know I am! I'm jealous! I want to be there. This is the exact kind of weird, unexplained shit that they'd talk about on one of the podcasts I listen to."

"You mean your true crime podcasts? Your *murder* podcasts?"

"They're not always about murder. Sometimes they're about alien abductions or unsolved disappearances."

There's a pause while I let her think about what she's just said.

"Oh, come on, Mattie," she urges. "Remember how you told me you want to be more assertive?"

"Breaking into someone's apartment isn't what I had in mind."

"You have to start somewhere. You're nervous, right? You feel uncomfortable. That's the first hurdle. Walking *into* a situation that makes you uncomfortable, rather than letting it walk all over you."

She's convincing me. Or maybe the wine's convincing me. Either way, I somehow find myself standing in my bedroom. And opening the door to my wardrobe.

"Yes!" says Margot. "Okay, flip the phone around so that I can see things from your point of view."

"Hold on, I just need to get some clothes out."

I put my phone on the floor of the wardrobe as I take down a handful of hangers. Then I pick the phone back up and turn the camera to face the panel in the back.

"This is it," I say. "It springs open when I press it, like this."

I reach with my other hand to press the panel open. But as it springs toward me, it knocks my phone out of my hand, which clatters back to the bottom of the wardrobe. When I pick it up, I've accidentally ended the call with Margot.

"Shit," I murmur.

I try to call her back, but for some reason, I can't get through. My phone's making the sound it does when I either have no service or the person on the other line has no service.

I look up, through the gap that I've opened again between the two wardrobes. It looks relatively unchanged from yesterday. The same clothes are still hanging from the rack. The same shoes are still sitting at the bottom. Unless . . . are those the same boots from yesterday or a different pair? I could have sworn the ones from yesterday were suede, but there's a chance I could be misremembering.

I hear a sound from beyond the wardrobe, and my heart hammers.

But it's just the black-and-white cat again. I can see it pad into view through the gap beyond the door. It comes and sits down right in front of the wardrobe, blinking its yellow-moon eyes at me.

Dammit. I hoped that, if Florence was right and the cat really was a stray that had somehow gotten in, it would have found its way back out again by now. But maybe it doesn't know how. Maybe I rescued the cat from the wardrobe only to keep it trapped in the empty apartment.

I pick up my phone to try Margot again, but I get the same no-signal beep.

The cat meows at me. It looks forlorn. Like it needs my help.

"Psst," I say. "Come here."

I rub my fingers together, beckoning the cat over to my side of the wardrobe.

The cat blinks and doesn't budge.

"Come on," I urge. "You're going to be stuck in there. No food or water. That doesn't sound very nice, does it?"

The cat blinks again. Then it gets up and jumps onto the bed. I can see that the folio is still lying there. It's this that the cat decides to nestle itself on top of, curling around it like it's a litter of kittens.

I consider my options. If I report this to our accommodation coordinator, someone might come to the apartment tomorrow to board the passageway up and let the cat out. If it really is stuck, another night might not be a big deal. Cats are self-sufficient.

But like Margot said, then the mystery wouldn't be solved. Then I might never know why this passageway exists and what's in that folio on the bed and why the cat keeps staring at me like it's offering an invitation. Or a dare.

I don't know what exactly it is. Whether it's the echo of Margot's encouragement ringing in my ears, the wine, the dream I had last night, concern for the cat, or something else entirely.

I think of the kids in that children's movie discovering their own secret passageway.

What would be your reaction? the director asked.

I'd just go in, the kids answered.

Before I can talk myself out of it, I'm squeezing myself through the door.

NINE

The first thing I notice is that the apartment smells like someone's been living in it.

I know that sounds strange, but it's unmistakable. There's that lingering scent of cologne on the clothes—something fresh and piney—as well as a leftover aroma of coffee and maybe toast.

This makes me uneasy. But a small relief is that at least it doesn't smell like anything the cat's left behind.

I emerge from the wardrobe and into the bedroom. This feels wrong. I'm acutely aware that I shouldn't be in here. It feels like I'm looking at someone naked—or more like I'm looking *inside* someone else's body. At something I shouldn't be able to see.

Still, I don't leave.

The bedroom is almost identical to mine. There's the small en suite bathroom in the corner and the closed door that leads out into the living area. The window across from the bed is shut.

All I really need to do is open the window. If I just open the window wide enough, the cat can jump out if it wants to. We're only one floor up, and there are plenty of trees for it to climb down. Which is probably how it got up in the first place.

But before I move to the window, I cast my eyes over the bed. The book that's resting on the nightstand is an old paperback western, the kind with a well-cracked spine and yellowed pages that you'd find in the back of a dusty secondhand store. It's a collection of short stories by

Louis L'Amour, who's one of my dad's favorites. The front cover features men riding horses, and there's a dog-ear marking a page somewhere toward the end.

The whiskey glass next to the book is empty.

I blink, staring at the glass. I know it had whiskey in it yesterday. Didn't it? I feel almost positive it did, but then again, memory isn't certainty. I heard somewhere that when you remember a moment, you're actually just remembering the last time you remembered the moment, not the original moment itself. So each new recollection will become a little more skewed than the last, like a child's game of telephone.

Maybe there was never any whiskey in the glass. Maybe when I saw the whiskey on set earlier this evening, my memory got distorted.

The cat meows, breaking my reverie.

"All right," I say, letting out a shaky breath. "Let's just focus on getting you free."

I move to go around the bed to the window. The cat stands up and slides its legs forward in a big stretch, pushing the folio off the bed.

A piece of paper from the folio slides out as it hits the ground, right at my feet.

I can't help it. I know it's not any of my business, but the words on the piece of paper catch my eye, and my pulse starts to pound in my throat. Before I know it, I'm reaching down to pick it up.

It's a wanted poster.

The words are stamped in siren red across the top of the page, eye catching and alarming. Below them is more text reading, **CAN YOU HELP? $5,000** REWARD FOR INFORMATION LEADING TO ARREST.

My eyes trail from the words to the photo below them. It's a police sketch of a young man with a clean-shaven symmetrical face, light-brown hair, a scattering of freckles.

My skin prickles. And then it goes cold.

Because I think I've seen that face before. In another photo that I held in my hands yesterday.

Austin Farrow.

Or at least, it looks uncannily like Austin Farrow. It's hard to tell, given the imperfections of the sketch. And the fact that the man in the photo has shorter hair and a cleanly shaven face. But it's the eyes. I remember the eyes that had looked down at me as I measured Austin's chest.

Then I notice something else. The jacket the guy is wearing in the sketch is a soft leather jacket. And it looks horribly like the jacket that's hanging up in the closet.

I drop the poster onto the bed and spin around. Am I standing in Austin Farrow's bedroom right now? Is my bedroom connected to Austin's by a secret passageway? Is Austin Farrow a clandestine *criminal*?

My head is reeling with all this, but my thoughts freeze completely when I hear a sound from beyond the bedroom.

It's a key turning in a lock outside.

Nothing about this night has gone the way I expected. But if I can be sure of one thing, it's that I don't want anyone—be it Austin Farrow, a squatter, a fugitive, or otherwise—to catch me standing here in a bedroom that's not mine.

I pick the folio up off the ground and toss it back onto the bed. The cat meows at me one last time, but I ignore it, as I dart back into the open wardrobe. I'm face-to-face with the leather jacket, the one that's identical to the one in the photo, and the earthy smell of it fills my nose. A sneeze rises behind my nostrils, and I hold my breath, willing it to stay in.

I can hear the door opening in the living room beyond. Someone's coming into the apartment. Into the apartment that no one's meant to be living in.

As I pull the wardrobe door behind me, a part of me is tempted. A part of me is tempted to stay in here, peering through the crack, waiting for the person to enter the bedroom. I know that's what Margot would want me to do.

But the sneeze is getting harder to hold in. And any moment now, it's going to rush out in an audible burst, revealing my presence.

So I bend down and duck back through the passageway. As I turn around to close the panels behind me, I catch a glimpse of the bedroom through the sliver in the wardrobe door I've accidentally left open in my haste.

I see the bedroom door creak open, pushed by a toned T-shirt-clad arm. I see the tip of a brown boot on the carpet and a peek of honey-colored hair . . .

But then the sneeze becomes impossible to hold in. I slide the panels shut, fall backward into the clothes pile spilling out of my wardrobe, and sneeze three times in quick succession.

After, I hold my breath. I listen for any sound from next door that might indicate that whoever just walked in heard me or saw me. I wonder if they're standing by the wardrobe right now. I wonder if it's Austin.

I can't hear anything, but I feel a strange presence. My skin is buzzing, almost like there's electricity in the air.

My phone starts to ping then, with messages coming through. They're all from Margot. She's been trying to call me back but was getting an out-of-service beep too. Maybe service was down for some reason.

I slide the belt back through the handles of the wardrobe. Then, for good measure, I jam the chair from the corner of the room under the handles too. And I grab a knife from one of the kitchen drawers and place it onto my nightstand. Just in case.

I still have no idea what I've found on the other side of the wardrobe, but there's definitely *someone* in there. Someone who owns the same jacket as whoever is on that wanted poster. And regardless of who they are, I don't want them crawling through my wardrobe. Which is hypocritical of me, I know.

I clamber into my bed and draw the covers tightly around me. I need to let Margot know that I'm alive, but there's something else I have to do first.

I pull up my web browser and type Austin Farrow's name in again. Maybe there was something I missed when I searched the other night.

I try a combination of different searches: Austin Farrow + wanted. Austin Farrow + criminal. Austin Farrow + police sketch. But nothing comes up. I trawl through all the images I can find of Austin online, but nothing's exactly matching the sketch on the wanted poster I just found next door.

When one of the links directs me back to Austin's filmography, a thought occurs to me. Of course. Austin is an *actor*. The wanted poster could be a film prop.

But as I rescan the list, I can't find any roles where Austin played a criminal. He hasn't been in any crime dramas or mysteries or thrillers. I even go so far as to find a link to one of his indie movies and scroll through it on triple speed, but there's no sign of a wanted poster with his face on it. There is one scene of him with his shirt off at the beach, and I resist the temptation to slow down to regular speed for that one.

Then there are the two other things that also aren't making sense. The first is that it would be odd for Austin Farrow to be staying next door to me, anyway. There are tiers of accommodation for cast and crew, and it would be highly unusual for a supporting lead like Austin be put up in the same apartment complex as a wardrobe assistant like me. More likely he'd be in the same hotel as Hayden King and Kandace Connolly—the nice one by the gardens in town.

The second thing, of course, is the secret passageway. Nothing I've found tonight has helped me to understand why that passageway exists. In fact, it's just made everything even more confusing.

I type and delete about a dozen messages to Margot. I want to explain to her what's happened, but I haven't told her anything about Austin Farrow yet. I know she's my best friend. I know I can normally tell her everything. But she'll have a hundred questions, and I don't feel ready to answer them.

So, I message her an abridged version of my trip through the wardrobe instead. I tell her about the Louis L'Amour book and the empty whiskey glass and the fact that I heard—and half saw—someone coming into the apartment. I tell her that I'm fine, albeit shaken and still confused as hell.

Margot messages me back with a string of links about people finding secret passageways in their houses. Some of them led to panic rooms or bunkers. Others to hiding places for valuable family heirlooms or illegal goods.

Which makes me think of fugitives again.

But the problem with these possibilities is that, given the spatial layout of the apartment complex, I just don't think my passageway can lead anywhere other than the apartment next door. I can see the balcony to number nine adjoining mine outside. There's nothing between our two walls that would allow for any kind of hidden room. And the room beyond the wardrobe simply looks like someone's bedroom. But whose? And why? Those are the questions.

Once I've finished messaging with Margot, I lie back in my bed with my heart thumping and my head spinning.

It takes me a few moments to realize that the energy coursing through my body isn't exactly fearful, despite the kitchen knife on my nightstand.

I think about how I felt, crouched in the wardrobe, daring myself to stay and keep watching. It's a thrill I haven't felt for a while. The kind of thrill that Margot talks about when she's planning her next death-defying adventure.

It's the thrill of being close to danger and narrowly avoiding it. Jumping off a cliff attached to a rope. Holding a defanged snake in your hands. Swimming in a cage surrounded by sharks.

You know how close you've come to something dangerous, something that could go terribly wrong.

But as soon as it's over, you want to do it again.

TEN

When I arrive at the production office the following morning, I find our travel and accommodation coordinator, Val, at her laptop furiously typing away while concurrently checking something on her phone and on a piece of paper next to her. Which seems like an impossible feat, given that she doesn't have three sets of eyes. But somehow, she's managing it.

This is Val in her element. Valentina Gallo is in her early thirties—beautiful and brilliant, with long dark hair and an almost clairvoyant knowledge of everything to do with Casey River and its surroundings. She lives in the area and is always the go-to for travel and accommodation needs when productions are filming here.

"Sorry to interrupt," I say, knocking on her desk like it's a door.

"No worries at all," Val says crisply. "How can I help?" Val has a background in the hotel industry, and it shows.

I pull up a stool next to Val and sit down on it. Then I scoot closer to her desk, hoping that no one else will be able to hear what I'm about to ask.

"Sorry if this is a weird question," I say. "But I'm just wondering if anyone else from the production is staying in the same apartment complex as I am."

Val frowns at her laptop screen.

"You're in that complex off the river path, right?" Val says. "The one near the forest and the trails. Nice spot."

"That's right," I reply.

I watch as Val opens a detailed spreadsheet on her screen.

"Nope," she says. "It's just you in there. I think there were two rooms available, but then Loren and Heidi from hair and makeup decided they wanted to stay together at Heidi's place. Which shaved quite a bit off the budget, thank God."

I nod slowly. "Okay," I say. "Thanks."

"Why are you asking?" Val continues. "Is everything okay with the place?"

I hesitate. This would be the prime opportunity for me to tell Val about the passageway. Val is one of the most efficient people I know, and she'd have it sorted in half an hour, most likely. And she'd do it in a no-fuss manner too, as if a secret passageway were akin to a faulty hot water system or a leak in the roof.

This is the sensible thing to do. The *safe* thing to do. A stranger potentially has access to my bedroom. Surely I need to rectify that.

"It's fine," I find myself saying instead, like my mouth's in protest with my mind. "It's great, actually."

"Fantastic," Val says. "It's always been popular when I've put crew there in the past. It's the best you can get at that price point, and I gave it to you because you're one of my favorites."

I force myself to smile at this. It's a lovely compliment, of course, but all I can think is that if the apartment's been popular with crew in the past, then obviously no one else has ever alerted Val to the existence of a secret passageway.

Val's phone starts to ring then, and I thank her quickly so that she can answer it. It sounds like Kandace Connolly's husband has decided to come visit last minute and she needs a room upgrade, so that's Val's new fire to put out for the day. I don't need to bother her with anything else.

I head to our wardrobe room, trying to reset my thoughts after that conversation. If no one from the production is staying next door to me, then it can't have been Austin Farrow I saw walking into the bedroom last night. Maybe it wasn't even his face on that wanted poster. I have been thinking about his face more than I'd like to admit since our meeting the other day. Maybe my brain superimposed it on there. Our minds are fallible, after all.

Thoughts of Austin's face are still flitting around my head when I enter the wardrobe room.

And I find Austin himself, sitting on a chair next to our clothing racks.

He has a tablet open in his lap with what looks like a script pulled up on the screen, and his brow is furrowed in concentration as he reads it. But when I pause in the doorway, he looks up from the screen and smiles at me.

"Mattie with two *t*'s," he says.

"Hey," I reply weakly.

I knew Austin would be here sometime this morning. He starts filming his first scenes as Mitchell today. We were expecting him later, though, and I hadn't yet decided whether I was brave enough to handle him again or if I was going to ask Henry to take over this time.

Now, it seems like my decision's been made for me.

"I'm a bit early, sorry," Austin continues. "Traffic was surprisingly good coming in."

I take a moment to compose myself. *Be professional,* I remember.

But I also realize—despite this perhaps being the opposite of professional—that I might be able to use this opportunity to my advantage. I have questions about Austin I want answers to, and now I have the man himself sitting here in front of me.

I think about what he said. *Traffic was surprisingly good coming in.* That means he drove into town.

"Where did you drive from?" I ask lightly, as I set down my bag and head over to one of our desks.

"I've been staying out with my brother, on our family's orchard," Austin replies. "I can drive it in less than an hour if I get a clear run."

"Your family's orchard?" I repeat.

"Yeah, it's where I grew up." Austin has a small, wistful smile on his face. "But I'll be staying in town from tonight, which is kind of a relief, because my brother keeps trying to put me to work while I'm there."

"Family, right?" I say.

"You know it. Speaking of family, I told my niece—Maddie with two *d*'s—that I met another Mattie the other day. She was very excited."

My body warms at the thought of Austin talking to someone about me. Saying my name when I'm not around.

"That's cute," I reply, trying to press down my smile. "How old is Maddie with two *d*'s?"

"Five. An age of endless questions. For starters, she wants to know where the name Matilda comes from. We established it's not from *True Grit*."

He also remembered my full first name. I move over to the comfort of the clothing racks, hiding myself behind them, steadying my hands in the fabric.

"It's from a song," I explain. "An old Australian folk song, called 'Waltzing Matilda.' I don't actually know it that well, but there's something in there about a man camping by a tree, and he's on the run from the law, maybe. And there's a sheep, I think?"

Austin starts laughing at this.

"It's not as cool as it being from *True Grit*," I continue. "But my parents met in Australia, and it had significance to them, so . . ." I shrug.

"Okay, first, I need to hear this song." Austin types something into his tablet. "But also, that's a funny coincidence, because my name also comes from where my parents first met."

"Really?"

"Yep. They met in Austin. At a country music festival, summer of '89. It became a special place for them."

"So, your name's a tribute too."

"Exactly. I guess our parents are all romantics."

I try not to blush. "I mean, I think the guy in the Australian song dies in the end. So, I'm not sure how romantic that is."

"Spoiler alert," Austin says.

He starts playing "Waltzing Matilda" on his tablet and grins down at the screen.

"I like this," he says. "It reminds me of an old-school country song."

"So, you're into country music too, like your parents?" I ask.

"Oh, a hundred percent. Fully into all that cowboy stuff."

Austin's nodding along to the song, like it's a certified jam rather than a tinny old folk song.

I have a thought.

"Have you ever been in a western?"

This is my chance to delve into Austin's acting history, to try to get to the bottom of that wanted poster. I know he hasn't been in a western, of course, because I'm becoming an expert on his filmography. But he doesn't know what I know, and this is a good thread to start tugging at.

"Oh, man," Austin says. "Not yet, but how did you know that's my absolute dream?"

"I can see you as a cowboy," I reply.

"Do I have a face for a Stetson?"

Is he really making me look at his face more closely? I set my jaw. I have to get used to this. Part of my job is to look at Austin. It can't be an ordeal every time.

"Sure," I reply. "I'd probably go with a wide brim for you, with a round crown."

"Why's that?"

I wave my hand in his general direction. "You have a square jaw. Curves and soft shapes offset that."

Austin nods. "Okay, so seeing as you're someone who knows aesthetics . . . next question is, Do you think I could pull off a Sundance Kid mustache?"

I tilt my head. "I'd actually say that you have more of a Paul Newman look than a Robert Redford look."

"Wow." Austin puts his hand over his heart. "What a compliment. I mean, I'd take either. I would die happy if I could be in a remake of *Butch Cassidy*. I'd even be an extra if I had to."

My mind flicks to the collection of Louis L'Amour short stories I found on the nightstand in the room next door. Stories about the Old West, about cowboys. It seems like way too much of a coincidence, and yet, I *know* that book can't belong to Austin, because he's not staying in that apartment. He and Val have both confirmed that.

I stay on track, determined to glean something from this conversation other than more questions.

"So," I say. "If you like cowboys, you must like morally gray characters."

"Every actor loves morally gray characters."

"Who's the most morally gray character you've played?"

What I really want to ask is *Have you played a character whose face appears on a wanted poster?*

"That's the problem," Austin replies. "My agent worries I'm getting typecast as 'the good guy.' I keep playing nice dudes. And everyone likes a nice dude in real life, but it's not as fun—"

He's cut off when Loren, one of our makeup artists, appears in the doorway.

"There you are," she says to Austin. She looks over at me, her brow creased, and then back to Austin. "We're ready for you now."

"Oh, sure," Austin says.

He gets up from his chair and stretches his arms above him.

"Wait," I say. "We're not dressing you now?"

I swipe up a call sheet from a nearby table and can see that our schedule does indeed have Austin getting his hair and makeup done before he's due to get into his costume.

"Like I said, I got here early," Austin says with a shrug. "We can continue this cowboy chat when I'm back."

He tucks his tablet under his arm and sidles to the door, where Loren is still standing with an incredibly suspicious look on her face.

Loren loves gossip just as much as Henry, and I feel a desperate need to tell her that I didn't *lure* Austin in here or anything. He was just waiting here when I arrived.

It's only once they're both gone that the reality of this hits me.

Austin arrived at the production office early, and he was supposed to be with hair and makeup first.

Yet he came here, to my department, to wait.

A hot flush rises to my cheeks. This doesn't necessarily mean anything. We have comfortable chairs in the wardrobe department (at Deidre's insistence), it's quiet, and it's close to the entrance of the office. It's as good a place as any to wait. That's all it is. It has nothing to do with me, probably. Austin wouldn't have even known that I'd be here. It could have been Henry or Deidre who walked in first.

I can't think about it being anything more than that. I can't go to that place in my head. There's the secret passageway and the wanted poster to figure out still. And there's also the fact that the last time I let myself believe a guy thought I was something special, it all went terribly wrong.

ELEVEN

The beginning of my relationship with Jack was dazzling. In the true, dangerous sense of the word, like looking straight into the sun or the headlights of an oncoming car.

When I first met him on a group camping trip, he had a girl-friend. She wasn't there on the trip, but I knew she existed. Though you wouldn't have thought it by the way Jack treated me.

I told myself I was imagining it at first. I'm honestly not the type to assume a guy is interested in me, especially when he has a girlfriend. I can barely convince myself a guy is interested in me even when he's completely single. I surmised that Jack probably just looked at everyone the way he looked at me—like I was the most interesting person in the world, like every joke I made was hilarious, like every silly story I told was incredibly charming.

But on the second day, I realized it wasn't everyone. It was just me. He swam out with me all the way to the center of the lake that morning, farther than I'd normally go on my own. As we lay on our backs looking up at the sky, our legs accidentally brushed against each other, and he laughed as if we were sharing a joke. As if we had been for some time.

Our mutual friend who invited me on the camping trip noticed. Because she told me over campfire beers that night to be careful. But I already knew that. I couldn't help how I felt—it was a physical reaction, like a sickness—but I wasn't going to do anything about it. Jack had a girlfriend, and I could certainly be a fool sometimes, but I wasn't a home-wrecker. I'd just keep it all in my head instead. I was good at that.

But then, a couple of weeks later, Jack didn't have a girlfriend anymore. And when we were having our first drink together, he told me how he'd felt on that camping trip. It had lit a fuse that had led to him breaking up with his girlfriend, but that wasn't the final explosion. No, it was just the beginning.

At the time, it felt like the closest I'd come to fate in a long while.

———

Austin and I don't actually get a chance to continue our "cowboy chat." When he returns to get dressed later that morning, Deidre's in the wardrobe room, working on some of Raquel's costumes. Austin stops to talk to Deidre first, and I notice that he has a good friendly rapport with her too—she even *smiles* at something he says. And *laughs* at something else. The only other person I've seen make Deidre laugh is her wife, Eleanor.

See, I tell myself. *Austin's just a friendly guy. He gets along with everyone.* Exactly like I thought, there's no special dynamic between us. And thinking there is will only make me a fool again.

Our first costume for Mitchell is a forest green flannel that I've tailored to fit Austin's measurements. He comes out of the fitting room wearing it, and I'm stunned for a second time by how well it matches the color of his eyes.

"What do we think?" Austin asks, extending his arms to show off the outfit.

Deidre glances up from the table. "Perfect," she says. "Just need to roll up the sleeves."

This is an instruction for me. I take a step closer to Austin. There's unfortunately no method for me to roll up Austin's sleeves without touching him, so I just need to go for it. I've done this many times before. It's actually an important skill—Deidre has a very particular way she likes men's shirt sleeves rolled up to a specific point just below the elbow.

I reach for one of Austin's arms and undo the button on his wrist. This close to him, I can smell his sweet, woodsy cologne.

My fingers catch on the button when I realize it's eerily similar to the one I could smell in the wardrobe next door.

But it's likely a common brand of cologne. And Deidre is here. And it shouldn't be taking me this long to roll up a damn sleeve.

I continue, folding up the material to reveal a generous portion of Austin's golden forearm. I force myself to pretend this is someone else. I imagine it's Hayden King instead. I don't feel this way when Hayden's around. And it's just a forearm. *It's just a forearm.*

I move quickly to the other arm. When I brush my hands against Austin's wrist, I see the muscles in his hand tense.

"Sorry," I say. "It's not too tight, is it?"

"No," he says, and maybe I imagine his voice sounds softer than normal. "No, it's great."

I take a step back. Such a large step back that I crash into one of our clothing racks. Deidre looks up at me sharply, just as I manage to steady the rack with my hands.

"This is actually really comfortable," Austin says loudly, like he's deliberately saving me from Deidre's glare. "Can I keep it?" he jokes.

"If you behave," Deidre says dryly. She stands up and comes over to him. I'm amazed at the ease with which she places her hands on him, smoothing out the shoulders of the shirt. I wish I could be so cool.

"I always behave," Austin replies. "I'm the good guy, right?"

He smiles at me as he says this, and I'm so relieved that Deidre's looking down at his shoes in this moment instead.

"I think you're ready to go," Deidre says, as she straightens back up.

Please, I add in my head. *Get out of here.*

Once Austin's gone, I feel like there's an invisible clock ticking in the room as I wait for Deidre to say something. And when she finally beckons me over, I brace myself.

"What do you think?" she asks, gesturing to two sketches she's done of adjustments to one of Raquel's dresses. "Left or right?"

I let out a breath. Then I contemplate the sketches.

"Right," I say. "That peplum style is great for Kandace's body type."

Deidre gives the smallest hint of a smile. It's not the same one she gave to Austin, but still, it's something.

"I thought so too," she says. "Thank you, Matilda."

"Anytime," I reply.

If Deidre has noticed me acting differently around Austin, she doesn't say anything more. Of course, she could just be silently noting it. Filing it away in the list of pluses and minuses I imagine she has against my name, somewhere in that impenetrable brain of hers.

I launch myself into the rest of the day, trying to be more focused. I'm out on set for half the time, so it's impossible to ignore Austin as he's filming his scenes. But I feel like I manage to strike a healthy balance of not looking at him too much, but also not *not* looking at him too much, because he's an actor and I'm a wardrobe assistant who should be looking at him. Professionally speaking.

Magic Season is coming together. The leads have settled into their roles, and I can start to see the story taking shape in the patchwork of scenes that we film mostly out of chronological order and more in an order that suits the complex logistics of our production schedule. The scenes we're filming today take place when Raquel first arrives in her hometown to care for her sick aunt and escape the job she's ruined back in the city. After meeting Grant at the tailor, she runs into Mitchell—her high school sweetheart, the *good guy*—in the street, buying Christmas presents. The tension between her old life and her new life becomes tauter. And so on and so forth, until her aunt passes away, she has a number of enchanting holiday epiphanies, and she ends up deciding to live happily ever after with Grant.

As I watch the scenes being filmed, I can't help but think about my own story. I've never considered myself the leading lady type. I can see Margot in that role—trekking through the wilderness on her own, having adventure after adventure. But I can't deny that finding a secret passageway is the kind of thing that normally happens to the protagonist. Unless, of course, the protagonist is the person on the other side of the wardrobe instead. The one I got a glimpse of last night. Who can't be Austin Farrow, because he's been staying out on his family's orchard. And who can't be anyone else from the production, according to Val. In fact, they shouldn't actually be anyone at all, according to Florence.

I consider for a moment that maybe this is why I hesitated to tell Val about the passageway. This is the first time in a while I've felt like my life might be interesting enough to rival the films I work behind the scenes on.

I want to go back through, I realize. I want to go back through the passageway and crack this case. I know it's risky, but I don't think my brain will be able to settle until I figure this out. It's almost like the wardrobe is calling to me, like a strange siren song that plays in the back of my mind all day.

But when we're winding down later and I'm back in the production office packing up, Henry comes to find me and interrupts my evening plans.

"We're going for drinks," he declares.

I glance up from the accessories I've been sorting. "Who's we?" I ask.

"Loren, Heidi, Val, me, you, and anyone else who desperately needs an alcoholic beverage. So probably half the crew."

"Where are you going?"

"*We*," Henry emphasizes, "are going to the brewery up on the corner. Three Pines Brewing Co. All local beers."

He can see me mulling this over.

"Come on," he insists. "We have a late call time tomorrow. And you know our rule."

I wouldn't say it's a *rule* exactly, but a few of us who've worked on a couple of productions together like to go out for a quick dinner or drink together at least once a week, normally on a day when we wrap early and start late the next day. It helps keep us sane, remembering there's a world outside the production.

Normally I'd be clamoring for a drink, but I still feel that tug inside me, pulling me to the wardrobe instead.

"Mattie," Henry says sternly.

"What?" I ask.

He comes over to me and places both hands on my shoulders, like he's a coach pumping me up for a race.

"You need a drink," he says to me.

"Why?"

"Because. You've seemed a little high strung lately."

"No, I haven't," I immediately say.

Henry raises an eyebrow.

"Have I?" I end weakly.

"I mean, you're still amazing. But yeah, a little." He narrows his eyes. "That guy's not bothering you again, is he?"

"What guy?"

"You know, the one we hate."

I pause for a moment before saying his name. "Jack?"

"See, my brain literally wiped his name out of existence," Henry says. "That's how much I dislike him."

"Well, no, he can't bother me anymore. I blocked his number ages ago."

"That's the energy we love to see."

I give a small smile. And all of a sudden, I feel like Henry's right. Maybe I do need a drink.

"Give me ten minutes," I say.

TWELVE

Three Pines Brewing Co. is in an old converted warehouse by the river, just on the outskirts of town. There's a snug garden out back bordered by pine trees (suspiciously more than three), which are draped in strings of gaudy lights. Summer twilight casts a dreamy haze over the scene, and it feels like it could be one of our film sets.

I'm seated on an Adirondack chair, talking to Val, who's managed to negotiate cheap drinks for all of us through her local connections. The pilsner in my hand is going down way too well.

"I mean, on the one hand, I feel like I know what I want," Val is saying. "But then on the other hand, I'm totally confused."

Val and I have been deep into a conversation about her relationship with her long-term boyfriend for the last fifteen minutes. He's her college sweetheart, and they both grew up in Casey River. Lately, her boyfriend's been feeling restless, and Val can't decide how she feels about it.

"Let's break it down," I say, taking a generous sip of my pilsner. "What's the main dilemma?"

"Okay, the thing is, I've always been a homebody," Val replies. "I like being comfortable, you know. I honestly think I'd be happy being a housewife—two kids, some chickens, baking bread every day. That kind of thing."

"Some days I see the appeal," I agree.

"And I always thought he wanted the same thing. But now he's suddenly decided he's hell bent on traveling the world."

"People can change their minds about things," I say gently. "Does he want to travel the world *with* you?"

"Yeah, of course. He's practically begging me. But that's the problem. I'm comfortable here."

"You could compromise," I suggest. "Like, you could travel with him for a bit and see how it goes. He might get his fix and come back ready to settle down. Or maybe you'll love it, and you'll change your mind. You'd make a killer itinerary, at the very least."

Val laughs. "Thanks. But I've always preferred to make grand travel plans for other people. Not myself."

"Our travel and accommodation coordinator really doesn't like to travel?"

Val shrugs. "I'm indifferent. I like a vacation. But I have no desire to spend months overseas." She sighs. "Maybe we're just not compatible. Maybe our relationship has run its course."

"Do you have to decide anytime soon?"

"Probably. He doesn't want to do another winter here. So I only have a few months to figure out if I want to go with him or not."

Val picks at the label of her drink.

"I hate making decisions," I empathize.

"I'm normally good at it."

"Good at what?"

Henry's come to join us, pulling up a spare Adirondack chair and forming a little circle.

"I'm trying to decide whether to break up with a guy who might be my soulmate," Val says dramatically.

"Well, if he was your soulmate, you wouldn't be struggling to decide whether to break up with him," offers Henry.

He has a point.

"Maybe I don't even believe in soulmates," Val muses.

"I do," Henry declares. "But I think you can have more than one."

"Doesn't that defeat the purpose?" I ask.

"No," says Henry. "I think you have different soulmates for different times in your life. It's like fashion, right? Your favorite outfit right now wasn't your favorite outfit ten years ago. You outgrow things. Your style changes. Makes sense for your soulmate to change too."

"That's a good point," Val says.

"People aren't clothes," I challenge.

Henry laughs. "Try telling Deidre that."

"Besides," I continue. "My favorite item of clothing is a blouse that I bought in my last year of high school—literally ten years ago. It's been with me through a lot; it doesn't have a single rip or hole, and it gets more comfortable with age. It still fits, and I'm going to want to wear it forever."

"So that blouse is your soulmate," says Val.

"It's served me better than any guy I've dated, at least," I joke.

I can feel myself getting lighter with every sip of beer I take. Things that seemed serious earlier today don't seem so serious anymore. Henry was right—I really did need a drink.

I finish my pilsner way too quickly and need to go to the restroom shortly after. So I leave Val and Henry to their soulmate debate and head into the brewery.

Three Pines is understandably busy, given that it's one of the only bars in Casey River, save for the dingy sports bar where we filmed our *Magic Season* scenes and one very expensive wine cellar. I push through the crowd of bodies, struggling not to get entangled in more conversations with fellow crew who are already on their second or third rounds.

Once I've finished in the restroom, I touch up my makeup, taking the opportunity to dab concealer under my sleep-deprived eyes and add a swipe of lipstick. Then I head to the bar to get another drink. I know the sensible thing to do would be to finish the night early and catch up on sleep, but that pilsner was too good, and we do have a late call time tomorrow, after all. So I head up to the long bar and place my elbows on the counter as I wait for the bartender to notice me.

"Just another pilsner, please," I say, when he finally turns around.

"Coming up," he says, making his way over to the taps.

"Make that two," says a voice next to me.

I feel an effervescence in my gut, like my stomach is full of bubbly champagne rather than beer.

I didn't know Austin was here. I thought I would have noticed. It's the way he always seems to take up so much space in my vision, despite his standard measurements. He's wearing an olive-colored T-shirt tonight, which matches his eyes so beautifully that I contemplate telling Deidre we need to incorporate it into Mitchell's wardrobe.

"Oh, hi," I say stupidly.

"Hi," Austin replies, leaning his elbow on the bar next to me. He smiles, and I truly have no idea what to do.

"They do a good pilsner," I say, continuing with the useless comments.

"Right?"

The bartender has set our two pints on the counter, and Austin's handing over a couple of bills. I realize too late that he's paying for mine as well.

"Oh, no," I say, reaching into my purse. "I've got mine."

"Don't worry about it." Austin lightly pats my hand down. "What goes around comes around."

"You don't have to do that," I insist.

The bartender looks between the two of us, holding the bills.

"It's fine," Austin says to both the bartender and me. The bartender opens the register and starts serving the next customer, while Austin turns back to me.

"This doesn't mean you owe me or anything," he says. "I've just had enough drinks bought for me in my life, I feel like it all balances itself out in the end."

"I'll buy you one at the wrap party or something," I offer.

"Two problems with that," Austin says. "One, all good wrap parties should have an open bar. Two, wrap's a while away—you really think we won't be having drinks together again before then?"

I can feel a flush rise to my cheeks. What an audacious comment. At least, it would be if I'd said it, but Austin still seems so casual, I wonder if I've misheard.

"I don't know," I decide to say. "Our schedule's pretty packed."

"All the more reason to make sure we're staying hydrated, right?"

He doesn't seem fazed by my discouraging response. Instead, he raises his glass to mine, and I tap it against his in a cheers.

"Are you with the crew outside?" Austin asks, as he peels himself off the counter and starts to head toward the garden.

"Yeah," I say. "What about you?"

"Yeah, I came with a couple of the stunt guys. I've worked with them before."

"Out with the stunt guys. That could go one of two ways."

"Oh yeah?"

"Well, I've found that some of them are fitness freaks. So they don't drink at all. And the rest are absolute liabilities."

Austin laughs. "Accurate," he agrees. "Unfortunately—or fortunately—it's the liabilities out tonight."

Outside, the evening has grown even more beautiful, with the persistent purple light of dusk lingering. I can see that my chair next to Val and Henry is still vacant, waiting for me to return. In the other corner of the garden, I spot the stunt guys locked in a game of what looks like very competitive cornhole.

"Oh God," Austin groans, following my gaze. "I'm terrible at that game."

"Really? You seem . . . sporty."

"I do?"

"Moderately. Or maybe that's just all the baseball hats we're making Mitchell wear."

"I *was* decent at baseball in school, but then I gave it up because it clashed with theater and guitar lessons. To think, life could have turned out so differently."

"Yeah, maybe if you hadn't given it up, you'd be over there dominating cornhole with your perfect aim."

"Or maybe I wouldn't be here at all. It's baseball season now."

"What, Casey River doesn't have a major-league team?"

He throws his head back in a laugh. "Depends what kind of alternate world we're talking about."

For a moment, both of us look between where the stunt guys are and where Val and Henry are sitting. They've spotted me talking to Austin, and Henry is eyeing us with razor-sharp interest. I consider just downing my pilsner and disappearing right now so that I don't have to suffer through his inevitable questioning.

But then something even more disconcerting happens. Austin starts heading over in Val and Henry's direction.

"You coming?" he asks, when he sees me still rooted to the spot.

"You really hate cornhole that much?" I ask.

"Oh yeah," he replies. "Plus, I figure I should mingle."

I gather myself. "Okay," I say, looking around. "Sure, I'll find you a seat."

But he's already sweeping up a nearby Adirondack chair and carrying it over to the circle, where he places it next to the vacant one. The one that's waiting for me.

I look down into my glass. This wasn't how I expected the night to go. Coming out for drinks was meant to relax me, not set my nervous system on edge the way it is now, the way it has been since Austin appeared at the bar.

But just like last night, when I went through the wardrobe, I realize that the sensation isn't exactly an unpleasant one. My pulse is quick and my head is light and life is feeling a lot like one big dare lately, one big, open door waiting to be stepped through. Isn't this exactly what I've been wanting?

Besides, it would be rude now to walk away. Especially when Austin's just bought me a drink. So I head on over to the circle and slip into my chair and the conversation, like this is exactly where I'm meant to be.

THIRTEEN

Henry and I talked a while back—after a nightmare day on our last production—about how strange it is that actors are put on such a pedestal in the hierarchy of the industry. Don't get me wrong; it takes a hell of a lot of skill to do what they do, and they're integral to the success of any project, but making a movie is a massive team effort. Everyone's role is important, and everyone works extremely hard to get these stories on screen. But no one will ever know my name or Henry's or recognize our faces the way they know Kandace Connolly and Hayden King. Our weekend activities won't make it into the gossip magazines. On the rare occasion we might be invited to an awards show, no one will care what we're wearing.

This was all exacerbated by working with an actor on that film who didn't like anyone in the crew making eye contact with him because it distracted him from his work. Never mind that the effort it took for us to constantly worry about whether we were accidentally making eye contact was a distraction from *our* work. *He* was more important.

Fortunately, most actors—especially on the type of productions I work on—don't play into the hierarchy. They're normal human beings, albeit always somehow a little shinier and more charismatic than the rest of us. Sometimes, they'll end up good friends with the crew. I've even heard of a famous actress who ended up marrying the camera assistant from one of her films. It's no more outrageous than any other workplace romance, really.

Not that I'm actively thinking about workplace romances. Mostly, as I sit in my Adirondack chair in the garden and sip my pilsner, I'm thinking about how normal Austin seems. He and Val have been chatting about people they both know in Casey River, given that Austin grew up nearby. It turns out that Val's uncle used to own a grocery store in town that the Farrow orchard supplied apples to. And that Val and Austin were both guests at Val's cousin's wedding the previous year.

"That happens around here," Austin says to Henry and me with a shrug. "My dad always says that we've got the best of both worlds—big landscapes, small communities. So everyone kind of ends up knowing everyone else."

"See, that's why I love this place," Val says. "That's why I don't want to leave."

"You're leaving?" Austin asks.

Val takes a breath in and explains her conundrum to Austin, about her boyfriend wanting to travel and her wanting to stay put. I watch Austin out of the corner of my eye as he listens intently, his finger stroking his bottom lip, genuinely invested in what Val has to say.

"That's a tough one," Austin says when Val's finished.

"So, what would you do?" Val urges. "Say, for example, you were offered your dream role. But your girlfriend wanted to move to the other side of the world instead. What would you do?"

"Well," says Austin. "To start with, I don't have a girlfriend."

I can't be one hundred percent sure, but I feel like, in this moment, Austin glances at me briefly out of the corner of his eye. I have a mouthful of beer, which I swallow too quickly and then have to pretend I'm not choking on, as Val continues.

"All right, but just pretend for a moment. You have a girlfriend. You've been offered your dream role. You have to choose between her and the role. What would you choose?"

Austin bites his lip.

"Actually, I've kind of been in this situation before," he says.

"Really?" Henry scoots forward in his seat, like a kid at story time.

"Yeah," Austin replies. "Only it wasn't a girlfriend."

Val raises an eyebrow. "A boyfriend?"

"No, it wasn't a romantic thing at all. It was my brother, Parker."

To my distress, Austin glances directly at me here.

"Parker is Maddie's dad," he explains, still looking at me.

"Excuse me?" Henry asks in bewilderment.

"Not me, obviously," I say. "Maddie with two *d*'s."

Austin laughs at Henry's clear confusion. "My brother, Parker, has a daughter, who's also named Maddie," he explains.

"*Interesting*," Henry says, looking at me pointedly. He can obviously tell that Austin and I have already discussed this, and I wish my Adirondack chair would sink into the ground and take me with it.

"Okay, so back to the story," Val says, with typical Val efficiency. "What was the situation with your brother?"

"I'll try to keep it short," Austin continues. He looks away from me now and back to the circle. "So, this was about seven years ago now. I'd just moved to LA, start of my career, doing audition after audition. Nothing was landing, but finally after about six months, I was cast in a role in this crime show. *Water Street Files*—not sure if you remember it. It ended after three seasons. My part wasn't huge, but it was the kind that's normally a springboard for bigger things."

He looks around us, as if making sure we want him to continue, but of course we do. We'll listen to anything he has to say.

"So, we're in prep, due to start filming in a couple of weeks. When Parker turns up at my door. He's suddenly booked this round-the-world trip, and he wants me to go with him. Which is unexpected, to be honest. Parker's not the spontaneous type. He'd just finished agricultural school and was all set to start managing the orchard, which had always been the plan. So this was pretty out of the blue."

"But you couldn't go," says Val. "Because you'd finally landed a real role."

"Ah, yeah." Austin runs a hand over his face. "You'd think it would have been an obvious decision. But . . . like I said, this was out of the blue. I was worried about Parks, like worried he was having some kind of breakdown or quarter-life crisis. I called my parents, and they were worried about the same thing. He hadn't been acting like himself. We thought the weight of taking on the business might be getting to him."

"So did you talk to him about it?" I ask quietly.

Austin turns to look at me again. "I tried," he says. "I explained to him that this *Water Street Files* role was pretty important to me but that if he wanted to hang out in LA for a couple of months with me until I finished filming, then we could travel after. I tried to ask him why he was suddenly so desperate to get away. But Parker's never been the type to talk about his feelings. He just insisted on leaving, then and there. With or without me."

"So what did you do?" Henry urges.

Austin sighs. "I called up the studio and backed out of the role. And I went traveling for six months with Parker instead."

"No!" Henry exclaims.

"I know," says Austin. "It should have been the nail in my career coffin—as a new actor, you really shouldn't be turning down any offers. But I was too worried about Parks to let him go on his own. And I was right to be. Over those six months, I realized that he really had been on the verge of a breakdown. He'd needed that trip. And I think he'd needed me there too. We've always been pretty close."

"That was a big sacrifice for you, though," I say.

Austin fixes me with a gaze I'm starting to find familiar.

"Maybe," he says. "But you do these things for the people you care about, right? And it all worked out in the end. Parker actually met his wife toward the end of our trip—I wingmanned for him at a beach bar in Thailand. He brought her back here and she loved the orchard life, so Parker was ready to take it on with her. He's still there now, married to his soulmate, with a cute kid and cute cat, perfectly happy."

Val lets out a breath.

"Sorry," says Austin. "I didn't mean for that to be such an intense story. Like I said, it all worked out fine in the end." He laughs, uncharacteristically self-conscious for a moment, and takes a large sip of his beer. "Basically, my advice is . . . just go with your gut."

"But what about you?" Val asks.

"Me?" Austin says.

"Yeah. You made it sound like you had to choose between your brother and your career. But you obviously still made it as an actor."

Val gestures at Austin and all around us, as if the lights on the pine trees were stage lights. We know what she means. Austin's acting plans obviously didn't come to a total end all those years ago; otherwise he wouldn't be here in Casey River filming *Magic Season*.

"Oh yeah," says Austin. "I went back to LA after traveling and started from scratch. It was hard, especially because the studio that did *Water Street Files* refused to cast me in anything. But eventually, I started landing some roles. And now here I am, with all of you."

There's something niggling at me. Something about Austin's story that has stuck to me, like lint to black cotton. Even as the conversation changes direction, I still find myself running over it in my head.

Suddenly, it comes to me. And the beer has made me bold enough to ask.

"What was the role?" I ask.

Austin turns to look at me. I've blurted the question out, almost rudely, while they were in the middle of talking about Val's uncle's grocery store again.

But Austin doesn't look affronted. He still has that ever-lingering smile on his face, those calm green eyes.

"Which role?" he asks.

"The one you turned down. In the crime show, *Water Street Files*. What role were you supposed to play?"

"Oh, man." He runs a hand through his hair. "It was a while ago. I've read for so many parts since then. But from what I remember, the character was this son of a rich businessman or something like that, who got caught up in the wrong crowd. He was the getaway car driver for this bank robbery that went wrong and became an accessory to murder. Then his rich father tried to cover it all up."

"The getaway car driver," I repeat.

"I know . . . the closest I've ever come to playing the bad guy," Austin says, referring back to our earlier conversation.

I can feel my heart thudding in my throat. I know the next question is going to sound oddly specific, but I'm too close to back down now.

"Was there a wanted poster with the character's face on it?" I ask. "In the show?"

"Yeah, that's right," Austin says, clicking his fingers. "I remember, because that's how the dad finds out what his son has done. Why—have you seen it?"

I haven't seen a single episode of *Water Street Files*, but I find myself nodding anyway, slowly, automatically, like I'm a puppet and someone else is pulling the strings.

"Please don't tell me what you thought of the guy who did end up with the part," Austin continues. "I don't want to know what I missed out on."

FOURTEEN

Back in my apartment, the first thing I do is find season 1 of *Water Street Files* and cast it to the television in the living room.

We stayed at Three Pines Brewing Co. for another half an hour after the conversation with Austin finished. Austin left shortly after it, saying that he'd promised to meet Hayden King for a nightcap before the bars in town closed.

I thought I imagined that Austin seemed apologetic about this. Like he didn't want to leave. Like his gaze lingered on me as he stood up from his Adirondack chair, twinkle lights reflected in his eyes.

Henry seemed to notice this too. Because he rounded on me as soon as Austin left, looking as giddy as a kid on Christmas morning, poised to attack me with a dozen questions I definitely wasn't equipped to handle. But then Loren and Heidi from hair and makeup came to join us, along with one of the stunt guys who's attractive in a way that's definitely Henry's type. And his attention was pulled away from me. Thankfully.

Because I've got more important questions on my mind now. Like whether the wanted poster I found next door is connected to Austin's would-be role in *Water Street Files*. And how, if he turned that role down, his face still ended up on the poster.

The storyline Austin described with the bank robbery gone wrong doesn't start until the end of the first episode of the series. When it does, the actor who appears on screen playing the getaway car driver isn't Austin, clearly. This actor's hair is dark and wavy, his eyes blue, his face more chiseled. But they're similar enough that I can see how Austin could have been cast in the role—a charming, easily molded kind of guy.

I watch the show on double speed so that I can get to the part where the wanted poster appears. There it is, at the start of episode 3. The character's dad is gawking at it on a lamppost in the downtown business district.

I hit pause on the television and stare.

It's the same poster that I found next door, no doubt about it.

Words stamped in bright red across the top of the page.

A caption reading, **CAN YOU HELP? $5,000 REWARD FOR INFORMATION.**

Only the face sketched on the poster is different. It's not Austin Farrow. It's the actor who took his place.

Beer and curiosity roil around inside me, making my head pound.

Making it reckless.

The next thing I know, I'm standing in front of the wardrobe in the bedroom, with my fist raised against the panel in the back. And with the same surprising lack of inhibition that's led me here so far, I put my fist to the panel, and I knock.

Now that I've done it, there's no going back. I just have to wait and hope there's no response.

Or hope there is one?

Moments pass, and nothing happens. I hear no footsteps, no meows. The compartment stays shut.

But it's like I'm under a spell. I can feel a tug inside my chest. It could be heartburn from too many beers. But it feels more like there's an invisible rope hooked around part of my rib cage, and someone is pulling on the other end.

Before I know what I'm doing, I'm opening the door for a third time.

The sight and smell of the wardrobe next door seem almost familiar now. I press my body through the hanging jackets and the neat T-shirts. For the first time, I realize that they're not exactly Austin's size. They're about a size or half a size smaller. Though the shoes are a match. And I can smell that sweet yet earthy cologne, which jolts me back to being with Austin in the wardrobe room earlier today.

I can't stop now that I'm here. I walk into the bedroom and look around. I expect my heart to be hammering in my throat, the way it was earlier this evening as Austin talked. But instead, I feel strangely calm. Like this is all happening in a dream or a first-person-perspective scene in a film, where I'm in an unseen body and someone—or something—else is calling the shots.

The leather folio of papers that contained the wanted poster is no longer on the bed. But my eyes fall on the nightstand, and I see it resting there instead, next to the dog-eared copy of the Louis L'Amour story collection.

The whiskey glass is gone.

I move over to the nightstand and pick up the folio. The wanted poster isn't the first page in the folio. Instead, I find a miscellaneous collection of papers in no particular order—there are call sheets and concert tickets, crumpled contracts and airline boarding passes. The name on all these is unmistakable. *Austin Farrow.*

Behind the miscellaneous mementos, there's a stack of lined notebook paper scrawled with messy handwriting. I cast my eyes over it, but it's almost illegible. I can barely make out any full words, but from the structure of the lines, they look like poetry or song lyrics.

This suddenly feels too personal. Before, I could trick myself into thinking I was merely visiting a set or a stranger's house. Now, I'm almost certain I'm standing in Austin Farrow's bedroom. Which of course, still makes no sense, because he's not supposed to be here. But why else would I be holding a folio full of his personal files?

I tell myself I need to close the folio. I need to close the folio and back out of here. But instead, I keep looking. I pull out a creased trail map of Casey River. Behind the map, I feel a thicker piece of paper between the notepaper sheets. As I slide it out, I see that it's a funeral booklet with a prayer printed on the back.

With an unsteady hand, I move to turn the booklet over.

Then something causes me to freeze.

"Don't move," comes a voice from behind me.

There's no need to tell me. As if under a hex, my feet feel rooted to the ground and my limbs are numb. I'm not sure I could move even if I wanted to.

I didn't hear anything to warn me that someone had come into the room. Not the door opening, not the footsteps on the carpet. But then again, I'd been busy swiping through the folio. The folio that doesn't belong to me, in the bedroom that doesn't belong to me.

And now I've been caught red handed.

By someone with a voice that sounds awfully familiar.

"This isn't what it looks like," I say, still facing the nightstand. "I can explain."

"Turn around," says the voice.

FIFTEEN

I turn around slowly until, for the third time that day, I'm face-to-face with Austin Farrow.

Only, he doesn't look exactly like the Austin Farrow I know.

It's subtle, but the Austin standing there in the bedroom looks . . . faded. There are dark circles under his eyes, and his hair is haphazardly tousled, making it seem longer. He also appears gaunter than I remember, but that's not possible. No one loses weight in a matter of hours.

That's when I realize Austin's pointing something at me that makes my heart rate spike for a second.

But it's just the handle of a guitar, the body of which is tucked firmly under Austin's arm.

"It's heavier than it looks," Austin says, following my gaze to the guitar. "It would hurt, if it hit you. I don't want to hit you, so please just stay where you are."

We were sitting next to each other on those Adirondack chairs, sipping beers together, mere hours ago. His gaze was soft, his smile sparkling.

But Austin isn't showing any signs of this now. He isn't showing any signs of recognition at all. Then again, the bedroom is lit by little more than moonlight, and this is a very different context than the others we've met in. This isn't the wardrobe department or a busy bar. This is his bedroom. Which I haven't been invited into. No matter which way you look at this, I'm not supposed to be here.

"I know this looks very, very weird," I say, trying to keep my voice calm. "But I can explain. It's me, Mattie. Wardrobe assistant Mattie."

I step closer and Austin takes a step back.

"I have no idea what you're talking about," he says.

"Mattie with two *t*'s," I say. "Like your niece's name?"

Austin's frown deepens. "I don't have a niece."

I falter. "But you said . . . your brother . . ."

Something dark flashes across Austin's face.

"How do you know about my brother?" he says, and his voice is dangerously hushed.

"You told me," I say.

I don't even know how I'm getting words out at this point—my throat is paper dry, and everything seems to stick.

Austin narrows his eyes at me and tilts his head a fraction.

"Wait," he says. "I do know you, don't I?"

He lowers the guitar and closes some of the gap between us. As he moves forward, I smell whiskey. And I realize that Austin might be more intoxicated than he was at Three Pines. His movements are shaky, and there's something vacant in his expression. It's almost like behind his eyes, he's a different person.

"You're the girl from the bookstore," he says.

I frown. "No," I reply.

"Yeah," Austin argues. "I remember you now. You were there behind the counter today when I went in."

"You must be getting mixed up," I say. "I don't work in a bookstore."

"I'm not mixed up," Austin says through gritted teeth. "I remember now. I . . . I *noticed* you. I remember."

A flush has risen to his cheeks, behind his stubble, and I don't know if it's frustration or embarrassment or something else. I'm reminded of someone much older, someone who's grown to doubt their own mind, insisting they remember their own name.

I'm becoming surer now that Austin's really out of it. I don't know how many beers he had at Three Pines before I started talking to him.

He seemed fine, but I was also tipsy. Then he went for a nightcap with Hayden King. And in the hour or so since then, it smells like he's consumed more whiskey.

He must be so wasted that he doesn't even remember where he knows me from. My stomach grows leaden, and I know I have more urgent things to be thinking about right now, but I can't ignore the dark disappointment I feel realizing that the Austin Farrow I thought I knew isn't the real Austin Farrow at all.

"Did you . . . follow me home?" Austin asks.

"No," I reply. "Jesus, no, I didn't follow you home. I'm staying in this apartment complex too. Next door to you. Our wardrobes are connected by a secret passageway."

I don't know if it's terrible timing or great timing, but the black-and-white cat chooses this moment to pad through the bedroom door. It meows and comes right over to me, curling itself around my legs, like I'm an old friend.

"Boots," Austin says, his voice gentler when he speaks to the cat. "Come here, buddy."

"See, he knows me," I say, as the cat—Boots—presses his head against my calf. "He's the reason I found the passageway. I heard him meowing one night, and that's when I found these panels that connect our two rooms. Our neighbor told me that no one was staying in here at the moment, so I thought the cat might be stuck. I was just trying to help."

This is a little lie. The first time I came through the wardrobe, perhaps, I was trying to help the cat. This time, it was unhinged curiosity that brought me through. But given the way Austin's looking at me right now, I need to find some way to soften the madness of all this.

"A secret passageway," Austin repeats.

"Yes," I reply. "You can see for yourself."

Austin walks slowly over to the wardrobe, keeping a still-wary eye on me. He pulls the door open, and when he sees the open panel in the back, he draws in a sharp breath.

"See?" I ask.

Austin reaches out a hand and swings the secret door back and forth, as if he has to touch it to confirm it's real. I wonder if he can see through into my wardrobe, to the dresses on the rack and the bras on the floor.

"Fuck," he says softly.

"I know," I reply.

Austin turns to me. For a moment, his expression softens, and he looks more like the Austin I saw earlier today. He hasn't come close to an eye-crinkling smile yet, but I can see the river green in them now.

"I've lived here for six months," he says. "And I didn't know this existed."

"You've lived here for six months? But I thought you said you've been staying at the orchard."

"No," Austin says. "I only go to the orchard on weekends to help Dad out, but . . . wait, how do you know about the orchard?"

"You . . . also told me that?"

"At the bookstore?"

I don't know how to reply to this. I thought that maybe if we talked more, Austin would remember where he knew me from. But he's still sticking with his bookstore story. And I feel afraid to question him. I clocked the way he gritted his teeth and insisted he wasn't misremembering where we know each other from. He must get frustrated with himself when he drinks too much. I don't want to stoke that fire. I don't want to make this any worse than it already is.

"Look, I'm sorry for alarming you," I say. "And for coming in here uninvited. It's not normally the kind of thing I'd do. I'm normally very sensible."

Austin's mouth twitches.

"I just needed to make sure," I continue. "You know, that there wasn't anything dangerous in here."

"Well. I'm a lot of things, but I'm not dangerous."

Both of us realize that he's still holding the guitar then, and he places it down on the bed.

"I kind of lied," he says. "It's not actually that heavy."

"Depends how strong your swing is, I suppose."

For a brief moment, this all almost seems comical. I have to press down a feverish laugh, and the first glimmer of something like a smile also flashes across Austin's face.

"If it makes you feel better," he says, "I'll get some nails, and I'll board up that passageway from my side. So you won't need to worry about it anymore."

"Okay," I say, nodding. "Thank you."

"No problem."

I swallow. "I guess I should go, then."

"I guess so," Austin replies.

I want to ask more. I want to ask how much whiskey he's had to drink, and why that wanted poster has his face on it, and if he remembers me rolling up his shirtsleeves today.

But I know that there's nothing worse than overstaying a welcome that was never even extended in the first place. So, I turn to head back through the wardrobe.

As I do, Austin places a light hand on my arm. My skin sears where he's touched me. He drops his hand quickly, as if he's felt it too.

"It was Mattie, right?" he asks.

I nod. "With two *t*'s."

"Mattie with two *t*'s," Austin says softly.

I hold his gaze, hoping that he might be remembering me. But the shadow stays on his face, and eventually he gives me a final nod. And I'm forced to bundle whatever dignity I have left and carry it with me, out of Austin's bedroom and back to my own.

SIXTEEN

Up until last year, I always considered myself a stable person.

Almost to a fault. Almost to the extent of being dull. "Basic bitch" is an insult, after all. That's me. I'm basic. I like fashion and movies and books and wine and hiking; I grew up in the suburbs, my parents are still happily married, and I have a small but strong group of friends. In terms of my love life, I had a steady relationship in college that ended when he moved overseas, and a handful of flings and situationships after that. And while I was always invested in the guys I dated, I couldn't even say it was to a particularly deranged level that might at least make me interesting.

Then there was Jack.

The thing is, stable girls aren't meant to fall for honey traps. I've read and watched stories of women who got swindled by con artists and cult leaders, and I always carelessly suspected that there must be something twisted or broken or missing within those women to begin with. That's why they were targets. That's why it worked on them.

I had no guard up before Jack. Because I never needed to before. I came from a boring, stable family. All my past relationships ended with a whimper, not a bang. Nothing truly bad had happened to me in my life. And this was an absolute privilege, of course.

But having no shell or thick skin means that your flesh is pretty much there for the taking.

The way Jack picked away at my brain was subtle, at first. It took me longer than I like to admit to figure out what was happening.

I thought I was just having a good time at that party, but when we got home, Jack told me I was embarrassingly drunk. "You always get like this," he said, as if it were a recurring problem. I watched what I drank after that, even though Margot told me she'd never worried about my drinking.

I thought that having a relatively solid career working in the film industry was something to be proud of. But as Jack pointed out, I was still just an assistant. Surely once you hit your mid-twenties, you shouldn't be an assistant anymore. That was true. Maybe I was letting the perceived glamour of the industry blind me to the fact that I was going nowhere.

I'd always thought that I was a critical thinker. But Jack told me I came across as too opinionated. It was unattractive sometimes, he said. I could tone it down a notch. So I did.

Little scratches, bit by bit, gradually stripping off my soft skin. I didn't even realize until the bone started to show.

It was the first time in my life that I really started to doubt my own mind.

It sticks with you. And even once you start to heal and feel stable again, basic again, you're still sometimes struck with the thought that your mind isn't a sanctuary anymore.

———

Like always, Margot helps me feel sane.

My encounter with Austin through the wardrobe last night took on a dreamlike quality. Everything was blurry around the edges thanks to the beer and the moonlit room and my mortification over being caught intruding. Austin's strangely skewed appearance and his mis-memory of me plunged the whole thing even deeper into the land of the surreal.

Just like a dream, I have to record it before it slips away, like holding water in your hands. And Margot is my vessel.

I tell her everything this time. Including the parts about Austin and all our encounters at work so far. I don't need to worry about her probing me about whether I'm attracted to him. Because that feeling has to disappear now. I can't still feel that way after what's happened.

"All right," Margot says over the phone, when I relay all this the next morning as I walk into town to clear my head. "This guy clearly has a drinking problem. Like, a blackout drinking problem. He must have hidden it when he was with you guys at the bar but then unraveled later. Poor dude."

"I just don't get it," I say. "He seemed so normal during the day. He didn't seem like he had any kind of problem."

"Mattie, babe," says Margot. "I don't want to be the one to say it, but you're not exactly . . ."

"The best judge of character, I know." I sigh.

"However, in your defense, I'm looking him up now, and you're right—he does come across as very normal. Very stable."

Very stable. We'd almost be a match made in heaven if we'd met under different circumstances.

"Also, pretty damn cute," Margot adds.

"He's an actor," I say quickly.

"Is that an explanation for his attractiveness or for his drinking problem?"

"Both? The thing I still don't get, though, is that wanted poster. Regardless of whether Austin has a drinking problem, I still don't understand why he had that poster with his face on it if he never even played that part."

"Could the poster be from another role?"

"He's never played a character like that, according to his filmography. And according to him, because he told me himself that he doesn't play bad guys."

"Okay," says Margot. "Okay, well, let's think about it. Austin was originally offered that part in the show . . . what's it called again?"

"*Water Street Files*."

"Yes. Actually, I think I binged that in a week once. It was . . . not very good, from memory."

"Your bar for crime shows is too high."

"It is. But back to the important part. If Austin was originally cast in the show, maybe they'd already created those posters before he pulled out. And maybe he kept one, for some reason. Like, as a reminder of what he missed out on."

"That's . . . a semiplausible theory," I admit.

"It's either that or the wanted poster isn't a prop at all," Margot continues. "And Austin's actually a fugitive."

"I mean, I know he's no Hollywood A-lister, but he has a public profile. It would be pretty hard to be on the run from the law and be a working actor."

"Maybe it's not current. Maybe he *was* on the run from the law, at some point in his past. Maybe that's connected to why he has a drinking problem."

"There's no evidence of that in anything I can find online."

"Okay. Well, as disappointed as I am that we're likely not dealing with a criminal case here, I suppose that's good news. Given that he has access to your room."

I think back to Austin's face when I told him about the passageway, when he touched the doors between our rooms.

"I honestly think he didn't know about that," I say. "I mean, I know he's an actor. But he really did seem surprised. And anyway, he said he was going to board the passageway up from his side. So we won't need to worry about that."

"Okay, good. You still sound worried, though."

"Well, I have to see him today."

This thought has been running through my mind since I got out of bed this morning, not that I got much sleep anyway. I have no choice but to see Austin at work today, and I don't know what to expect. I'm not sure what will be worse—if he remembers last night or if he doesn't.

"What if he tells someone he found me hanging out uninvited in his bedroom?" I continue to Margot. "What if I lose my job over this?"

"That's a lot of what-ifs," Margot replies. "Mattie, you're smart and measured and you're good at your job. You just need to turn up and see what happens. You'll be able to handle it."

Always the fire sign to my earth sign, Margot recognizes when the ground underneath me is starting to crumble. And she helps to fuse it back together.

I'm on the edge of the town square now, a block from our converted bed-and-breakfast production office. I can already see the crew milling around on the street outside. So I say goodbye to Margot and brace myself.

I don't really have a choice. There's a *chance* that I'll turn up to the production office and be fired. But if I don't turn up to the production office at all, there's a *certainty* that I'll be fired.

And even though I've been questioning lately whether I even like this job, I realize that I don't want to be fired. It could be my persisting desire to please Deidre, or perhaps the fact that I'll be financially screwed if I don't get this paycheck. Maybe it's even something more than that. I don't know anymore.

Whatever it is, I grit my teeth and open the door to the office gingerly, like a bomb is going to detonate when I walk in.

Inside, everything is normal.

And by that, I mean that it does kind of look like a bomb has gone off, but it's the organized chaos you always expect inside a production office.

Nothing seems awry. Everyone gives me the standard greeting. There's no air of tension or awkwardness. Those who were out for drinks last night are moving a bit more slowly than normal, but that's it.

Val gives me her regular wave from her desk, which is the moment when I feel my breath steady. Val would know. If Austin had reported any of this, then Val would definitely know, given the link to our accommodation. But she obviously knows nothing. She just grumbles about why I let her have that extra drink last night, before her phone interrupts us again.

It's much the same with Henry, who stayed out even later than I did and is clearly regretting it. He's drinking a bottle of Coke instead of his regular coffee, which he never does, and is wearing jeans and a plain T-shirt, which he also never does.

"I think that shirt's ironed enough," I tell him, as I start getting our bits and pieces ready for the day.

Henry's been steam ironing the same spot on a shirt for about five minutes, clearly thankful for the repetitive motion. At my comment, he sighs, puts down the iron, and finishes his Coke.

"Why is catering serving *granola pots* for breakfast today of all days?" he mumbles. "I need something with bacon in it."

"You're a vegetarian."

"Now you understand the direness of the situation."

This is great. I thought *I* had a cloud of regret and embarrassment hanging over my head from last night, but it's simply blending in with everyone else's cloud of regret and embarrassment. Maybe, just maybe, I've gotten away with all this.

But then Deidre walks in, and the straight set of her lips causes my heart to drop into my stomach.

"Matilda, can I have a word please?"

Oh God. My relief was premature. This is it. Deidre knows. Austin came to his senses and complained to her about finding me in his room last night. I'm done for. It's all over.

I follow Deidre out of our main wardrobe room and into a small alcove under the stairs in the hallway that Deidre has recently commandeered as her own private office. Her laptop is open on a small desk, and Deidre walks over to check something on it before straightening back up and looking at me.

I've always admired Deidre Dotto's style. It's like a thermostat. She can turn the temperature up and down perfectly to suit the occasion. She knows how to stun at parties and awards shows, in glittering gowns and feathered jackets, with earrings the size of saucers and shoes that could kill a man.

On set, she turns it down to a warm, comfortable temperature. She wears athleisure leggings and cashmere sweaters, loose-fitting jeans and expensive sneakers. Today she's wearing an organic cotton T-shirt tucked into high-waisted linen trousers.

There's no such thing as a bad outfit, she told me once. *Only one that's wrong for the occasion.*

She always looks so good. It's why she scares me. It's why I admire her. It's why this next part is probably going to hurt more than I expected.

"I need your help," Deidre says.

I blink, thrown. "Oh," I say.

"I know this isn't technically part of your job," Deidre continues. "But I need to buy a gift for my sister-in-law—Eleanor's younger sister—who's your age, and I just have no idea what to buy her. She doesn't like clothes."

I stare at Deidre, trying to process the whiplash of thinking I was about to get fired, and then getting this instead.

"She doesn't like clothes," I repeat, like an idiot.

"Well, she wears clothes," Deidre points out. "But she's not interested in them. Or jewelry. Or anything else that I'd normally have an opinion about."

I try to gather myself.

"Okay," I say, nodding slowly. "Okay, well, what else do you know about her?"

Deidre sighs, like this is a supremely difficult question.

"She's in her thirties," she repeats. "She's outdoorsy. I think she likes hiking. You know about that, right?"

"A bit. I mean, I'm no expert, but I know a little. It might be risky to buy her any technical gear, though. People can be picky about that kind of stuff." I know this from the agony of having to find a present for Margot every year.

"Right, okay, well, what else do I know? She's just moved into a new apartment. We helped her move her sofa."

Something stirs in the back of my mind.

"Oh!" I say, getting an idea. "When I moved into my apartment, someone bought me a coffee-table book about '90s fashion. Which I loved. Coffee-table books are always a safe gift idea, especially if she's just moved."

Deidre clicks her fingers. "That's a good idea."

"There's a cute bookstore in town," I say. "I can go have a look in there for you later today if you'd like?"

"That would be wonderful. I appreciate it."

Deidre bustles off then, leaving me standing in the alcove, recovering from the huge weight that's been dropped from my shoulders.

I'm so relieved about the bullet I seem to have dodged that I don't even make the connection right away. It's not until I'm in the bookstore later that day that I remember.

This is where Austin mistakenly thought he'd recognized me from last night.

And I only remember because, as I'm turning into an aisle of books, Austin's walking out of it.

SEVENTEEN

We literally collide.

I'm distracted looking at a coffee-table book I've spotted on a high shelf, and Austin's distracted looking down at a book in his hands. Our collision presses me into the shelves, and Austin places his hands on my shoulders to steady me.

"Woah," he says.

When I register who I've run into, my heart speeds up and my hands grow clammy.

Austin looks down at me. He appears to realize then that he basically has me pressed up against the bookshelf, and he takes a step back.

I wait for his eyes to narrow when he remembers our encounter last night.

I wait for his lips to turn down when he remembers he found me standing uninvited in his bedroom.

But instead, his face breaks into a warm smile.

"Mattie," he says. "Hey."

He's smiling at me. Austin's voice is light and friendly and he's smiling at me, revealing no leftover tension or awkwardness from the night before. In the sunshine that's streaming through the bookstore windows, he also looks normal. His eyes are bright and bagless. His hair looks tidier. He doesn't smell of alcohol. Henry looked worse than he does.

I realize that I'm staring, and I haven't even said hello back.

"Hi," I say, and my voice sounds like a different person's.

"How was the rest of last night?" Austin asks.

"Last night?" I repeat, panic rising.

"Yeah. How long did you guys stay at Three Pines?"

"Three Pines. Right. Um, not too much longer after you left. Maybe half an hour?"

"Great, so I didn't miss anything."

I shake my head. "How was your nightcap with Hayden?" I ask delicately.

"Oh, the usual. We shared a whiskey and chatted about work."

"Just one whiskey?"

I know I'm pushing it. But I have to.

"Just one," Austin replies. "I can't sleep otherwise."

"I see," I say.

I look into Austin's eyes, searching for a hint of a lie or deception. But there's nothing there. Only their regular sparkle.

"What are you here for, by the way?" Austin asks.

"Huh?"

Austin looks around us.

"Are you looking for a book, or—?"

"Oh. Yeah. I'm in a bookstore, looking for a book. I was after this one, actually."

I'm grateful for a reason to turn around and reach up to grab the coffee-table book I've spotted on the top shelf, which is called *Wanderlust* and has an artful photograph of a sunlit mountain on it. I'm relatively tall, but even standing on tiptoe, I can't reach the book.

I feel Austin's presence behind me as he reaches up and over me and slides the book out from the shelf.

"This one?" he asks.

"Yeah. Thanks."

I look down at the book, and the photo of the mountain swims before my eyes. I feel completely disoriented by the fact that Austin seems to be acting like last night never happened. Margot must be right. He must have a severe drinking problem. To the extent that he's completely blacked me out. I don't know how he can manage to look so good after drinking like that, but like I said, he is an actor. They're a special breed.

"Is it for you?" Austin asks, nodding down at the book in my hands.

"This? No, it's a gift. For Deidre's sister-in-law."

"Ah, cool. What's it about?"

I start flicking through the pages of the book, revealing glossy photographs of mountains and rivers and trails.

"Deidre says she's into hiking and just moved into a new place, so I thought this would suit," I explain.

Austin moves his hand to pause a page I was about to swipe past.

"I think that's 'round here somewhere," he says, pointing at a photo of a mountain peak. "Look: If you squint, you can almost see our orchard."

He points at something in the background of the photo.

"And that's the lake that Casey River flows into," he says, pointing at a shimmering oval of silver blue. "And there are the campgrounds, where they have the Valley and Hills Country Music Festival every year."

"A country music festival," I repeat. "Like the one your parents met at?"

Austin grins, seeming pleased that I remember this anecdote. "I mean, this one's not exactly on par with the big one in Texas, but it's a cool little festival. One year, my brother and I played there as a surprise for my parents' anniversary."

"Like, you played music?"

"Yeah. It's crazy the things you have the confidence to do in your early twenties. Both of us are pretty average guitarists, but we got together and wrote a song as a gift for our parents. They have this tent where local musicians can book slots, like an open mic. So we told them to meet us there, and we surprised them with this song. It was probably terrible, but Mom cried and Dad pretended he didn't, so it had the intended effect."

As soon as Austin mentioned guitarists, my mind sped to the image of him brandishing that guitar at me last night.

"So you're a musician as well," I say, managing to keep my voice so casual I almost wonder if I should have gotten into acting myself.

Austin shrugs. "I can play. But I wouldn't exactly call myself a triple threat."

"You can't dance?"

"Depends how many beers I've had."

I smile, then stop myself. Joking so casually about beers doesn't seem like something an alcoholic would do. Or maybe it's exactly the kind of thing an alcoholic would do.

I don't know. I don't know what to do with any of this. Austin clearly has no memory of last night, no matter how much we keep talking. Or if he does, he's the greatest actor in the world. Just give him all the awards right now. Because I see absolutely none of that dark, weary shadow in him that I saw last night. None at all. There's not even a hint of a hangover. This is a different guy. This is the guy I met for his fitting. This is the guy I had beers with at Three Pines Brewing Co.

This is the guy whose gaze lingered on me as he left last night.

The guy who's looking at me now as if he wants to say more.

But then his phone starts ringing.

Austin pulls out his phone. I glance down briefly, without thinking, and see the name "Parker" across the screen. The name of his brother.

"Ah, this is my weekly call from my niece," Austin says, tapping the screen. "The other Maddie. Sorry, I gotta take this."

"Don't apologize," I say.

Austin gives me one final smile, before picking up the call and heading out.

Alone in the aisle again, I blow out a long breath and lean back against the shelf.

It's then that I remember something.

Last night, the Austin I met in the bedroom told me he didn't have a niece.

I spring back off the shelf and walk down the aisle to the store window. Outside, I can see Austin holding his phone in front of him, headphones in his ears, smiling at a young girl who definitely looks like his niece.

I can also see the book in his hand. It's a small paperback with a receipt hanging out of it. The cover is gray and features a man on a horse. I already know who the author is going to be before my eyes slide to the title.

Louis L'Amour.

"What the actual fuck," I murmur to myself.

"Can I help you?" asks a voice behind me.

I turn around to see the shop assistant standing in the aisle looking at me. I'm so flustered that it takes me a moment to realize that I know her.

"Florence," I say.

It's my neighbor. The one from number ten. With the red hair and the wooden pendant.

"Oh, Mattie!" Florence says, beaming. "I thought that was you. And who was *that?*"

She nods outside, to where Austin's back is still visible, disappearing into the small-town crowd. Her tone is suggestive and brazen, befitting older people who simply can't be bothered to beat around the bush.

"Oh." I think I'm blushing. "He's working on the movie too."

"He's interested in you," says Florence.

"No," I say too quickly. "No, we're just working together."

"That doesn't mean he's not interested in you."

"I don't think—"

"Trust me, when you get to my age, you can tell these things. Now, what else can I help you with today, my dear?"

I look down at the *Wanderlust* book. I only have five minutes left of my break, so that doesn't allow for a lot of browsing. I decide to just go with it.

As Florence rings the book up for me at the counter, I think of something.

"I didn't realize you worked here," I say.

"Just casually," Florence replies. "I'm supposed to be retired, but I get too bored."

"Fair enough. Do, uh, many other people work here?"

I'm remembering Austin last night, mistakenly thinking that he saw me behind the counter at the bookstore. I'm wondering if I somehow have a doppelgänger.

Florence shakes her head. "We're a small team; business isn't exactly booming. These days it's just Leigh—the owner—her husband, her nephew, and me."

"I see. And how old is Leigh?"

Florence frowns a little. "I've never asked. I want to say mid-fifties. Why's that?"

I shrug. "Just curious, I guess. So, there's not a girl my age working here?"

"Not at the moment. Why? Do you want a job?"

"No," I say. "I mean, sure, it would be a lovely job."

"It's certainly less stressful than yours seems to be."

"Mine seems stressful?"

"Oh yes, you film folks out there are always rushing around, on your phones, thinking of something else."

This doesn't come across as an insult from Florence. She's right, of course, like she seems to be about most things.

"Just before, though," Florence continues, nodding to the aisle where Austin and I stood. "With him, over there. Neither of you seemed particularly rushed."

Now I'm definitely blushing. I take the book, which Florence has placed in a brown paper bag.

"Thank you," I say quietly.

Florence gives a small wink. "Happy to help."

EIGHTEEN

When I get back to my apartment that night, I decide it's time to tidy up. I need something to clear my head, and maybe decluttering in real life will help declutter my mind, akin to the theory about making your bed every morning.

I start in the bathroom, where my makeup and toiletries are scattered across the counter. I carefully place them all back in their containers, wipe the counter, and open the window for some fresh air.

Back in the room, I get started on my clothes. I hang up the pieces that have been draped across the chair, and then I tackle the pile spilling out of the wardrobe. I hold up one of the dresses I made myself a few years ago—a long sky blue slip dress with a cute bow at the front. I think about how long it's been since I made my own clothes, or since I wore anything but the muted, dark colors we're always instructed to wear on film sets, so that we can blend into the background and not be a distraction.

I shake my head and hang it back up, alongside the rest.

Cleaning has helped a little, but I'm still feeling disoriented from my strange day. Nothing else major happened, but I had another few interactions with Austin on set. They were much like our conversation in the bookstore, like all our conversations so far. Friendly, familiar, and charged with an energy I can't quite describe but that Florence would have a lot to say about, I'm guessing.

There wasn't a single hint that last night I'd been standing uninvited in his bedroom while he pointed a guitar at me like a gun.

There are plausible reasons why someone might completely forget an entire interaction. Drinking, as Margot suspects. Or potentially some other kind of substance abuse or mental condition I don't feel informed enough to muse about.

I didn't overtly forget things when I was with Jack, but I doubted my memory of them. The version of events he presented to me was so different to the version I thought I'd experienced; it made my brain feel as though it had been put through the washing machine and come out with the dye stripped off. Often, there was no one else around to verify either of our versions, and Jack was so convincing that I was always the one who conceded. I must have been remembering wrong. My mind was no longer a fortress. No longer that sanctuary.

I know now that this had less to do with the weakness of my mind and more to do with the strength of Jack's strategic offenses.

But still.

What if it's not Austin who's misremembering last night?

What if it's me?

After all, I'm the one who opened the secret passageway. I'm the one who trespassed into someone else's space. Austin had stood there, in his bedroom, looking at me like I was the one to be worried about. Am I the one to be worried about?

I stare at my reflection in the wardrobe mirror. The distorted and chipped glass makes my face look almost like a stranger's, which doesn't help. I move forward and look deeper into my own eyes.

And then, in the safety of my own gaze, I feel the thoughts settle. I remind myself that I know me. I didn't lose my mind back then and I'm not losing my mind now. I know what I saw through the passageway.

And I know what I'm hearing from the other side right now.

It's not another meow this time. It's the sound of music.

I sit down at the edge of the wardrobe and press my ear against the wall.

From the other side, I hear the unmistakable strum of an acoustic guitar. Though it sounds muffled and warped, as if I were listening to it on a radio station with a poor connection. I can also hear the murmur of someone singing.

I think of Austin pointing the guitar at me last night. I think of him telling me today about the song he wrote with his brother. I think of the scrawled notepaper I found in the folio that looked a lot like song lyrics.

It must be him, playing and singing in his bedroom. This seems like a private thing, and I probably shouldn't wedge open the panel to listen more closely. But this is, of course, exactly what I do.

I can see the back of Austin's wardrobe through the panel, though his side of the passageway is closed. Even still, the open recess makes the music clearer. I can hear the distinct sound of Austin's voice now, singing along to the chords he plucks.

Austin has a compelling singing voice. It has a coarse, earthy twang to it but is also thick with sadness, a sadness that creeps into my chest and clings there like a lonely creature.

I listen closely, trying to make out the words. If I hold my breath, halting the hiss of it in my ears, I can catch some snippets.

> *It happens late at night sometimes*
> *With a drop or two cloudin' my mind*
> *I look back and see the crossroads, clear*
> *And the path I took that brought me here.*

There's a pause then, and a scratching sound, like the rustle of notepaper. Then the song starts up again. He repeats the previous verse with a few tweaks, then continues onto the next one:

> *The other one, it haunts me cold*
> *Wish I could go back down that road*
> *Where my brother rides right by my side*
> *Where our mama never had to cry*

Where my papa never had to lie
Where my brother never had to—

I can't tell if the line is meant to end there or if Austin can't bring himself to sing the next part. But either way, those lyrics crawl down from my chest, into the pit of my stomach.

I'm aware that Austin might be singing a song written by someone else. Or a song about a hypothetical situation.

But my thoughts are tugged back to the story Austin told last night at Three Pines. About his brother, Parker, turning up on his doorstep in LA, agitated and out of character. About how Austin turned down the role in *Water Street Files* to accompany Parker on his trip around the world because he was so worried.

Then I think about the funeral booklet I found in that folio. In the fray of everything that happened after, I almost forgot about it. I didn't see any details on it except the prayer on the back. But I remember the weight of it in my hands. The weight that felt like much more than paper.

Where my brother never had to—

But no. No, this doesn't make sense. Austin's brother is completely fine—Austin said so himself. After the trip, Parker ended up back on the Farrows' family orchard, happy and well, married with a cute little kid . . .

A cute little kid named Maddie, with two *d*'s.

The niece Austin was talking to on the phone today, when his brother, Parker, called him.

The niece that Austin claimed last night, as we stood in his bedroom, he didn't have.

My head swims. I press myself against the wall to steady the dizziness, waiting for Austin to start singing again, listening for answers.

But the strumming has become more distant now—it sounds as if Austin might have left the bedroom and is now playing in the living room or kitchen instead.

So I decide to go outside.

My balcony is connected to the balcony of number nine. I might have a better chance of hearing Austin from out there.

Outside, the night sky is strewn with stars, and I can hear that waterfall gushing in the distance, steadying the uneven beat of my heart. I look next door, at the balcony to number nine. It seems like it hasn't been used in a long time. The wicker furniture has faint cobwebs connecting its legs with the railings. Dried leaves are scattered across the tiled floor like abandoned toys. Maybe Austin isn't a sitting-on-the-balcony kind of guy.

But there's also no light streaming through any of the windows of number nine.

No music wafting my way.

Which doesn't make sense. Because I can see light and hear sounds from the other balconies of the apartment complex. There's Florence in number ten, clinking a teaspoon against a cup of tea, warm candlelight spilling onto her balcony. There are my other neighbors, listening to a loud action movie, the light of the TV flickering through the curtains.

Why does it look like no one's in number nine, when I heard Austin just moments before with my own two ears?

Puzzled, I head back inside to the bedroom and open my wardrobe back up. Through the wedge in the panel, I can definitely see light through the passageway. And I can definitely hear Austin strumming and singing from the living room now.

Adrenaline is coursing through my veins as I return to the balcony. I stare at number nine. It's still completely dark. Still completely quiet. Still completely at odds with what I've just seen and heard through the passageway.

This is something I wouldn't normally do in a million years. But the concept of "normal" seems distant right now, as far flung as those stars in the sky. So, I decide to roll with the absurdity of it all.

Before I can talk myself out of it, I'm clambering over the railing and onto the balcony of number nine.

My bare feet crunch in the dry leaves and accumulated grit on the balcony floor. I move toward the sliding door and see that the curtains have been left slightly open.

Inside the apartment, all is dark and quiet and untouched.

I rap my knuckles lightly on the glass door. I don't even care anymore about looking like a creep, standing on someone else's balcony. I'll be relieved if I see a light flick on and a figure carrying a guitar emerge in the hallway. I'll be relieved even if he calls the cops on me this time.

Because at least then, I'll know that he's real.

But no one comes.

I cup my hands around my face and peer through the glass, trying to make out any details of the apartment inside.

The living room is shadowed and silent. I can see past the empty sofa to the door of the bedroom. The door is slightly ajar, showing that the bedroom is also dark and empty.

And that the bed is in a completely different position than I remember it being last night.

I press myself away from the glass, as if I've been stung. I back all the way up until I hit the balcony railing and the cold metal bites my waist.

After a minute more of standing there, frozen, hoping that some sense will tumble out of the sky, I have my answer.

Austin isn't in number nine.

No one's in number nine.

At least not in the version of number nine that I'm standing in front of right now.

II: THE FANTASY

NINETEEN

There was a time in my life when I considered working in a bookstore.

It was the summer break between my second and third years of college, and I was on a weekend beach trip with a small group of friends. The rest of them went to swim for the afternoon, while I decided to stay behind and do some shopping instead. I found myself wandering through the backstreets of the little coastal town, which is where all the best vintage clothing stores are usually hidden.

It was there that I came across a cozy bookstore tucked down a winding lane. Inside, it was deceptively larger than the salt-white-and-aquamarine facade suggested—narrow and long, lined with shelves that groaned under the weight of books. It widened out at the end and extended into a small sunlit courtyard, where there was a wheeled cart serving coffee.

There was a sense of peace and simplicity in that bookstore I hadn't felt in a long time. The shelves created a cloister from the world. I didn't know anyone in there—no one was going to ask me if I'd lined up an internship yet or how my love life was or what I thought about the upcoming election.

I pulled down a memoir written by a famous actress from one of the shelves and sat at a table in the courtyard. I alternated between flicking through the book and looking up at the two women working in the store—one was making coffee and one was behind the counter. They were several years older than me and seemed at ease, soft smiles on their faces, movements unrushed.

Why did I feel so tired all the time? I was young and privileged and my whole life was before me, but still, I was tired. Of the city and crowds and public transport and deadlines and the economy and dating and climate change and worrying about what other people thought of me. I wanted my life to be smaller. I wanted to be one of these slow-moving women.

I think a lot of people have had a fantasy like this at some point in their lives. About moving away to a quiet, small town and getting a job in a bookstore or a bakery or a florist. These types of fantasies are exactly what the worlds of romantic comedies like *Magic Season* are built on.

It was only two weeks after that day in the bookstore that I was offered my first job as a production runner on that local show. Before I accepted the offer, I felt a small tug inside me, pulling me somewhere else. Pulling me back to that bookstore, back to the fantasy of a quiet, unhurried life in a distant town.

But only a twenty-year-old fool would turn down an opportunity for a paid job in the film industry. So I accepted the offer, severing whatever thread may have been pulling me toward another life.

——

Florence answers her door after three sharp knocks.

She's wearing a purple dressing gown and holding the mug of tea I heard her stirring only moments ago. Her face is stripped of makeup and looks reassuringly lovely and wise. I'm so glad to see her. She's real, at least.

"Mattie," she greets me. "Are you okay?"

"I don't know," I reply.

"What's wrong?" Florence says, craning her neck down our shared hallway toward my apartment. "Are you hurt? Is there a fire?"

"No," I reply. "I just . . . I don't know what's going on. I need to talk to someone."

"Of course, my dear. Come in."

Florence beckons me into her apartment. The candle she's lit smells of vanilla and cinnamon and pine, like eating warm cookies at the end of a cold October hike. Her apartment is full of paintings and books and knickknacks, with silver-rimmed mirrors and mosaics clinging to the walls. There's an old, ornate wooden chest by the television, and my eyes are strangely drawn to it, as if there's something inside I should know about.

"It's an antique," Florence says, following my gaze. "Locally made."

"It's beautiful," I say.

Florence gestures for me to sit down on a squishy sofa draped in patchwork blankets and beaded cushions and asks me if I want a cup of tea.

"Yes, please," I reply, feeling like a small child.

As Florence moves to her kitchen to make me a cup, I ask the question out loud.

"Do you believe in ghosts?" I ask.

"Of course," Florence replies, as if this is a standard question. "Why?"

"Is it possible that number nine is haunted?"

Florence blinks at me now. "Number nine?" she repeats. "Next door? Why do you ask that? Is this related to you hearing a cat in there the other day?"

I take a deep breath in and then spill out as many details as I can manage about the events of the last few days. By the time I've finished, the cup of tea is in my hand and Florence is settled on a maroon armchair next to me. Her expression is creased, but she isn't looking at me like I'm crazy.

"Well," Florence says. "Firstly, what you've encountered doesn't sound like a ghost. You say that the man you've seen inside that apartment is a man you've met in real life. I also saw him today, with my own two eyes. He can't be a ghost."

"Well then, what's happening?" I grip my teacup forcefully, to stop my hands from shaking. "What's the answer to all this?"

"What do you think it could be?" Florence asks calmly.

I take a moment to think, trying to articulate the theory that's formed in my head over the course of the night.

"It sounds crazy . . ." I start.

"As crazy as a ghost?" Florence points out.

"I don't know. I feel like a ghost would make more sense."

"But this . . . ?"

"This . . . is impossible. Completely impossible. But the only thing that makes sense to me is if the apartment I can see, and hear, through that passageway is . . . God, I don't even know how to say it."

"Go on," Florence urges.

I take a breath and force the words to come.

"It feels like it's a parallel world," I say. "Like, another version of this world. Some things are the same—Austin's here in Casey River; I'm here in Casey River. But other things are different."

"Like what?"

"Well, the Austin I saw next door swore he met me at a bookstore. So maybe, in that world, I do work in a bookstore rather than in the film industry. And maybe the reason Austin seemed so different is because his life also took a different turn."

"A different turn," Florence repeats in a murmur.

"Well, first, it looks like he's living, or staying, in the apartment next door, which he obviously isn't in this world," I continue. "But the most telling part is the song I heard him singing. He was talking about a crossroads in his life and wishing that he took another path, where his brother was still beside him. And the other night, the real Austin—I mean, the Austin in *this* world—told us that, when he was younger, he turned down this role in a crime show so that he could travel with his brother, Parker, instead. It seemed like it was a big decision for him at the time."

"Interesting," Florence says. I get the impression she knows where I'm going with this but is letting me talk it out, letting me be the one to say it.

"So then, what if . . ." I continue. "What if, in this other weird world through the wardrobe, Austin hadn't turned down the role? That would mean his face *would* have ended up on that prop wanted poster I found. And it would also mean that Parker ended up traveling alone. And maybe, if he was alone, something happened to him. Something bad."

Florence nods. "A decision that led to a different set of consequences."

"Exactly. The other Austin insisted that he didn't have a niece. Which makes me think that his brother, who's the dad of his niece in *this* world, isn't . . . isn't there anymore, in that world. And if that's because something happened to him on that trip, Austin probably wouldn't have been able to forgive himself for choosing his career over his brother. That's why he drinks and sings sad songs. God, when I heard him singing, his voice sounded so haunted. Just like the guy I met in that apartment. It was like . . . a different version of him."

Florence nods over her tea, as if I were telling her the details of a juicy breakup, rather than possibly the most inconceivable thing I've ever voiced in my life.

"Why is it impossible?" she asks eventually.

"What?"

"Why do you think it's impossible that the passageway in your wardrobe leads to an alternate world?"

"Because . . . because that defies the laws of our world as we know it?"

"Well, that's the key phrase. *As we know it.* There's much we don't know. All science was once something we didn't understand. And there are many scientists who are intrigued by the theory of parallel universes."

"Okay, but if parallel universes are just hanging around in people's wardrobes, then surely we'd know? People would go to the media or the government. Surely?"

"Will you?"

I hesitate.

"I don't think anyone would believe me."

"Precisely."

"But I have proof," I say, perking up. "There's literally a passageway, in my wardrobe. You can come see it."

If Florence thinks I'm losing it, she doesn't show it. She places her cup of tea next to mine on the coffee table and follows me out of her apartment and down the hall into mine.

I march resolutely into my bedroom and over to my wardrobe. I throw open the door, nervous for a moment that the panel isn't going to be there. But there it is.

"Curious," Florence murmurs, crouching down to look at the panel. "Very curious."

"Listen," I say.

We both stop and listen closely for a moment. But the sound of the music coming from next door has stopped.

"Okay, then look," I say.

I don't even care about what this alternate version of Austin might do when he sees me flinging open the panel and peering through the passageway into his bedroom again. I'm daring myself to find out, daring myself to prove that this extraordinary theory of mine is true. Especially when Florence is standing next to me, as a witness to the unfathomable.

But when I open the first panel in the back of my wardrobe, I can see that something's different.

Something's wrong.

There's no passageway.

No recess leading to the back of Austin's wardrobe.

There's nothing behind there but a solid wall.

TWENTY

I originally got into hiking to clear my head.

I knew I was never going to be an extreme hiker like Margot and her friends—I didn't have any interest in the type of tracks that involved ropes or crampons or hooking yourself to the side of a mountain to sleep. But after a few long day hikes, I realized how good it could feel to push yourself into that next level of consciousness. It wasn't just the clean air or the beauty of the landscapes or the adrenaline. It was the way my mind grew lighter, like taking off a pack that was too heavy for me to be carrying in the first place.

I began to recognize the stages my brain would go through on a hike. In the first stage, I'd be thinking of regular things, chatting with my companions, or listening to music if I was on my own. My thoughts would be shallow and comfortable and familiar.

In the second stage, I'd start to think about the hike itself. I'd notice the pain in my legs or my shortness of breath, check my watch to see how much time had passed or how much distance I'd traveled, counting down how far I had to go.

In the third stage, the deeper thoughts would come. This stage wouldn't always happen. Sometimes I'd spend a whole hike oscillating between stages one and two and never hit stage three. But when I did, stage three felt close to a spiritual experience. It was when I'd start to think about what it felt to have a body, what it felt to be a human connecting with nature again, what I was trying to walk away from, what I was trying to walk toward. This stage often felt close to enlightenment.

But the third stage wasn't the final stage. No, there was a fourth, even more unattainable level, that I only achieved once when on a particularly arduous overnight hike with Margot. After hours of hiking, we reached the ridgeline of a mountain, walking across it in single file as if tiptoeing along a dragon's spine. Because we had to walk in a line with space in between us, we couldn't talk. All we did was focus on one foot at a time, looking down at the earth and out at the expanse of mountains and forest and sky around us.

It was on this stretch of hike that my mind emptied completely. I lost all concept of space and time. It wasn't until we reached the end of the ridge and started our descent back down into the valley that I realized I had no idea how much time had passed or how much distance we had traveled. I had been thinking about nothing. And even though there was ground beneath my feet, I felt like I was walking on air.

Everything seemed brighter and clearer once I experienced that moment on the ridgeline. The pain in my legs felt earned, the birdsong louder, my pack lighter, even though it was full of the same things.

I'd always thought of an epiphany as gaining something. When in fact, an epiphany can sometimes be a surrender.

———

To her credit, Florence doesn't treat me like I've lost my mind.

After I've crouched staring at the wall for probably longer than is warranted, she invites me back to her apartment to finish my tea. She tells me she still believes me, even though I'm not sure I believe myself anymore. She tells me of several impossible things that have happened to her in life. Tarot readings that have prophesied future events. A vision of an aunt who died when she was a child, standing in her bedroom.

As I listen to Florence talk and I stare around her apartment, with its eclectic knickknacks and peculiar trimmings, I can only think of one thing.

"But why?" I ask eventually.

"Why what?" Florence asks.

"Tarot readings and ghost sightings," I say. "Hard to believe, sure, but I get it. They're connected to you, to your life, sending you some kind of message. But this? What does this have to do with me? Why would *I* suddenly be able to access an alternate world, in the apartment of this guy I've only just met. It feels wrong. These kinds of things don't happen to me."

"Well, why shouldn't they?"

"Because . . . I don't know, they seem to happen to a particular kind of person."

"What kind of person?" Florence looks mildly offended for a moment. "You know, we've got scientists and mechanics who attend our local tarot club. Are those the kinds of people you imagine these things would happen to?"

I don't reply.

"Apart from that, you're asking the right question, though," Florence continues.

"Which is?"

Florence fixes her gaze on me.

"*Why?*" she asks simply.

This question rings in my mind as I get ready for bed that night. I check the panel before I go to bed, but the passageway is still closed.

Then, just as I'm playing with the idea that maybe the passageway was never there in the first place, I notice something in the gap between the panel and the wall.

It's a piece of paper. And when I tug it out, I see that it's a creased trail map.

The creased trail map I found as I rummaged through the folio on the nightstand next door.

I hold it up triumphantly. The trail map isn't anything obviously magical. It's a map to the park behind the apartment complex, marking the trails and viewpoints along the way, along with information about local flora and fauna. It's not the wanted poster or the funeral booklet or the sheet of lyrics—nothing that could definitively prove this outrageous theory I've created in my head.

But it feels like enough. It's something solid, between my fingers, that I found in the world beyond the wardrobe.

I know it's easy to dwell on the how. *How* could this be possible?

But instead, it's that other question that sticks to my insides.

Why?

Why was I given access to another world?

And *why* did I see what I saw in there? Austin Farrow. An alternate, haunted, shadowy version of Austin Farrow.

What am I meant to do with this?

I place the trail map on my nightstand, and I try to get some sleep. But I'm still tossing and turning once dawn breaks. I figure that I could continue to chase sleep for another hour or two. Or I could take advantage of actually being awake early for once and try to clear my head the way I used to.

Early morning always takes on a surreal quality. If there was ever a time to believe in the impossible, I think dawn would have to be it. I can hear the first feeble peeps of birds starting to herald the day. The sky outside is still dark, but there's a faint glimmer on the horizon, a whisper of sunrise. The apartments around mine are silent, and the waterfall in the distance sounds even louder in the stillness.

I reach for the nightstand and am relieved when my fingers touch the creased paper. It hasn't disappeared in the night. It's still real. I pull out the map and scan the nearby trails. My eyes fall on a point on the map intriguingly called Fallen Tree Falls. That must be the rushing water I can hear. And it seems as good a destination as any to map my morning adventure around.

By the time I'm dressed and ready, water and coffee packed, the morning is lit with a golden glow. I step out onto my street and take a left turn where I'd normally take a right to head into town. There's a path down at the end of the street between two houses that leads to a leafy parking lot, and I find the trailhead on the other side.

Within two minutes of walking, I feel my shoulders begin to relax. The trees stretch up around me like guardians—this is an old-growth forest, a mix of fir and cedar and spruce. Early sunlight presses gently through the canopy; the birdsong grows surer as more birds rouse. I sip my coffee and step one foot after another along the mulch trail.

Here, in the forest, in the quiet secrecy of morning, I don't feel so much like I'm losing my mind. I feel like I'm reaching that musing, meditative stage far quicker than I normally would.

I used to believe in magical things. As a child, it's hard not to. I devoured books and glued myself to television shows where other, more interesting kids disappeared into distant lands via portals in trees and mirrors and brick walls. I entertained the possibility of time travel and world hopping and prophecies.

I don't think it's maturity that stops us from believing in these things. I think it's the simple fact that they don't end up happening to us. When you reach the age of twenty and you still haven't found your secret portal or magical talisman, it's better to believe that they simply don't exist rather than that maybe you just haven't been chosen.

Have I been chosen?

Like I said, I've never felt like the type to be chosen. I've always been better behind the camera than in front of it. A very flirtatious creative director I worked with on a photoshoot once tried to put me in front of the camera, and even he was somewhat baffled by the way I became muted and awkward once the lens was on me. He said I was a rare kind of person who looked better in real life than in photographs. Just like Austin had joked about the morning we first met.

All my creative pursuits so far have revolved around trying to make someone else the main character. Production running, wardrobe assisting, fashion design, even my brief interest in journalism. It's always been about other people's stories.

And in a way, my portal is too. After all, it wasn't my own life I glimpsed beyond the wardrobe. It was Austin Farrow's. I was *in* his life—a minor character he met in a bookstore—but that was all.

Why? Why, why, why? The word echoes in my mind, in rhythm with my footsteps.

Fallen Tree Falls isn't the most impressive waterfall I've ever seen. When I reach the viewpoint, I see that the waterfall is relatively short and narrow, though the rush of the water is strong. The flow cascades from a wall of mossy, weather-smoothed rocks, down into a round pool of water that meets a brook that must eventually connect with the Casey River.

Contrary to the waterfall's name, there don't appear to be any fallen trees around. Though there are plenty of standing trees, including one particularly impressive one that seems to have grown out of an old stump.

I wander over to the lookout that juts out over the pool to see if there's a sign or anything to explain the name and history behind the waterfall. But there's nothing at the lookout except for people's initials and the occasional crude word etched into the wooden frame. I ignore these and instead focus on a heart that's been jaggedly cut with a pocketknife. I press my fingers into the heart as I look out across the falls and let the cool spray of the water tickle my face. I feel like my thoughts are flowing into the pool, along with the water, and I'm reaching that airy peaceful surrender akin to an epiphany.

I still don't know why. I still don't have the answers.

But instead of feeling heavy, I suddenly feel light.

Instead of the portal being a burden, it feels like it could be an opportunity.

And for the first time in a while, I feel like a child again, playing dress-up, believing in magical things, daring to hope that, maybe, my story could be just as interesting as the ones I'm always helping other people tell.

TWENTY-ONE

Two days go by without the portal revealing itself to me again. I spend those days at work in a daze, untethered to reality, counting down the minutes until I can get back to the apartment and check the wardrobe. When the solid wall is still there on the second night, I start to get nervous. I don't question what I've seen, but I begin to worry that now that I've figured the portal out, it might have closed itself off to me. Story over. Mystery solved.

But that's not how stories work. I've made enough movies to know that they don't end after the first act. There's still more to come—I know it. I just need to be patient. If I'm going to believe in the impossible, then I need to trust in the impossible and the strange ways in which impossible things work.

Margot is away on a multinight hike, so I haven't told anyone except Florence about the portal. It's definitely not something I'm going to share with anyone I work with. Sure, the industry is full of people with wild minds, but I know how far-fetched this all sounds. Even if I do decide to quit after this gig, I'd prefer to leave with my reputation intact, rather than as the girl who lost it.

The biggest test for me is seeing Austin. I already found myself flustered enough around him before, and now I have the added factor of having magically glimpsed an alternate timeline of his life. Whenever I see him now, I can hear that drumbeat of *Why, why, why?* in my head. Once or twice, I even toy with the idea that maybe I'm meant to tell him. Maybe I'm meant to tell Austin that, for whatever reason, I witnessed another timeline where his eyes don't have that sparkle to them, all because of one decision he made differently that led him down a darker path. Maybe this will help Austin feel more grateful for the life he's living now.

But as I watch Austin on set, talking and laughing with the cast and crew in that easygoing, friendly way he has, I realize that this version of Austin doesn't need to be told any of that. This Austin already seems to be grateful for his life. He doesn't need a magical portal.

Besides, I'm sure if I confessed to Austin about the portal, it would go down *really* well. He'd believe me immediately, for sure. He definitely wouldn't think I was unhinged. I absolutely wouldn't get fired. My reputation wouldn't be irrevocably damaged. Definitely not.

I'm in our wardrobe room one evening readying our costumes for the next day when Austin comes out of the fitting room and hands me Mitchell's signature jeans and flannel. I thank him and take them over to our laundry section. This should be the extent of our interaction. That's normally all it is with the other actors. But as usual, Austin doesn't seem in a hurry to leave.

"I have a question for you," he says, leaning against one of our clothing racks.

"Okay," I say. "Go for it."

"You know how you're named after that song?"

"'Waltzing Matilda'?"

"That's the one. And I'm named after a place known for country music?"

"Austin?"

"Exactly. See, I've been thinking, there's this music theme going on here."

I think of hearing Austin's voice singing that song, and I suck a breath in to keep my features neutral.

"There is?" I ask.

"I think there is. And there also happens to be a country music festival coming up this weekend. Valley and Hills Festival, the one I told you about in the bookstore the other day."

"Oh, yeah," I say, wondering where this is going.

"*And* this weekend also happens to be one the crew actually has off. If I'm reading our schedules right."

I realize that my heart is pattering in a way it hasn't in a while. It's not stress. Stress makes my heart thud, like stomping on wooden floorboards. This is lighter, more like a dance.

I pick up two shoes and put them in a box together, despite them being from completely different pairs.

"We do have a day off," I confirm.

"Okay, so I think a couple of the stunt guys and maybe even Hayden are going to come to the festival. And I thought that, given this music connection you and I have, maybe you wanted to come too?"

I force myself to breathe normally. Austin isn't asking me out. This is a group thing. Several people are going. It's normal for the crew to do things together on our rare days off. This is all perfectly fine, and there's no reason for my heart to be doing this quickstep.

"Oh," I say. "That sounds like fun. Henry and Loren had talked about doing something on our off day. I can see if they want to come."

"Of course—invite them too," Austin says.

He runs a hand through his hair, and for a moment, I wonder if he looks a little nervous. He's toying with one of the dresses on the rack with his other hand: a deep-red dress with a bow on the front, like a Christmas present.

I feel like I need to do something to break the tension. My heart is about ready to jump out of my throat, and I've never seen Austin look anything other than cool and collected.

"That would suit you," I say, nodding down at the dress he's playing with. "Red goes well with green eyes."

Austin's eyes crinkle at the corners as he laughs. The tension breaks and I don't even regret making a semiflirtatious joke or knowing the color of Austin's eyes. It's part of my job, after all. I need to be intimately familiar with every actor's features—their skin tone, their bone structure, their eye color—for professional reasons. And professional reasons only.

"What goes well with blue eyes?" Austin asks.

"Other blues," I say automatically, as if I'm being quizzed. "They help the eyes pop. Pastels are also good."

"And yet you always seem to wear black."

I look up at Austin. Of course. He's talking about *my* eyes.

"Oh," I say, my cheeks hot. "Well, yeah. We're supposed to wear dark colors on set. So we're not a distraction."

Austin opens his mouth to say something, but then someone appears in the doorway.

It's Hayden King, the actor playing Grant.

"You ready, man?" Hayden calls in to Austin.

"Yeah," Austin replies. He turns back to me for a moment and explains. "Another nightcap. It was a tradition when we were in college together."

Hayden gives me a slight nod of acknowledgment from the doorway, in the polite yet distant manner that's typical of him. Hayden King isn't a diva, but he's nowhere near as friendly as Austin. I wonder what they talk about over their nightcaps.

"Have fun," I say.

Austin smiles at me as he leaves, and maybe I imagine it, but I'm sure Hayden raises his eyebrows at him at the doorway, as if in an unspoken question. But then they're both gone, and I'm left trying not to think about what other colors go well with green eyes.

TWENTY-TWO

The portal is open again.

I know it before I even open the wardrobe. It's like the feeling of walking into a seemingly empty room and knowing someone's there. As if the air feels fuller than it should. You can't touch it or hear it or see it, but you know.

I'm so relieved when I see the passageway beyond the panel, I feel like I could cry. I want to pump my fist in the air and shout out to no one, *See, I told you!* I knew it. I wasn't imagining things. I wasn't misremembering. It was real. It was all real.

But my feeling of triumph only lasts a few moments before the trepidation sets in.

Because of course, now I have to go through.

And this will be my first time going through with the knowledge that I'm stepping into another world.

There's no advice on the internet to prepare you for this feeling. No motivational videos on "How to Pump Yourself Up to Enter Another World." I feel like I'm standing on the edge of a precipice without the right gear, and in any normal scenario, my first instinct would be to take a step back. A few weeks ago, I would have taken a step back.

But how can I? Whether or not I believe I should have been chosen, I have been. One thing I've always been good at is doing what's asked of me, and right now, it's clear what I'm being asked to do. I'm being asked to answer the call.

So, I take a deep breath, and I move through the passageway.

This time, it feels different. It's like I can sense the air shift around me as I move from one wardrobe into the next. It's a sigh or a shrug—something subtle you wouldn't notice if you weren't looking for it.

The first thing I see is that this isn't the same wardrobe I stepped into before.

Austin's clothes are gone. In fact, there aren't many clothes hanging in this wardrobe at all. It looks like whoever's here is only here temporarily—there are a few women's blouses, a jacket, and a pair of heels. They're all high-quality pieces, the type I'd save on social media but then never bring myself to buy on a wardrobe assistant's salary.

I take a moment to process this. This isn't just a different world to the one I left behind. This appears to be a different world to the *other* world I visited as well. Which I suppose shouldn't be a shock. If a portal can lead to one world, who's to say it can't lead to multiple? Who's to say the worlds in the wardrobe can't swap and change like outfits?

I stay in the wardrobe listening for any sound from the bedroom beyond. When I don't hear any, I press open the door.

The bedroom looks eerily like the one I just left behind. The bedding is different, but the artwork on the walls is much the same. There's a suitcase over by the armchair in the corner—a small suitcase, appropriate for a weekend trip. A few clothes and accessories spill out of it.

On the nightstand by the bed is a stack of magazines. They're mostly shiny entertainment and culture periodicals. I flick through them for a moment but don't see anything particularly interesting.

In the Austin timeline, I didn't venture out of the bedroom. But after peering out the bedroom door and seeing that the living room beyond appears to be empty, I decide to wander farther into the apartment to figure out what kind of world I may have walked into.

Just like the bedroom, the rest of the apartment is similar to mine, save for a few different touches here and there—fresh flowers on the dining table, a basket of fruit in the kitchen. There's a clean citrus aroma that hangs in the air, mingled with a distantly familiar perfume.

In the living room, I notice that the TV is on. There's a pack of horses on screen, frozen mid-jump. Whoever was watching the TV obviously stopped it mid-scene, which makes me nervous. It implies that whoever's staying here might only be out temporarily, which means I don't have the luxury of time to poke around every corner of this apartment. I need to move fast.

On the coffee table in front of the TV, there's a notebook open to a page scribbled with notes. I look down at the page. As I cast my eyes over the scribbles, my stomach flips.

It's my handwriting.

There's no doubt about it. I recognize the slope of my letters, the way I sometimes forget to finish words or cross my *t*'s completely before I'm rushing onto the next thought. I even recognize the pen as my favorite kind that I always used when taking notes in college.

What I don't recognize is the notes themselves. There's a heading at the top that seems to say something like *UC PROFILES INT. PREP*. Underneath are bullet points that take me a while to decipher. The first bullet point is a date of some kind, and then the name of a town not far from Casey River. After this comes a set of questions, abbreviated into keywords: *Influences? Childhood? Genres? Directors? Technique? Ambitions? Funny stories?*

I flick back through the previous notes and can see that they're similar. The first bullet points always seem to be birth dates and places, then lists of things like record-album names, awards shows, film and TV titles, significant events.

It seems that I've been taking notes on artists or celebrities. But what for?

I look from the coffee table to the sofa and spot two more magazines open on the sofa's arm. I flip them closed and see that they're both copies of *Up Close*, a magazine that features poignant and well-written articles about artists, athletes, politicians, and other public personalities. It's the kind of magazine I would have been interested in writing for. If I'd pursued journalism. In another life.

My heart is racing as I flick through the pages of *Up Close*, poring over the bylines of the articles. I'm past the middle before I spot my name.

It's not underneath the cover story. But it's still a byline on a decent feature: a full two-page spread about an indie musician who's shot to stardom after releasing her music on a social media platform. The writing is well researched and self-assured. This obviously isn't my first byline. I'm obviously good at this.

I take a moment to feel proud of myself, which is a strange feeling.

Why is it easier to feel proud of myself in third person than it is in first person?

I stand up and look around the living room. I imagine for a moment that this is my life. I'm a journalist. I've come to Casey River on a work trip to research a story. Is this version of me proud of me? Do I feel accomplished? Am I happier here than I am in my life next door?

I think of the clothes hanging in the wardrobe. They're not exactly haute couture, but they're still more high end than what I can afford now. I wander over to the fridge in the kitchen and open it. I've obviously developed a taste for good white wine instead of midrange red in this timeline. The containers of olives and expensive cheeses also indicate upscale preferences.

That's when I glance out the kitchen window and down to the street below. And there on the footpath, illuminated by a streetlight, is the strangest thing I've ever seen in my life.

I thought I'd already experienced the pinnacle of surreal. I thought that nothing could get stranger than all the things that have happened over the last few days.

But I hadn't yet experienced the startling sensation of seeing myself in another timeline.

Until now.

There I am, down on the street below. I've just hopped out of a car that looks like a rental, carrying a bag of takeout from town. I look taller than I thought I was, my shoulders straighter, my face slimmer.

My hair is much the same as it is now—caramel brown with sideswept bangs—though it seems glossier, like I take better care of it.

It's so bizarre. In a normal world, no one would ever get the privilege— or the horror—of actually *seeing* themselves. In a mirror, yes, or in a photograph or video. But never there, in the flesh, unburdened by a glass screen.

I'm fascinated as I watch myself cross the pavement and step into the apartment building. So mesmerized that it takes a beat for me to realize that the other version of me is of course heading upstairs. To the apartment. Where I'm standing right now.

For a brief, delirious moment, I think about staying here. I think about watching my own face as I walk through the door and see a double of myself standing in the kitchen. It's terrifying yet thrilling, like the idea of pushing a button someone's told you not to, just to see what might happen.

But even though no one's explained exactly what's going on here, I feel like this would break whatever rules are at play. Most time-travel stories I know are about jumping back and forth in *vertical* time, not horizontal time—if that's what this is—but I figure some of the same rules apply. Like the importance of not interacting with yourself.

So I do the sensible thing. I leave the living room and head back to the bedroom. I'm standing in front of the wardrobe again when I hear the key turn in the lock outside. I feel that temptation again—that dangerous, electrifying wound coil inside my stomach, the one that keeps people like Margot doing the daring things they do.

In the end, I compromise. I head back through the wardrobe. But not before swiping one of the magazines off the bedside table and taking it with me.

Once I'm back in my own bedroom, I stand by my bed, panting like I've just run a marathon. My hands are shaking. I look down and am amazed to see my fist still clutching the magazine.

I sink down onto my bed and open the cover. This one is a travel-and-lifestyle journal with thick, glossy pages, owned by the same company as *Up Close.* I flick through the pages until I find what I'm looking for. There's another byline of mine on a feature about a new shopping precinct that's just opened in a city halfway across the country. This must mean that I often travel for work. Unless I've moved to another city completely? It's a life step I've thought about on occasion but have never taken.

I read the article over and over, until I have the words memorized. Like the article in *Up Close*, I'm impressed with my own writing. It's probably nothing particularly revelatory to anyone else, but it is to me. There's a confidence about it, like I actually know what I'm talking about. I have a weird urge to pick up my phone and message myself, congratulating myself on the piece. But of course, I can't do that. All I can do is sit here with the magazine I've pulled from another world with the same question pounding in my head:

Why?

Am I supposed to feel envious of the version of me in that timeline? She's arguably more successful. Bylines in well-known magazines are more impressive than credits in films that appear long after everyone's already left the cinema or turned off the TV. Right? I feel like they are. I'm obviously making more money in that timeline too, given the clothes in the wardrobe. Or maybe I get free clothes with my writing gigs sometimes. That alone would probably make me happier.

Is this alternate timeline meant to make me rethink my current life? If that's the case, it's doing the job. I think back to college, when I was studying journalism subjects alongside fashion and film. It always felt like the subject I was best at. The only reason I got into the film industry instead was because my professor got me that gig as a production runner.

I sleep with the magazine beside my bed that night, just like the alternate version of me did. I wonder if she'll notice it's missing. I wonder if she'll notice her notebook has been touched. I wonder what she was watching on TV, that scene with the horses mid-gallop, and if she enjoyed the rest of it with another glass of that upmarket white wine. I wonder if the interview she was preparing for will go well.

I wonder, if she could have a glimpse into this alternate version of her life, what she'd be wondering about me.

TWENTY-THREE

Over the next few days, I go through the portal two more times.

It becomes like a habit. Almost a ritual. Instead of watching TV or scrolling through social media when I get home from the production office, I visit an alternate world inside my wardrobe.

And each time, it's a different one.

It's like one of those retro CD carousels that holds six CDs at a time, and all you have to do is click a button to select the one you want to listen to. Only, I don't have a choice over what music, what world, I'm experiencing that night. The wardrobe does it for me.

First there was the Dark Austin timeline.

Then there was the Journalist Mattie timeline.

The next time I enter the wardrobe, the apartment next door isn't just similar to the one I'm staying in now. It's almost identical. I think for a moment that I've gotten myself turned around and haven't crossed through the portal at all.

But then I notice that the clothes in the wardrobe and the bedroom, while unmistakably mine, are even more scattered and far flung than the room I've left behind. This is still a slightly different world, even if it is eerily similar to my current one.

This is when I begin to understand that the apartment beyond the wardrobe isn't actually the apartment "next door" or even an alternate version of the apartment next door. It's an alternate version of the same apartment I'm staying in at the moment. It's never been number nine; it's been a twin of number eight all along, only in another world. In the first world, Austin lived in number eight. In the second world, it was a temporary rental again, which the journalist version of me was staying in on a work trip.

In this world, it also seems to be a temporary rental. And I'm the renter again. But I'm not the same version of myself that I was in the journalist timeline. I can tell, because the clothes in the wardrobe and scattered across the room aren't the same chic pieces. They're not even as nice as the clothes I own in my current world. These are older, faded items that I either threw out a while ago or might still have tucked into the back of my drawers back home—emergency backup clothes that I'd only wear if I forgot to do laundry. I can't see any of my handmade creations.

It's in this timeline that I discover call sheets and other crew documentation for *Magic Season* on the kitchen counter with my name on them, just like in the current timeline. Only, my name isn't in the wardrobe section. It's in the production section, low down the list. I'm listed as a production runner again. At age twenty-eight, I'm no further along my career path than I was as a recent college graduate.

Don't get me wrong; being a runner isn't shameful, and I respect the hell out of all the runners I work with. But most people start out as runners to work their way up the ladder, or they supplement running gigs with other freelance work. If the journalist timeline was a step above my current timeline, then this almost feels like a step back. I wonder what happened along the way to stop me from moving upward. I wonder what made me stall.

And I wonder again what I'm meant to be learning from all this.

The next time I enter the portal, it's a similar setup but with an added twist. There are two suitcases in the room this time—one I recognize as mine, the other I recognize as someone else's, though I can't immediately tell whose.

In this timeline, I hear laughter and music coming from the living room. I freeze in the wardrobe, weighing the risks of venturing out. Eventually, my curiosity gets the better of me, and I tiptoe to the door of the room and peer through the crack into the living room.

I see a familiar flash of curly red hair on the sofa and feel a welcome rush of comfort.

It's Margot.

My best friend, Margot.

She's pouring a stream of clear liquid from a bottle into a shot glass on the coffee table and clinking it against the glass of the person next to her.

That person is me. My hair is longer and my face is fuller, with bright gold glitter flashing on my eyes in a style I haven't worn since the early 2000s. I'm also wearing a cowboy hat, which isn't an accessory I think I've ever owned. I realize then that the music that's thudding through the apartment is country music, which also isn't something Margot and I would typically choose to listen to when we're together. Margot favors rock 'n' roll, while I'm more of an indie-pop kind of girl.

"This seems dangerous," the perplexingly cowgirl version of me says to Margot, as I down whatever's in the shot glass.

"Exactly," Margot replies.

"If you were to ask me last month what I thought I'd be doing right now, going to a country music festival with you out in the sticks wouldn't have been high on my list."

My brain stirs. Margot and I are here for a country music festival? Ostensibly the same country music festival I agreed to go to with Austin and the crew. Which isn't a festival I've heard of or attended before now.

"I know," Margot replies to the other version of me. "But who can say no to free VIP tickets?"

"How did you meet this guy again? The one who gave you the tickets?"

"That hike I did last month. He's hot in like, a tattooed, bearded kind of way, but he also knows it. That's probably why he's a good musician."

"So, he's hot and he gave you free VIP tickets . . ."

"He gave them to everyone in our hiking crew. I'm not interested. *However*, I did notice this photo he just posted with another musician friend who's playing on the main stage tomorrow."

Margot hands me her phone and shows the other version of me a picture that I can't see from here.

"Okay," the other me says. "Am I meant to know this other guy?"

"Not *yet*."

I can see Margot's devilish grin from here, as the other me rolls her eyes and hands back the phone.

"You've never been this determined to play matchmaker for me before," the other me says.

"I just think you need to have a little more fun. You're always, like, creating fun for the kids, but you need to have more fun yourself."

Margot's words clang inside my head. What kids is she referring to? Do I have *children* in this timeline? I press my face closer to the gap in the door, trying to catch a glimpse of my hands to see if there's a wedding ring on the left one. There isn't, though I could still have kids without being married. But who the hell would the father be? I've never even gotten close to having kids with any of my exes. At least not any of the ones I've dated in my current timeline.

"I have fun at work," the other me says to Margot now.

"Please don't just talk about work when you meet this guy."

"Hey, being a teacher is in the top five most noble professions, apparently. And plus, who says I'm going to even meet this guy? If he's playing on the main stage, he must be a big deal."

"Don't sell yourself short, Miss Bridges. Here, have another shot."

The other me obliges and takes another drink from Margot. Meanwhile, the real me feels my shoulders relax. I didn't even realize they'd tensed up at the thought of being a mother in this timeline. It sounds like the kids Margot was referring to are kids that I work with, in my job as a teacher.

Which, just like being a mother, isn't a pathway that feels particularly close to the one I'm walking now. I enjoyed working with kids on that children's movie, but I wouldn't say I felt a deeper calling to teach the next generation. How did I end up on that track? When did I get my teaching credential? Am I good at it? I have a dozen questions I want to shout out through the crack in the doorway, but instead I silently watch Margot and Mattie get steadily tipsier as Margot's pours become more generous and the music grows louder.

It's only then that I listen closer to the song that's currently playing. It's an upbeat, anthemic country track, the kind I imagine I could sing along to at a festival on the outskirts of Casey River as the sun sets behind the hills. And the vocals that pulse through the speakers sound familiar, though I can't quite put my finger on why. I know I haven't heard this song before.

Before I can figure it out, Margot clicks over to a new song, and the familiar voice disappears, replaced by the bass-heavy twang of a heavier country-rock tune. A different, deeper voice starts singing.

"This is him," Margot says, nodding at her phone. "The guy I met hiking."

"Even his voice is hot," the other me observes. "In a tattooed, bearded kind of way."

"Hm, okay, I mean if you want to go for him for a bit of fun, then I won't stop you. But I still think his friend is more your type."

"If you keep pouring like that, I'm not going to be in a state to go for *anyone*."

"The day is young."

"I need a bathroom break."

The other me stands up with a slight wobble and starts to head to the bathroom. Which is in the bedroom, where I'm still standing, entranced.

Once again, I'm forced to retreat into the wardrobe to avoid running into myself. But this time, I wait a moment before I go back through the other side. I watch myself through the crack in the doors as I walk into the bedroom, moving my shoulders slightly to the song that's playing.

And I'm struck with a strange feeling. Of wanting to go out there and hang out with this Mattie and Margot. Of wanting to put glitter on my eyes and head off to a country music festival, to dance and drink and maybe meet a cute guy. Of wanting to be friends with myself and my best friend.

Of longing for something that, when you really think about it, I maybe already have.

TWENTY-FOUR

Valley and Hills Country Music Festival has taken over a large campground near Carrickvale, about twenty minutes from Casey River. It's a place of green slopes, rugged fields, and smooth pines. The Main Stage is set up at the back of the campground, with a distant view of the mountains behind it. Three smaller stages are scattered around the site, and there's a large market on the western side, where colorful stalls and food trucks stretch over the trimmed grass, serving up local produce and hot street food.

There's also a large bar tent, which is where Henry and I head when we arrive at the festival. We've arranged to meet Val and Loren there, and I suppose at some point, maybe, probably, we'll meet up with Austin and the others. I don't actually have Austin's phone number in my personal contacts. This seems like a dangerous next step, one that shifts our connection from happenstance into design. I don't feel quite ready for that move.

I admit, I feel a little relieved that the three other timelines I've visited through the wardrobe haven't starred Austin Farrow. These timelines are more what I would expect from a portal that leads to alternate versions of my life—which is, of course, a situation you should definitely have preconceived expectations about. In these timelines, I've been getting glimpses into my own alternate universes: Journalist Mattie, Production Runner Mattie, Teacher Mattie. I still don't understand the why, but at least this gives me something to work with. I'm starting to wonder if maybe I visited the Dark Austin timeline as an error the first time. The portal showed me the wrong thing—the wrong CD inside the right case. Now it's corrected itself.

Today, however, I've told myself I need to push the portal into the back of my mind. Today I need to act like a normal girl who's attending a small-town country music festival with her work friends. I haven't put glitter on my eyes and I'm not wearing a cowgirl hat, but my spirits are high. It's a beautiful day—balmy and clear—and the bar's selling fruity hard seltzers in plastic cups that Henry and I sip as we wait for the others.

"Tom's attractive, right?" Henry says.

We're leaning against a standing table in the bar area, with a large beer-branded umbrella shading us from the sun. I can hear the music thrumming from one of the smaller stages nearby and the muted cheer of a crowd.

"Stunt Guy Tom?" I ask.

"The one and only."

"He's definitely in shape," I reply.

"He's a babe," Henry declares, as if he never needed my confirmation in the first place. "But he doesn't talk much."

"That's okay; you do enough talking for the both of you."

"Ha ha," Henry says dryly, sipping his drink. "He's here, you know. Tom and the other stunties."

"I think a lot of the crew is here," I say almost too casually. "Do you think Deidre is?"

"God, I hope not. I want to let loose today. However, I *would* love to see Deidre in a pair of rhinestone cowboy boots."

Henry has opted for a rhinestone look himself today, in a black western shirt with a stylized yoke and a smattering of small silver jewels, which he'd somehow found yesterday in a boutique store in town, being the eagle-eyed shopper he is. I've gone for a more understated option—a cute plaid crop I made from end-of-roll fabric I found on discount once, paired with high-waisted denim shorts and a good belt.

I shake my head. "Deidre wouldn't be caught dead in rhinestones."

"You're right. She'd go for real diamonds. Ah, and speaking of classy . . . look who we have here."

Henry nods at the entrance to the tent, where Loren and Heidi from hair and makeup have entered with Val. Loren and Heidi are wearing pink cowgirl hats and tight jeans, and even if they don't exactly look *classy*, they do look hot, which I respect. Val, however, looks like she's actually from around here, in bootcut jeans, a T-shirt, and a look on her face that implies she regrets coming with the other two.

"Thank God you're here," she says, lunging for Henry and me.

"She's embarrassed by us," Loren explains. "We look like *city* people."

"Preposterous," says Henry. "I fucking love those hats, by the way."

"I actually grew up riding horses," Heidi explains. "And I've literally helped a cow give birth. I just like pink."

"And so you should," I encourage her. "It suits your skin tone."

Heidi beams at my compliment. Val, meanwhile, checks her watch.

"My cousin's playing at the Locals Tent in ten minutes," she says. "I promised I'd go see him. Are you guys coming?"

Val knows how to navigate this festival far better than any of us does, so we follow her lead, like we always do. The Locals Tent is the closest one to the bar—a small yellow tent draped in bunting, with a thin crowd milling around inside. Val's cousin is on stage doing a sound check when we get inside, and she drags me over to meet him and his wife, who's also his bandmate. We exchange niceties for a few moments, before they have to head backstage.

When we turn around to rejoin the rest of the group, I can see that they've met up with some of the other crew at the back of the tent. There's Tom and a few of the stunt guys. And Austin.

Austin grins when he sees me, and I swear he wasn't smiling at the others like that.

"You made it," he says to me.

"I did," I confirm.

"Having fun so far?"

"We've only been here for about half an hour, so we haven't checked out any of the bands yet. But Val's cousin's next up here."

"Yeah, I actually know these guys, through family friends. Val and I were both at their wedding last year."

"That's right—you were talking about that at Three Pines. Everyone really does know everyone around here."

"I also know one of the guys playing on the River Stage next. And the guy running the bagel van and the woman selling ice cream. As well as three of the bartenders." Austin's counting on his fingers. "Oh, and two of the security guards."

"That could come in handy."

"Why, are you thinking of doing something bad?"

Austin raises his eyebrows at this, and I feel heat flush through my cheeks and my chest. I glance around us, but everyone else is wrapped up in their own conversations.

"No, I'm a good girl," I reply.

It comes out more playful than I expected, and Austin looks momentarily disarmed.

"Just like I'm a good guy," he says quietly, when he's recovered. "Always."

I don't know if it's a welcome or inconvenient disruption, but Val's cousin and his wife walk onto stage then, waving at the crowd and carrying their guitars. When they start strumming, it's too loud to continue any conversation, so Austin and I both turn to the stage to watch.

We stand next to each other for the whole set. I try to pay attention to the music, but I'm vividly aware of Austin's presence beside me. My shoulder is in line with his chest, and when someone jostles past us, I'm pressed into him for a moment. He places a hand on my waist to steady me but then drops it quickly after. I don't dare look at him. I keep my eyes firmly on the stage until the lights swim and the colors blur.

When the set is over, the group splits. Henry's flirting with Tom, the other stunt guys go for a drink, Heidi and Loren have been approached by some guys, and Val's talking to her cousin. Austin takes a moment to say hello to the duo as well. And then suddenly, it's just the two of us, facing each other.

"Do you wanna come see my friend on the River Stage?" Austin asks.

For a moment, I can see it in my mind's eye—that fork in the road, where the path splits into two separate directions. It almost makes me dizzy.

But I told myself I wouldn't think about the portal today. Today is for lightness. For fun. For saying yes, rather than *What if?*

"Sure," I reply.

Austin leads me out of the Locals Tent and back into the crowd. As we leave the shade of the tent, I touch his shoulder.

"Yeah?" he asks.

"I meant to ask . . . Was this where you and your brother played the song for your parents' anniversary?"

Austin smiles and looks up at the tent.

"Sure is. It's gotten even bigger since then. And I don't think this is the actual tent—pretty sure that got blown away in a storm a few years back. But otherwise, yes."

"Are they here this year?"

Austin shakes his head. "Parker's busy on the orchard. And my parents are traveling right now."

"So, it's just you."

"And you."

Austin bumps my shoulder lightly with his, and I force myself to keep walking.

We stop by the bar and grab more hard seltzers before hitting the River Stage. Austin attempts to buy my drink for me, but I elbow him out of the way and remind him about the pilsner he bought for me at Three Pines. He rolls his eyes and tries to insist, and eventually the bartender—one Austin knows—gives us both our drinks for free to shut us up.

The River Stage is the second-largest stage at the festival, smaller than the main but bigger than the Locals Tent. The crowd is unexpectedly thick, spilling out onto the walkways.

"Is your friend a big deal?" I ask Austin, as we look out at the crowd.

"He's blown up recently," Austin answers. "One of his songs was in the season finale of a TV show a month or two ago, and it kind of went viral from there."

"How do you two know each other?"

"We went to theater school together, back when we were kids. We fell out of touch, but then we ended up moving to LA around the same time. He was doing the music thing, and I was doing the acting thing, and we ended up at a lot of parties together."

"I'm sure you did."

Austin cranes his neck over the crowd.

"Come on," he says. "I think I can get us up front."

He grabs me gently by the crook of my arm and starts to lead me through the crowd. It grows heavier and rowdier the closer we get to the front. When we become separated for a second, Austin reaches back for me again, but this time, his hand finds my hand and his fingers twist with mine.

Warmth rushes up from our connected palms, flooding my whole body. I worry for a second that people might see us, but then I realize it doesn't matter. We're in a crowd at a music festival. No one's paying attention to anyone else. No one's looking down at our intertwined hands. The heat rising from me isn't visible, even though it feels hotter and brighter than a sunburn.

We reach the front left of the crowd, where there's a barricade separating a VIP area from the rest. I don't hear what Austin says to the security guard, but within moments, we're slipping into the VIP section. It's still crowded here, but it's calmer and has a good view of the stage. We probably don't need to still be holding hands. But I don't let go. And neither does Austin.

Austin's friend takes to the stage then. He's a good-looking guy with a sleeve of tattoos and dark hair. But he could be a three-eyed extraterrestrial for all I can comprehend right now. As he strums the first chords on his guitar, the VIP crowd presses in more tightly.

That's when Austin drops my hand. But I don't have time to feel his absence, because he touches my hips instead and guides me in front of him, so that I can see better. And then he rests his elbow on the barricade next to us, so that his arm is almost around me.

"Are you okay?" he asks, his mouth right by my ear.

I'm not okay. I feel like I've climbed higher up a mountain than I expected to and found myself on a slippery rocky outcrop with no way of getting down. But the view is stunning, and I don't think I'm ready to get down, anyway.

"I'm fine," I say weakly.

"Good," Austin replies.

I have no solid grasp on how long Austin's friend's set lasts. It's all a blur of amplified sensations—the thrum of the music, the hot glare of the sun, the murmur of the crowd, the buzz of the fruity seltzer in my system, and Austin's arm by my side. My head is already swimming, and then we arrive at the final song of the set. The one everyone's been waiting for, the viral one.

As the bass-heavy twang reverberates through the crowd, I realize I recognize this song. It takes me a moment to remember where from, and then I do.

It's the one I heard earlier, through the portal. Margot had said it was by the guy she met hiking. The one who had given us the VIP tickets and was apparently hot in a tattooed, bearded way—just like the guy on stage right now.

Blood rushes to my head as I try to piece this all together. And this must be the thing that tips me over the edge. Because suddenly, the storm of sensations brewing inside me reaches a dizzying high. A physically dizzying high that makes my head light and my body weak.

I see white spots in my vision, like incongruous stars in the daytime. And I feel Austin's arm tighten around me as I start to slip to the ground.

TWENTY-FIVE

I really should know better. I know about the risk of dehydration. Heat, alcohol, and a lack of food and water form a dangerous combination that I'm normally sensible enough to avoid. When I hike, I keep a hydration pack filled with water and electrolytes on my back like a crutch, sipping it so frequently I normally get a cramp. There's always a steady stream of small snacks. I know the rules, and I almost always follow them.

But today, I've been so caught up in the festival and Austin and all the surrealness of the last week that I've forgotten to be sensible. I haven't had anything to eat since breakfast, and those hard seltzers have gone down far too easily. Plus, a part of me also wonders whether traveling through the portal has weakened me in some way. I haven't stopped to consider before now the effects this might have on my body as well as my mind.

What I do know is that, rather than enjoying the festival, I'm now sitting on a patch of grass by the water-refill stations, feeling like a child who can't look after herself.

"I'm sorry," I say to Austin.

He's crouched next to me with his hand on my back.

"Please stop saying sorry," he murmurs. "*I'm* sorry. If I'd known you weren't feeling well, I wouldn't have dragged you into the crowd."

"I was feeling fine," I insist.

Austin's eyebrows are furrowed as he looks me over.

"Have some more," he says, easing another cup of water into my hands.

Val turns up then. I don't know if she was deliberately looking for us or if she just happened to be walking by, but in typical efficient Val fashion, she's exactly where she needs to be.

Even though I keep insisting to both of them that I feel totally fine now—albeit incredibly embarrassed—Val tells Austin that I probably need sugar and food. And he disappears into the crowd to do her bidding, which is the power Val has.

"Tell me again what happened?" Val asks, commandeering Austin's spot by my side.

"I just had a head rush and fell a little bit," I say. "I didn't completely black out or anything. It was just a dizzy spell."

"And has this happened before?"

"Like, once when I was a teenager and was on a bad diet. It's not a big deal and it doesn't happen often. Honestly, I'm fine."

Val regards me with a slightly different look on her face to Austin's.

"What?" I ask, taking another sip of water.

"Where were you?" she asks.

"What do you mean?"

"Where were you, when it happened?"

I feel myself flush. "Watching an act on the River Stage."

"With Austin?"

"Yeah," I mumble.

"Just Austin?"

I take another gulp of water.

"Mattie." Val places a hand on my knee. "I'm not a snitch."

"There's nothing to snitch about," I insist.

Val shakes her head but doesn't push the issue. She settles down next to me, with her back against one of the fences.

"This used to happen more often," she says. "People passing out at the festival. That's why I insisted on putting free water stations in, the year I worked here."

"I didn't know you worked for the festival."

"I wear many hats. How's your head feeling now?"

"It's fine. Do you wear an EMT hat too?"

"I do have my level three first aid certificate."

We sit there talking for a few more minutes. The topic of Austin doesn't come up again, and I'm glad it doesn't. I'm almost hoping he doesn't return from the crowd. I feel mortified that I essentially collapsed in his arms. I haven't even come to terms with what happened there in the crowd—the hand holding, his arm beside me, his mouth by my ear—and what it all meant, but now I probably don't even need to stress about it. Because it likely won't be happening again anytime soon.

But whether I want him to or not, Austin does return. And his arms are laden with food options.

"I got you a bagel from the bagel van, as well as a salad, in case you're vegetarian or gluten intolerant," he explains. "And some fries, because fries always help. And ice cream from Virginia's ice cream truck, because it's the best ice cream in the world."

I can feel Val looking at me, trying to gauge my reaction to this, but I deliberately don't look back at her.

"Thank you," I say to Austin.

"I'll eat whatever you don't," he says.

He settles himself on my other side and spreads out the mountain of food in front of the three of us. Val starts picking at the fries, and I reach for the ice cream.

"The best ice cream in the world, you say?" I ask.

"I might be biased," Austin replies. "Because it's made with apples from my family's orchard."

"Virginia's famous apple pie ice cream is made with your apples?" Val asks.

"I don't know if I'd call them *my* apples," Austin says. "Parker can take credit for that these days."

I pick up the small wooden spoon and have a taste of the ice cream. The sweetness of the apple balances perfectly with the spice of cinnamon and nutmeg, and there are even surprise chunks of pie pastry in there, like cookie dough. As the sugar rush hits me, I feel myself perk up.

"You were right," I say.

"Who was right?" Austin asks.

"Val was right that I needed sugar. And you were right that this is the best ice cream in the world."

Austin blesses me with one of his eye-crinkling smiles.

"Virginia used to have a shop in downtown Casey River," he explains. "Parker and I would fight over who'd get to go with Dad on delivery days so that we could get free ice cream."

"Her shop was across the road from my uncle's grocery store," Val adds.

"That's right," Austin says. "They closed around the same time. But thank God Virginia kept selling ice cream out of her truck. I would have taken it up, otherwise. Forget acting. I'd be an ice cream peddler."

"Maybe you missed your calling," Val says.

I wonder if there's another timeline floating around out there where Austin became an ice cream seller instead of an actor. As I think about this, and take another spoonful, I realize that, while I'm feeling *better*, I'm still not a hundred percent. My head still feels slightly detached from my body. And I think my hands are shaking.

"You still don't look great," Val says to me, noticing the same thing.

This is exactly what I want to hear when Austin's sitting beside me. That I look terrible. Though maybe that's a good thing. Maybe it's better if Austin's repelled by me. Maybe that's safer than whatever reality we were hurtling toward, back there at the River Stage.

"I was thinking of heading home soon," Val continues. "I've seen all these acts before, anyway. And I haven't been drinking. I can give you a ride back."

I don't even mean to, but my eyes slide to Austin's. I see a flutter of something in his, beneath his furrowed brows. Something like disappointment.

"That might be a good idea," I tell Val. "If it's not too out of your way."

"Not at all," she replies.

Austin opens his mouth, then closes it. Then opens it again. Just as his phone starts ringing.

I glance down and see Hayden King's name flashing on Austin's screen.

"Oh yeah, Hayden's been looking for you," Val says, seeing the call too. "I think a few of them have VIP spots at the Main Stage."

Austin doesn't answer Hayden's call.

"I feel like I should be looking after you," he says to me instead.

"You're as sweet as your family's apples," says Val. "But I've got her."

Austin keeps his gaze fixed on me, as if waiting for my response.

"I'll go home with Val," I say. "There's no reason for you to miss out."

Austin sighs as his phone starts ringing again.

"Honestly," I say. "Go."

Austin is just cool enough to not insist. Even so, he doesn't leave in a hurry. He waits until I've finished the ice cream, half the bagel, and another cup of water. He waits until I stand up, watching me carefully to make sure I'm not going to keel over again. He waits until Val's distracted fishing around in her bag for her car keys. Then he reaches for my phone and punches his number into the keypad.

"There," he says. "Let me know later that you're all right, okay?"

I nod. "Okay. Thanks for the food, by the way. I guess I owe you again."

"No, you really don't."

He reaches out and squeezes my shoulder. But then Val's beside us again. And Austin slips his hand into his pockets, as if to stop them from doing anything more, and backs away into the crowd.

TWENTY-SIX

When I get back to the apartment, I fall into a deep sleep.

I didn't realize how much I needed it. Between the long working hours, being kept awake by portal musings, and my fainting spell today, my body is practically clamoring for rest. I think I have strange dreams, but I don't remember any of them. When I finally wake up, I struggle to remember anything at all. Night has fallen, thick and dark, outside. I wade through those first discombobulating moments after a nap that started in daylight and ended in evening, trying to recall how I got here.

When I remember the festival, the fainting, the food, I groan into my pillow.

My phone screen is full of messages. Val, Henry, and Loren are all checking if I'm all right. There's nothing from Austin, but he doesn't have my number. I have his. The ball's in my court. I should let him know how I'm doing, but my thumb hesitates over his name on my screen. Eventually, I message the others instead. I assume the word will get back to Austin. Or maybe I'll message him later. When my head has righted itself again.

I feel like I need some fresh air, so I pour myself a glass of water in the kitchen and step out onto the balcony. I look over at number nine, which is as dark and quiet as always. On the other side of number nine, the sliding door opens and Florence steps out onto her balcony, carrying a cup of tea.

"Evening, my dear," she calls out when she sees me. She raises her teacup at me. "Care for a cup?"

Actually, yes. A cup of tea with Florence is exactly what I need right now.

Moments later, I'm settled on the balcony of number ten next to Florence with a mug of hot chamomile in my hands. Florence has the same effect on me she always seems to have. I'm telling her too much, and before I know it, I've relayed almost everything that happened at the Valley and Hills Country Music Festival.

"I told you," Florence says simply, once I've finished.

"Told me what?" I ask.

"In the bookstore. I knew that man was interested in you."

The tea catches in my throat. I thought Florence might be more concerned about my fainting spell, but she's dived right into the matter of Austin, because of course she has.

"He didn't . . ." I say. "We didn't . . ."

"The thing about men, Mattie, is that they're not very inclined to do anything they don't want to do. If he invited you and you alone to join him at that stage, and if he held your hand, and looked after you when you fainted, he did those things because he wanted to. Because he likes you."

"He's a friendly guy," I say. "A good guy. He wasn't going to abandon me after I collapsed."

"Was he holding your hand in a *friendly* manner too?"

"He was making sure we didn't get separated," I say.

Florence's eyebrows are raised as she sips her tea.

"Anyway," I continue. "I don't get it. I don't get why he'd be interested in me. He hangs out with actresses all the time, and he used to date the lead singer of this girl band who has really nice hair."

"You're as pretty as any actress, Mattie, but more importantly, you have a kind and gracious aura that compels people to be around you. And for what it's worth, you also have nice hair."

Now it's my turn to raise my eyebrows, always unsure how to react when someone gives me a genuine compliment.

"Thank you," I say quietly.

"You're very welcome. But it's not a big mystery. The bigger mystery here, of course, is what you've been seeing through that wardrobe."

I mentioned to Florence the song I recognized, but I haven't run her through the other timelines I've discovered in detail yet. I take the opportunity to do this now, grateful to steer the conversation away from Austin.

Florence seems fascinated as I give her a thorough update. She steeples her fingers and looks out into the dark forest, digesting it all.

"Fascinating," she says.

"Fascinating or crazy?" I ask.

"I don't believe in crazy."

We sit there in comfortable silence for a few moments, listening to the night birds wake up in the trees.

"Have you noticed anything about these different timelines?" Florence asks eventually.

"Apart from the fact that they shouldn't be possible?"

Florence waves her hand. "Oh, we're past that now. I mean, have you noticed if the timelines have anything in common with each other?"

I think for a moment.

"Well," I say. "I guess the common factor is me. I'm in all of them. Even the first one I entered, the one with Austin in it . . . I was still there, in the background. He said he'd met me at the bookstore."

Florence nods. "Anything else?"

I frown, thinking.

"It's quite obvious," Florence says eventually.

"What?"

"Well, what else do the timelines have in common? What's something that you've done in every single one of those timelines so far?"

I feel like I'm back in college, struggling to understand a concept that my professor thinks is a no-brainer.

But then it comes to me. As I focus in on the sound of the waterfall in the distance—Fallen Tree Falls—it comes to me. Florence is right. It is quite obvious.

"I end up in Casey River," I murmur. "In all the timelines, I end up in Casey River somehow. In most of them, I even end up in the same apartment."

Florence sits back in her seat. "Yes," she says.

Until now, I hadn't thought that Casey River was a particularly significant place in my life. I've only been here a couple of times before: once as a child for a late-summer vacation with my parents and another time for one of my college friend's birthdays.

I've always found Casey River a charming town—potentially a nice place to retire or to live out that small-town, romantic fantasy that pops into my mind every now and again. But apart from that, I've never given Casey River a great deal of thought. I wouldn't say I felt a tie or cosmic connection to this place.

But, for the first time, I consider that maybe this is why this portal exists here for me. Maybe this place is a crossroads. It's a place where the different paths of my life interconnect. Maybe everyone has a place like this somewhere—where they end up in the same place at the same time, no matter what path they've taken to get there—and if they're lucky, the portal appears there for them. A brick wall, a secret garden, a circle of stones, a rabbit hole.

"A crossroads," Florence says, when I try to articulate this to her. She claps her hands together like a child. "Oh, I like that."

"It's the closest I've come to any kind of explanation for this," I admit.

Florence tilts her head to the side.

"This town does have an energy running through it," she says. "Some people say it comes from the river, but I think it's more than that. I think it's tied to the history of the town."

"What history?" I ask.

"Well, to start with, do you know where Fallen Tree Falls gets its name from?"

Florence gestures out into the dark of the forest, to the cascading water we can hear in the distance.

"No," I reply. "But I have been wondering."

Florence nods sagely. "True to its name, there was once a fallen tree at the falls. And that tree was crucial to the founding of Casey River as we know it."

"A tree?"

"Indeed. As the story goes, the Casey family—who named the town—was only meant to be traveling through these parts on their way east. They were headed into the interior for an assignment Edward Casey had with a mining company. But Edward Casey's young wife, Annette, grew enamored with this place when they stopped for the night. The forests, the river, the hills. Some of the records say she had a touch of the clairvoyant about her, that she could also pick up on unseen energies. She suggested to her husband that they put down roots here instead."

Florence pauses to take a sip of her tea. I feel hypnotized by her story and the melodic sound of the falls in the distance.

"Of course, the Casey family wasn't the first to travel through here—Indigenous people had been passing through these parts long before anyone with the name Casey came along. But the river could be difficult and perilous to cross in those days, and so most people stuck to the other side, which was closer to the settlements farther north. And that was a problem for the Caseys too. They had no way of crossing the river safely to get to the flat, unsettled land they could see on the other side—the land that seemed to be calling to Annette."

I think I'm starting to see where this story is going, but I listen as Florence regales me with the rest: about how a storm shook the Casey camp that very night, striking the infamous tree and causing it to fall across the rush of the river, right by the waterfall.

"It created a bridge," I say softly.

Florence nods. "A bridge that led the Caseys to the other side, and to the founding of the town as we know it. If that storm hadn't come, or if it had struck elsewhere, you and I probably wouldn't be sitting here in this apartment today."

"We'd be somewhere else," I say. "In a different timeline."

Florence nods. "This is a town built at a crossroads. Not a physical crossroads, like a railway line. But a crossroads in time. Two forking paths, linked by a fallen tree."

I swill these thoughts around in my mind like the tea left in my cup.

"I guess maybe, in a completely unscientific, unverifiable way, that starts to explain *how* this portal might exist," I say. "If that fallen tree created some kind of . . . mystical power here." It sounds ridiculous even as I say it. These aren't words I ever imagined I'd be bringing up in serious conversation. "And I guess it makes sense that I've found it, if this is also a crossroads place for me. But I still don't feel like it explains *why*. Like, what I'm supposed to do with all this."

"No," Florence agrees. "That's still not entirely clear. But I feel like you might be getting closer."

TWENTY-SEVEN

I've begun to form a collection of souvenirs from my trips through the wardrobe.

There's the trail map to Fallen Tree Falls from the Dark Austin timeline.

The magazine from the world where I'm a journalist.

The call sheet from the one where I'm still a production runner.

A small bottle of eye glitter I swiped from the world where Margot and I were getting ready for the country music festival.

I have them all on my nightstand, and I stare at them when I get back from Florence's, as if hoping they'll speak to me or shed a sudden spotlight on the answer to all of this. I flick through the magazine again, and I scan the call sheet. I press my finger into the bottle of eye glitter and rub it on the back of my hand, watching it sparkle. I open the trail map and look at the line to the falls, the place where the tree fell all those years ago, creating this magic.

These objects might be charmed in their own way, but they don't speak to me. I don't think my answer is going to fall from the sky. I'm going to have to find it myself.

I stand up from the bed and walk over to the wardrobe. It's only when I get this close that I can hear murmured voices coming from the other side of the panel.

A soft female laugh. A teasing male voice.

Someone's in the bedroom beyond. More than one someone.

My hand pauses before it opens the passageway. I've always felt like I'm intruding when I go through the portal, but this feels worse than normal.

I press the panels as gently as I can, to prevent them from making any sound. When I finally get a glimpse beyond, I hold my breath.

It's like I knew what I was going to see before I saw it.

Me. And Austin.

Austin and me.

On the bed.

I'm wearing the same outfit I wore today—the plaid crop, the denim shorts, the nice belt. Austin's also wearing the clothes he wore to the festival. He's sitting on my bed, leaning back against the pillows, and I'm sitting next to him. Dangerously close. He reaches his hand out and tucks a strand of my hair, unkempt from a day at the festival, behind my ear. And even though it's a different version of me, I feel like I can feel it.

I reach up and touch my own cheek, as if I might meet Austin's fingers there.

But there's nothing there. Because it's not me that Austin's touching. It's the other version of me. The version that's now starting to lean in closer.

The version that kisses him. And that he kisses back.

I'm stunned, staring through the wardrobe, trying to comprehend what I'm looking at right now. I'm watching myself kiss Austin Farrow. Part of this feels like a movie. But then another part feels distressingly real.

I realize that the world I'm witnessing through the crack in the wardrobe must be a world that splintered off from this one at some point earlier today. Maybe I remembered to eat food and drink water and I didn't faint. Maybe we went somewhere else after the Locals Tent, rather than the River Stage. Or maybe something else transpired over the last few weeks to change the dynamic between us, to put things on fast-forward, to make me bold enough to do what I'm doing right now in this other world.

Maybe, maybe, maybe. I don't know and might not ever know, but what I *do* know is that I'm watching Austin and me kiss. More than that—I'm watching Austin's hands roam over my hips and up to the edge of my plaid crop . . .

I shut the panels, as fast and silently as possible.

Then I go to the bathroom, and I take a long shower.

For some reason, it's easier for me to contemplate different time-lines that deviated from my current one further back into the past. This one is too close to home. This one is too easy to visualize, running alongside my current track, like parallel trains that are bound for different destinations.

The idea that different universes are potentially being created every day, with almost every movement I make, suddenly makes me feel dizzy again. Is there a world out there where I didn't decide to step into the shower just now? Am I manifesting another timeline right this very moment, by staying in the shower instead of getting out? Is it the small decisions we make that matter just as much as the big ones?

I feel like I can suddenly see all the threads hanging there in the steam from the shower—a hundred of them, a thousand, an infinite number.

I thought I was feeling better after the nap and the tea and the talk with Florence, but now my head's spinning again.

And I'm forced to ponder the smaller yet somehow more startling reality.

That there's a world out there where I brought Austin Farrow home with me from the festival.

Where I leaned in and kissed him, like the main character in the story rather than the one watching from the sidelines.

Once I've stood in the shower for what feels like over an hour, I finally emerge, warm and wrinkly and dazed. I sit gingerly on the bed and stare at the pillows, where Austin sat in the other timeline.

I pick up my phone, and I pull up Austin's number again. And then, inspired perhaps by my brashness in the other timeline, I type a message letting him know that I'm recovered.

Which isn't quite the truth, of course. But it's taken enough for me to message him. I don't want it to be a bigger deal than it needs to be.

Austin's response comes alarmingly quickly.

Thank God. I've been waiting up all night, wondering.

I press my fingers to my lips. Then I type back.

Haven't you been up all night because you're having
fun at the festival?

His response:

It wasn't as fun after you left.

My heart patters in that now-familiar dance, as I type back.

Thanks again for looking after me.

Of course. Do you need anything? I know it's late, but I could do
an ice cream run.

My fingers freeze over the phone. I think of inviting Austin to my apartment. Of replicating what's happening next door right now.

I know there's a version of me where I'm brave. I saw it, moments ago, through the wardrobe. And I know it comes out sometimes, in the small, flirtatious things I say to Austin, without even meaning to. *Red goes well with green eyes. No, I'm a good girl.* I didn't drop his hand. I didn't shy away from his arm by my side.

I know what I want.

And yet, I still find ways to convince myself I'm wrong.

There's the fact that we work together, for one.

The fact that he's an actor with a chaotic schedule in an industry I've been thinking of leaving anyway.

The fact that I've seen things through the portal that Austin hasn't.

The fact that I feel like maybe I don't deserve this.

The fact that Jack made me afraid.

This last part tugs a heavy cloud over me, and anything brave I thought I might be able to say vanishes.

I'll probably dream about that ice cream tonight. But I think I'm okay. Thank you, though.

It is dream-worthy ice cream.

There's a pause then, and I wonder if Austin's feeling spurned. I wonder where the limits of his niceness lie. Surely, he can sense my hesitation. And just like at the festival, when I decided to go home with Val, I don't think he'll push it. There are only so many times he can offer his hand.

Will you be back to work tomorrow? Or do you need more rest?

Good one. I think I'd need to be hospitalized before I called in sick on Deidre. Maybe not even then.

I would cover for you.

How?

I can spin a good story sometimes.

Have you ever thought of making a career out of that?

Ha ha.

Thank you, though. But honestly, I feel fine. I'll be at work tomorrow.

So . . . I'll see you then?

You'll see me then.

Another pause. A bubble that indicates Austin's typing something. Then the bubble disappears. And is followed by a longer pause.

Eventually, I realize that it's me who has to close the conversation off. Austin's given enough.

I should let you get to bed. Good night, Austin.

The bubbles start and stop about three times. And then, finally, a simple reply.

Good night, Mattie with two t's.

As I fall asleep, I try not to wonder what else Austin wanted to say.

TWENTY-EIGHT

The production office is in a frenzy again.

This time, it's not because our director's made another impulsive change. It's because of the weather forecast. There's a front expected to come in a couple of days, which could turn into a storm. A big one.

We're no strangers to weather disrupting our schedules on a shoot. We always have contingency plans in place for just that. But still, tensions seem to grow when we're forced to rearrange things—voices become high pitched, phones trill more often, bodies move faster through the rooms of the production office.

Within half an hour of me arriving at the office the next day, the decision has been made to bring forward the hiking scene with Raquel, Grant, and Mitchell that was originally scheduled for next week. If the storm's as bad as they're saying it might be, our location out in a nearby regional park might become unfilmable, so it's better to get that in the can now. We'll head out there tomorrow.

I'm in charge of checking and sorting through our hiking wardrobe to make sure it's ready. My head is feeling clearer today, and I'm able to focus on my work. Which is lucky, because I notice that the jackets we have for Raquel are likely the wrong size. I know from my own hiking adventures that this particular brand runs notoriously small. I also know there's an outdoor supply store at the end of Main Street, so I head out to find a better size and pick up a few extra accessories when I'm there.

I look up at the sky as I'm walking back. It's crisp and blue today, and it's difficult to think that it might soon become a roiling mess, wreaking havoc on these currently sun-soaked streets.

My mind is tugged to Austin, the way it has been approximately every fifteen minutes since yesterday. I realize that bringing forward the hiking scene might mean that Austin ends up wrapping earlier than he was originally meant to.

These last few weeks, I've been feeling stirrings of the old me again. The me who used to love watching romantic movies and reading fairy tales. But it's not a complete revival, I realize now. There's a tug-of-war happening within me.

Between Jack and working in this industry, the last few years have tied knots in my heart. Romanticism is now tangled up with cynicism. I can't watch a kissing scene in a movie anymore without thinking about the costumes and imagining the crew standing right there, watching every move. I can't feel a flutter in my heart without thinking of all those flutters in my heart at the beginning with Jack, which ended up being warning signs that I was too foolish to detect.

I can't think about Austin without thinking of all the reasons I shouldn't be thinking of him. And now, there's the reality that in a couple of weeks, he'll be somewhere else. Maybe playing a cowboy in a desert somewhere, flirting with another wardrobe assistant who has far more interesting costumes to dress him in than the same old jeans and flannel.

Casting my eyes up at the blue sky again, I realize that actually, yes, I can very much imagine it turning to gray.

When I'm back at the production office, Deidre calls me aside. Despite being vaguely in her good books lately, I still feel uneasy about the way she jerks her head for me to follow her into her alcove office, the straight set of her lips as she turns to face me.

Today, Deidre's wearing high-waisted black jeans and a steel gray T-shirt, one of those soft pima cotton ones that you think might cost twenty dollars from a basics store but likely costs $120 instead. It was Deidre who taught me why you should always wear dark colors on a film set. Whites can unintentionally reflect light onto the scene, and bright colors can be a distraction to the actors. There are so many rules I've learned over the last few years, and something about the way Deidre is standing, looking at me, makes me rehash all of them in my mind. I feel suddenly certain that I've broken one.

"Henry tells me you went and got a different size for Raquel's hiking jacket," Deidre says.

My uneasiness intensifies. I knew it. I've done something wrong.

"Um, yeah," I say. "I know that brand, and I know the sizes run small, so I thought we would need a larger size to offer. I'm sorry; I didn't even think about the fact that Kandace might be offended that we got her a larger size. Like, maybe we're implying . . ."

Deidre holds up a hand to cut me off.

"Most assistants would check in with me before doing that," she says.

"I know, I'm sorry. I just knew you were busy with the schedule change, and . . ."

"I like initiative, Matilda. I like it when my team knows the difference between the big decisions they need to run by me and the small ones they're able to make themselves. You did just that."

I have my mouth half open to apologize again, but then Deidre's words fully sink in.

She's not upset with me. She's not smiling, of course, but she's also not upset with me.

"Oh," I say.

"I need more of you," Deidre says, with a sigh. "You can teach someone to sew, but you can't teach the right attitude, you know?"

I nod slowly. "Yes," I say. "I mean . . . thank you?"

"The reason I'm telling you this," Deidre continues, "is that I have a supervisor position available on my next shoot."

My heart rate speeds up. On a large project, a wardrobe-supervisor role is normally one step below the costume designer. Above the assistant position I'm in now. In other words, it's the kind of job that anyone in the wardrobe department should aspire to, second only to being a costume designer like Deidre herself.

I know Deidre isn't just telling me this as a fun fact. I know what she's trying to say.

"I'm already signed up, and it will roll soon after we wrap on this one," Deidre continues. "I'd like for either you or Henry to consider stepping into the role. I'm planning on giving Henry the same heads-up. Just so you're aware."

She says it so matter-of-factly. So typical of Deidre Dotto.

"That's . . ." I say. "That's really nice of you. Thank you."

"Yes, but obviously the supervisor role is only for one person," Deidre continues. "Fortunately, I'd like to bring you both along anyway. Whoever works the assistant position can shadow the supervisor, and then there might be opportunities to step up in future. That's how these things work."

I nod and swallow. Yes, I know that's how these things are meant to work. If you're serious about a lasting career in the film industry, a supervisor role is definitely an opportunity to be excited about. I should be excited.

But I remember where my head was when this shoot began. I was considering taking a break after *Magic Season*. Taking some time to figure out if this was really what I wanted to do. If that's how I feel, then it makes sense for me to cede this opportunity to Henry. He'd be great at it. I think it's exactly what he wants.

But somehow, suddenly, it doesn't seem that easy. My life has been turned on its head in the last few weeks. How I felt then isn't quite how I feel now. I can't put my finger on how exactly I do feel, but all I know is that things are different.

"Matilda," Deidre continues. "I've been working with you for longer than Henry, and you have potential. You're sharp and organized and you keep a clear head when things don't go according to plan. You have initiative, like you showed today. And I think you have a good creative eye too, but your problem is you lack the confidence to really go for it."

I don't know how to respond to this. On the one hand, I think Deidre has just given me a clear string of compliments, which is unheard of. On the other hand, she kind of tied it all up with an insult.

"If I'm being honest, you would be my first choice," Deidre continues. "But I can't help but feel that you've been somewhat distracted on this shoot."

The hits just keep on coming. Nothing Deidre is saying is wrong—in fact, everything she's saying is entirely correct—but I feel somewhat staggered to hear it spoken out loud, so bluntly. Even if that is what Deidre's good at.

"I'm sorry," I reply, my cheeks hot. "I've had some things going on, but—"

Deidre holds up a hand. "You don't need to apologize. For the most part, it hasn't affected your work. But it has made me question what you want your next steps to be."

She clasps her hands together, the simple gold rings on her fingers glinting.

"I won't need to make my decision for another two weeks," Deidre continues. "That gives both of you some time to think as well."

I nod. "Thank you," I say. "I really appreciate the opportunity. Honestly. And I'm sorry again if I've seemed distracted. I'll try—"

Deidre sighs, and I realize I've apologized again when she told me not to. I have to press my lips together to stop myself from apologizing for apologizing.

"Here's some advice, Matilda, if you'll take it," Deidre says. "Though it might not be my place to say it."

"I appreciate any advice," I say softly.

"I'm not normally in the business of commenting on my team's personal lives, but I feel it's my duty . . ." Deidre clears her throat, and for the first time ever, I think she might seem uneasy, her cool, calm demeanor shifted slightly left of center.

"All I'll say," Deidre continues, "is be careful of that young man, all right?"

I look up, stunned. Of all the things I expected Deidre to say, that was definitely not it. I open my mouth to respond, but I can't find any words.

Deidre doesn't seem to need a response. She simply nods at me, places a hand on my shoulder briefly, and then sweeps out into the hallway.

TWENTY-NINE

Deidre's words echo in my head all day. Austin arrives to get ready for his scenes, and I leave Henry to dress him. I make sure I'm not anywhere near our wardrobe room when he's in there, because I know I won't be able to look him in the eye and act normally.

I have to assume, of course, that someone told Deidre about the festival. Or maybe she really *was* there—her diamonds blending in with the rhinestones—and saw Austin and me together with her own eyes.

What I don't exactly understand is what Deidre's warning me about. It would have been one thing for her to remind me to be professional. But that's not what she said. She said to *be careful*. Which is confusing, because everyone loves Austin. Deidre seems to love Austin. He's everyone's friend.

For the first time in a while, I think about the version of Austin I met through the wardrobe that first night. I know the reason that Austin was a marred version of the Austin I know. Losing a sibling would change you irrevocably.

But I'm conscious that this means there must be a dark seed in Austin, buried deep. A seed that has the potential to grow if watered with tragedy.

Maybe that's why I found that first timeline. As a warning. Just like Deidre's.

But even then, it's not like Austin was evil. He was a hollow, haunted, whiskey-reliant version of himself, sure, but he still didn't seem like a bad guy. He didn't swing that guitar at me. His room was neat. He was channeling his pain into his songwriting. If that's the worst that Austin gets, it's not too bad.

So, what exactly do I need to be afraid of?

I'm not entirely sure. All I know is that when Austin makes his way over to me when we're having a break on set later that evening, my heart is hammering in an unpleasant way again. Not dancing on floorboards this time. Stomping.

"There you are," Austin says in his easy, friendly way.

We're standing on Main Street, outside our bar. This scene follows a previous scene where Mitchell has tried to convince Raquel to stay at his family's farm for Christmas. Raquel and Grant have had a disagreement, so this is the pivotal moment when Raquel decides whether she's going to take Mitchell up on his offer, which represents the small-town life she grew up with, or if she's going to make up with Grant and spend Christmas with him instead, in the sprawling manor that's been in his family for generations.

We've run through the scene multiple times—in which Raquel ultimately turns Mitchell down—and now the camera and lighting team are resetting for a different angle. Austin's costume is fine. Makeup has already touched him up. He doesn't need to come over here to talk to me. And yet he has.

"Here I am," I say to him now.

"You're looking much better," he says.

"I'm feeling much better."

"Good." Austin slips his hands into his pockets and looks up at the sky. "This storm's getting everyone pretty riled up, huh?"

"Yeah. It's a pity our producers haven't figured out a way to pay someone to control the weather yet."

Austin smiles. "If they could, they would. And they'd probably try to negotiate a discount."

I can't help but laugh at this. Austin meets my gaze and holds it.

"Anyway," I say loudly. "Sounds like we'll be moving the hiking scene forward. You might be wrapped early."

"I know." Austin casts his eyes down. "Which is a shame."

"Really? More time off."

"I dunno. I'm enjoying it here."

"I guess it is close to home for you."

"It's not just that."

Stomp, stomp, stomp.

"There's also Virginia's ice cream truck," I offer weakly.

Austin holds my gaze. "It's not that either."

"The pilsners at Three Pines?"

"Mattie . . ."

"Austin, we're back on," calls out one of the assistant directors.

Austin turns back to look at me. He leans in and lowers his voice.

"Pretend you're fixing my collar," he murmurs.

"What?" I ask.

"I think there's something wrong with my collar," he emphasizes. "It feels crooked."

Almost out of obligation, I reach up to Austin's collar to fix it. There's nothing there to fix, of course, but it brings me close to him, so close that only I can hear when he says into my ear, "Do you think maybe we could go for a drink tonight? Just me and you?"

Stomp, stomp, stomp.

Be careful of that young man.

"We'll be finished really late," I say weakly. "I'll be done even later than you."

I can see Austin's Adam's apple move up and down. My lips are right by his collarbone. I think about what I saw through the wardrobe last night, and heat flushes my body.

"Okay," Austin murmurs. "Then what about tomorrow morning?"

"A drink in the morning?"

"Doesn't have to be a drink. We can go for a walk or something."

I hesitate.

"Mattie," Austin says softly.

And his voice suddenly sounds different. Its regular playfulness is gone. He sounds serious. Almost pleading.

"I just think," he continues, "that we should talk about this."

My eyes lock with his. In my peripheral vision, I can see someone walking over to us.

I could continue playing dumb. I could ask Austin what he means. But I know. We both know—if I can see it in Austin's eyes, then there's no way he can't see it in mine. And maybe he's right. Maybe it's best if we did talk about this.

I nod. "There's a nice trail by my place," I say. "I'll message you."

"Mattie," says the assistant director, walking over to us. "Is there something wrong, or are we good?"

"We're good," I say. I step away from Austin, feeling like a child being scolded.

"Austin?" the AD says.

"Yeah, coming," Austin replies.

He looks at me for a moment longer, but when I give him nothing in return, he makes his way back to set, where the director is waiting for him.

I notice a few of our fellow crew members giving me funny looks and raised eyebrows, and I kind of wish the sky would open up right then and there and rain down hailstones—anything to take the attention off me and cool the heat I know is showing on my face.

I'm the epitome of professionalism for the rest of the afternoon. I almost go over the top with it, refusing to crack a single joke or full smile until we're finally wrapped for the day and back in the production office.

I haven't properly seen Henry since the festival. We've been like passing ships today, and I'm grateful for it. If Deidre knows about Austin—and the rest of the crew seems to suspect it, given the looks I was getting—then Henry definitely knows.

Unfortunately, I can't avoid him forever, and I inevitably find myself cornered in our wardrobe room at the end of the night. I'm caged in by racks of clothing on either side of me and Henry between me and the door, with no escape.

"*What*," he declares, "is going on?"

"Nothing," I say too quickly.

"There's a rumor going around," Henry continues. "Can you guess what it is?"

"That Kandace is divorcing her husband?"

"Come on, Mattie . . ."

"That you have a crush on Stunt Guy Tom?"

"I actually got over that. Turns out we have nothing in common. But speaking of . . ."

"I also heard from Loren that there's a theory—"

"*Mattie*. Stop. And tell me, what's going on with you and Mr. Austin Farrow?"

I laugh, but it's way too high pitched. "What?" I say. "Nothing."

Henry rolls his eyes. "Please. Val told me about yesterday. Glad you're okay, by the way."

"Thank you?"

"Val said Austin was very sweet to you. Very caring."

"He's a nice guy."

"And it's not just Val. Other people have noticed. *I've* noticed. There's a hundred percent something there."

"Am I being interrogated?"

"By me? Never. It's just that I recall a particular conversation the other week in which you scolded me about being professional."

"I am being professional," I insist. "Just as professional as you hanging out with Stunt Guy Tom."

"Oh my God, Mattie." Henry drapes himself over one of the clothing racks, exasperated. "I'm not trying to get you in trouble. I just need to *know*—you know I need to know things like this! What's going on?!"

I sigh and slump against the wall.

"Honestly," I say. "Nothing's happened. We've chatted here a bit, obviously, and then there was the festival. Everyone else was doing their own thing, so I went with him to watch his friend play. Then I fainted, and he was nice about it. That's it."

"I don't think that *is* it."

Neither do I, and Henry can tell.

"Well, even if it's more than that, what's the point?" I continue sharply. "He'll be leaving soon."

"So? You're in the same industry, he's an absolute babe, and he *is* a nice guy. What's the problem?"

I fix my gaze on Henry. "There are a lot of problems," I say. More than Henry can imagine.

Henry sighs. "Well, for the record, I think you should go for it."

I roll my eyes and shake my head. "It's not that easy."

"It could be. If you wanted it to be."

"I don't think Deidre would be happy," I admit.

Henry softens his expression then.

"She told you too, didn't she?" he says. "About the supervisor position?"

"Yeah. She did."

"Game on, I guess?"

I shrug. "If you really want it, you should have it."

"You're infuriating, you know that?"

"Why?"

"You're much better at this than I am. You should have that job. The problem is you don't seem like you want it."

"Maybe I don't."

"Why not?"

I sigh. "I don't know. I know it's a great opportunity. I'm just not sure if this is the right career for me."

It feels like I can be honest with Henry. I know he gossips, but he's not vindictive. And he's infuriatingly good at seeing right through people anyway.

"Okay," he says. "So, what do you want to do instead?"

"If I knew that, it would be easier. I guess I could explore a different part of the fashion industry . . ."

"You know fashion people can be the absolute worst, right?"

Henry's right. If the cutthroat nature of the film industry exhausts me sometimes, then fashion is hardly going to be any better.

"Or maybe journalism," I say. "I've always been interested in journalism."

"Kind of a dying career these days, isn't it? With social media and all that?"

"Right, well, who knows?" I throw my hands up in the air. "Maybe I'll stay in Casey River and get a job working in a bakery or a . . . bookstore . . . or something."

"And make minimum wage?"

"Why are you being such a downer?"

"Because." Henry leans against one of our plastic boxes full of rain ponchos. "I'm trying to make a point. There will be a downside to any job you have. Any industry you work in. You'll get sick of anything after a while. Plus, if you switch careers, you'll probably have to start from scratch. At least here, you have a reputation already. You have a *good* reputation, even if you would never say it yourself."

"Do *you* not want that supervisor role? Is that why you're trying so hard to persuade me that I want it?"

"No. I do want it. But a competition is always more satisfying to win when your rival is actually trying."

Henry tries to arrange his face into an evil grin, but he doesn't quite manage it.

"I just have some things to think about," I say. "That's all."

Henry straightens up and comes over to me. He places both hands on my shoulders.

"Just remember," he says. "The grass isn't always greener on the other side."

"You're so inspiring. You should start a podcast."

"I have thought about that, actually."

"Of course you have."

Henry turns to leave then, but he pauses in the doorway.

"You know where the grass is greener, though?" he says.

"Where?"

"On an apple orchard. Probably."

"Shut up," I groan.

Henry winks at me and then disappears.

THIRTY

I don't like what I find through the portal that night.

The atmosphere is off as soon as I step through the wardrobe. I can smell a sour aroma in the air—like spilled beer—and hear bass-heavy dance music thudding from the living room. There's absolutely nothing hanging in the wardrobe except for the bare hangers, but when I peer through the crack, I see men's clothes strewn across the room and empty bottles on the nightstand.

Something about this feels ominous. I almost want to turn back around and close the door behind me. But I stay.

It definitely doesn't look like I'm occupying this version of the apartment. I know I can go through messy phases, but I would never let my living space look this bad.

I wonder if this is another Austin timeline. Maybe in this world he's sunk even lower than the first one. It could be another warning, another red flag from the universe telling me to run in the opposite direction.

I step tentatively into the bedroom and start to poke around. There's an air mattress on the far side of the room with some sheets and a blanket haphazardly draped over it. A duffel bag with men's clothes spilling out of it is at the foot of the mattress. In the bathroom, it's a similar story. There are two men's travel cases by the sink. Toiletries in the shower. A blue glass bottle of cologne by the window.

I pick up the bottle. It looks vaguely familiar. And when I uncap the lid and bring it to my nose, the scent hits me like a punch to the face.

I know that scent.

That's when I hear someone come into the bedroom and close the door behind them.

This time, I'm not in the wardrobe. I can't just escape to the other side. I'm trapped. I can hear the person take a few more steps across the carpet. My heart is pounding. The footsteps stop. And then there's the squeak of bed springs as the person sits down on the bed.

I can hear the faint dial sound of the person calling someone. After a few rings, a voice on the other end of the line says, "Hey. What's up?"

It's my voice. I'm the one on the other side of the call.

"Where are you?" says the person sitting on the bed.

And my fears are confirmed. I knew it as soon as I smelled the cologne.

It's Jack. Jack's on the other side of the door. Jack's in the bedroom. Jack's calling me, asking me where I am.

"I'm at the winery with the girls," my voice replies. "The one where we're staying. We're having dinner at the on-site restaurant."

"Just you girls?"

"Uh, well, actually . . ." I can sense the nervousness in my voice, even from here. "We've run into some of my friends from work. They're filming a movie out here at the moment, and they ended up coming here for dinner too."

"Isn't that convenient?" Jack says, his voice tight.

"Yeah, I mean, we didn't plan it or anything. But it's nice to see them."

"Who's them?"

"You know, Henry and Loren. I've talked about them before. Then there's Val—she's a local."

"Is that it?"

"Uh, there are some of the stunt guys here too. And one of the actors."

"Which actor?"

"Why are you asking so many questions?"

"It's just, this is meant to be a girls' weekend. That's what you told me. And yet Hannah posted that photo of you earlier, and it's not just girls, is it?"

"We ran into some of my coworkers, that's all . . ."

"Ex-coworkers."

"Huh?"

"Ex-coworkers. You're not doing the film stuff anymore."

"Yeah. I guess. Anyway, how's your weekend? How was golf?"

Jack doesn't respond right away. I take a deep breath and venture to peer through the crack in the bathroom door.

I haven't realized until now that the sight of Jack actually frightens me a little. It's funny, really, the way the butterflies of a new relationship feel very much like a stress response. Your heart rate increases, your stomach tightens, your mouth goes dry, you forget how to speak. Somehow, you convince yourself this feels good, and maybe it kind of does. I remember what Margot told me about good kinds of stress.

But ideally, that feeling will thaw out into a healthy feeling of comfort. Your heart rate slows to the rhythm of the dancing on the floorboards, rather than stomping.

Not with Jack. No, now I realize that the butterflies never settled with Jack. His broad shoulders, his gray eyes, the way he runs his hands over the stubble on his chin and blows an infuriated sigh out of his thin lips as he looks down at his phone . . . all of it causes my hair to stand on end.

"Golf was fine," he says tersely.

"And what are you up to tonight?"

"Just having drinks at the apartment."

"It's a pity there aren't any strip clubs in Casey River, huh?"

My voice isn't accusatory. I can tell that I'm trying to be cool and lighthearted, always trying to make Jack crack a smile when he's in a mood like this—sulky and suspicious about something small I've done: a too-friendly conversation with a stranger at a café, a message from an old friend who happens to be a guy.

"What do you mean?" Jack challenges me.

"You know . . . Isn't that what guys do at bachelor parties?"

"Are you trying to say you don't trust me?"

"No, I'm just making a joke. It's, like, a pretty universal thing for guys to arrange strippers for a bachelor party, isn't it?"

"Is that what your friends have done for you?"

My stomach is suddenly churning. The dots are connecting in my mind.

Jack's away with the boys. I'm away with the girls.

It can't be. I wouldn't have been that foolish.

Or would I? I was foolish throughout that entire relationship. I eventually woke up to it.

But what if I didn't?

"Of course not," I reply. "The cheapest bottle of wine at this place is fifty dollars. It's not the kind of place a male stripper's about to come waltzing into."

"But there is a good-looking actor there."

"Oh, come on . . ."

"Come on what?"

"I'm not doing anything wrong. I'm just out celebrating with my friends, like you are. I'm allowed to do this."

"Fuck, Mattie, I never said you weren't *allowed* to. You're always talking like this, like a child, about what you're allowed to do."

"Because that's how you make me feel!"

My voice on the other side has become less casual, less cool. I'm starting to fight back. I realize the version of me here in the bathroom is pressed against the door, anxiously waiting to see what happens next.

"I don't make you *feel* like a child," Jack retorts. "I don't make you feel like anything. You talk like you don't have control over your own emotions."

"I do. It's just . . ."

"It's just what?"

"It's just . . . nothing. It's nothing."

No, I think. Don't back down. Keep fighting.

Jack blows out a sharp breath.

"I knew this was a bad idea," he mutters.

"What?" I ask, my voice smaller now. "The weekend? Or . . . the engagement?"

No, I think, as the churning feeling in my stomach speeds up to turbo mode. *No, no, no.*

"I don't know," Jack says. "Bachelor and bachelorette parties are so stupid. If you need to celebrate your last week of freedom, why do people even do this? Why do people even get married?"

"You told me you wanted to get married."

"I don't know what I want."

The worst kind of déjà vu comes washing over me.

I remember this. I remember this too well.

THIRTY-ONE

In my timeline—my real timeline—Jack broke up with me three times in total. The first time was about three months in, when I'd been working on a production out of town. It was only going to be a couple of weeks away, but I noticed Jack grow distant and sulky in the lead-up to it. He said it was because he was going to miss me, but the vibe quickly grew resentful. I started to worry that I was being selfish for going away for so long. Maybe I should be looking at only taking jobs that didn't require me to travel? But I knew that was ridiculous. In the patchy, unpredictable work of film, you take what you can get.

Jack's communication with me was off for the whole shoot. And then, on the last night, at our wrap party, he called me. He told me he'd been having second thoughts and wasn't sure if the relationship was going to work. Things didn't feel the way they had at the beginning, he told me.

Blinking back tears, swallowing down the nausea I felt, I tried to tell him that it was normal for things to change in a relationship. It didn't mean things were *bad*, just different. I felt like the world's most pathetic lawyer, desperately pleading my case. But it didn't matter what argument I put forward. Jack had made up his mind.

I left the wrap party early and went back to the motel room I was staying in and literally cried myself to sleep. I woke up with my eyes half swollen shut, reaching for my phone to make sure it hadn't all just been a bad dream.

But then, when I was back from the shoot and back in town, I heard from Jack a few days later. He was missing me. He'd made a mistake, he said. Could we catch up for a drink and talk?

Once we got back together, I told myself that I'd be more careful this time. Jack was a special person with unique needs—that's what made him so electric, so exciting to be with. But he was also vulnerable, and I needed to understand that. I was good at paying attention to other people and what they needed. I could do this. I could be the perfect fit for him.

Six months went by of tumult and confusion and brief bright patches of fun and passion, which were all that kept me clinging on. During the low points, I'd pull those memories out of my mind, like pulling jewelry out of a trinket box, reminding myself of how good things could be when they were good. I told myself that it evened out in the end. It was better than being in a boring, passionless relationship, like so many other people I saw around me.

The second breakup happened the day before my birthday. I was planning a get-together at a local bar, and I was excited for Jack to finally meet and mingle with everyone I loved, because he hadn't been able to meet many of my friends or family yet. But yet again, he grew sulky in the lead-up. He wasn't sure why I needed a big party—he'd wanted to take me out for an intimate dinner, just the two of us. I told him that was a really sweet idea, and we could do that as well, maybe the night before, if he wanted to. But he told me it wasn't the same and that he just felt like an afterthought.

I ended up hating my own birthday party, wandering around like a ghost with swollen eyes again.

This was when I confided in Margot. I kept a lot of it to myself originally, but this time I told her everything. She admitted that she knew, and she was worried about me, but that she didn't want to be too overt about it in case it pushed me away. She'd already noticed I'd grown distant from her and the rest of our friends, even though I hadn't noticed yet. It was like when you go swimming in the ocean and get caught in a tide, then don't realize how far you've drifted from shore until you look back again.

When I took Jack back for the second time, I was nervous about telling Margot. I remember the way she hid her sigh and told me she'd still be there for me, for anything.

The next three months were faded, like a printer running out of ink. It's like I knew the truth but still didn't feel strong enough to face it. When he broke up with me the third time, just before our one-year anniversary, I didn't even have the energy to cry myself to sleep.

I went for a long hike with Margot and her friends after that. A long, grueling, mind-emptying, epiphany-rich hike. When I came back, I booked in to see a therapist that one of Margot's friends recommended. The ache in my limbs and the blisters on my feet faded, but the clarity I'd gained on the hike remained. My eyes weren't swollen anymore. They were finally open.

And when the inevitable call came from Jack, I bundled all my newfound strength around me like armor. I let the call ring out. And the next one. I called Margot instead, and she came and sat by my side and watched as I blocked his number.

It felt like reaching the summit of a mountain I didn't even know I'd been climbing.

———

In this timeline though, I must have answered the call.

I must have slid back down the mountainside and taken him back again. And now here I am, trying to plead my case over the phone once more, when I should be ordering multiple bottles of that fifty-dollar wine with my girlfriends.

"It was your idea," I hear my other voice saying. "You said getting married was the right thing to do. The right way to show how committed we are to each other."

"Yeah, I know I said that. You don't have to repeat what I said to me."

"I thought this was what you wanted."

I hear Jack sigh. "Yeah, well, I guess it's you that I worry about."

"Me? About what?"

"About your commitment."

"Jack, I'm going to marry you."

"Yeah, but you also said this was a girls' weekend. And you didn't keep your word about that. I just don't know if you mean what you say sometimes."

"I told you . . . look, should I get a taxi there? Maybe we should talk about this in person?"

I don't know what makes me do what I do next. Maybe two weeks ago I wouldn't have done it at all.

All I know is that it's somehow much easier to defend other people than it is yourself.

I've always been a nonconfrontational person, to the extent of almost being a pushover. But the few times in my life when I've felt brazen anger and made it known, it's been because of someone else's suffering—not mine. Some kids throwing rocks at a stray dog in the park. A colleague who was making fun of someone on set. A friend's boyfriend who was treating her terribly . . .

I don't know where that fire goes when it's me who needs the defending. I've been treated badly at work, in relationships, in friendships, and I just flounder and let it happen. I make excuses, talk it down, or else combat the conflict with passive-aggressive techniques like silence or complaining behind someone's back instead of to their face.

But now. Now I've been given the extraordinary, never-in-a-lifetime opportunity to defend myself as a third person.

And before I know what I'm doing, I'm bursting through the bathroom door.

Jack's jaw drops at the sight of me standing there in the bedroom. He stares down at his phone and then back up at me.

"What the fuck?" he says.

"We're not getting married," I announce.

"What . . . who is that?" my voice through the phone asks.

I stride across the room and yank Jack's phone out of his hand while he's still sitting there frozen.

"Mattie, it's me," I say into the phone. "I mean, it's you. I'm a different version of you. I've come here from a different timeline. One where you walked away from this toxic bullshit months ago."

Jack stands up, and I brace myself, but he doesn't move toward me. He moves away, backing against the wall.

"What the fuck is happening?" he asks.

"Yeah, I'm asking myself the same question," says the other version of me. "Who is this?"

"I told you, I'm you," I repeat. "I'm here to tell you that you can't marry this guy. Under any circumstances. If you really think about it, you don't even want to. You don't really want him. You don't want this life."

"What is this twisted game you're playing?" Jack says, still pressed against the wall, his face a pale, fearful gray that gives me intense satisfaction.

"You're the one playing a game," I say to him. Then I direct my voice at the phone again. "And it's an unwinnable game, Mattie. Nothing you do is going to make him happy. Nothing you do is going to make him feel less insecure about himself. I think you know this already. There's nothing you can do except leave. Trust me."

Jack's phone flashes with a notification, telling me the other Mattie is requesting to video chat. I take a deep breath and accept.

When the other version of me sees me on the screen, all blood drains from her face. But this gives me less satisfaction than it did with Jack.

"What the . . ." the other version stammers. "This is . . . I don't understand . . . oh my God, has someone spiked my drink?"

"No," I say. "This is real. I'm real. I'm another version of you, from a different life. And I'm happier. I might not realize it every day, but I'm so much happier now that I'm not chained to this relationship, pushing it uphill every damn day only to start at the bottom again the next morning. You have to believe me, Mattie. You have to believe yourself."

I can see the glint of tears in my eyes. Both versions of them.

"This is fucked up." Jack pushes himself off the wall and lunges toward me. He grabs his phone out of my hand, where it clatters to the ground. "Have you completely lost your mind?"

"No," I say. "I think I've finally found it."

Jack steps toward me. His hands reach for my shoulders.

But I'm too quick for him. I back away, all the way to the wardrobe. The last thing I see before I disappear back through the portal is the slant of Jack's eyes—sharp and gray like knives.

THIRTY-TWO

I don't bring back a souvenir from this timeline. At least not a physical one. But this timeline burrows into me deeper than any of the ones that came before it.

I interfered. I interfered with the natural course of events. What does this mean? Am I going to be punished? Is the portal going to close to me forever as a reprimand for breaking its unwritten rules?

Or did I do exactly what I was meant to do? Is this the reason I've been given access to these other worlds—to change something? To make a difference?

It does feel exhilarating, in a way. I stood up for myself. It was another version of me, sure, but *I stood up for myself.* I looked Jack in the eye, and I didn't flinch. *I* scared *him*, for once.

Hindsight is twenty-twenty. It's so obvious now, listening to the way Jack talked to me on the phone, how manipulative he was. Making me feel like I did something wrong or had been deceitful, just because I happened to run into my film friends at the winery. Then trying to twist it around on me and tell me I was acting like a child for feebly trying to defend myself. This was how all our arguments went. I ended up feeling so lost, as if I'd waded deep into the woods and didn't even know what path I'd taken to get there. I always ended up conceding. Worried that if I didn't, he'd just break up with me. Like he'd done before.

It's easy to look back now and think, *Why? Why did I stay? Why did I go back? Why is there a timeline where I agreed to* marry *the guy, for God's sake?*

But I remember. At the beginning, it had been attraction. A deluded belief that I'd been chosen, that we were special together.

But then when the cracks started to show—turning into gaping chasms—I think it was the game of it that kept me. The belief that maybe, if I played all my cards right, I would win him. The real, whole, true version of him, which I only ever got glimpses of. A version of him that wasn't real, of course. Not in any timeline.

The unwinnable game.

I'm a different person now. I know that relationship changed me, and for a while now, I've been wondering if it changed me for the worse. Now I can see that, even if I'm battle scarred, I'm stronger. I'm happier, even if I don't always realize it.

And maybe that's the invisible souvenir I carry with me.

———

I'm feeling brave when I meet Austin the next morning. We meet on the street outside my apartment. The morning is gray, with a light rain starting up. Austin and I are accidentally matching, in waterproof jackets and baseball hats. We exchange a joke about this as I lead Austin toward the trail to Fallen Tree Falls, which I figure is as good a place as any to take a walk to this morning. Perhaps the best place, given the story that Florence told me about the falls the other day.

This place is a crossroads.

"I know this trail," Austin says, as we enter the glistening, rain-soaked cloister of the trees.

"You've been here before?" I ask.

"Yeah, I ran it just the other day. I came in from the trailhead closer to town, though. It leads to the waterfall, right?"

"Fallen Tree Falls," I confirm.

I wonder what day Austin ran the trail and if it was the same day I came for my walk. We might have missed each other by moments.

Now, we walk side by side on the damp trail. Our elbows knock occasionally, as we navigate around ruts and puddles, but otherwise, we don't touch.

"We'll be on the other side of the park later today," I say. "For your hiking scene."

"I'm looking forward to that. Hopefully the rain eases up."

"It's supposed to in the afternoon. Then it gets bad tomorrow."

We're talking about the weather. Dammit. I can feel the tension between us, hanging in the air like electricity from the impending storm. Austin seems more serious than usual. He cracks a couple of jokes, but they seem muted. When we come to a spot on the trail where a large puddle is forming, we have to walk single file to get around it. Austin guides me in front of him, his hand on the small of my back for the briefest moment, before he lets go.

We arrive at the lookout to the falls right when we've run out of small talk. We both lean against the railing and listen to the water gushing for a moment. The rain has eased temporarily, and I shake some stray droplets from my jacket. I want to do the same for Austin's, but I'm afraid to touch him.

"You know the other day at the festival?" Austin says eventually.

Here we are. We've arrived at the reason he wanted to meet up today. I can see Austin steeling himself, the way he does when he's getting ready for a scene.

"Yeah?" I reply.

"I'm sorry if I came on too strong," Austin continues. "Or any time before that too. I hadn't even stopped to think about it, until I talked to Hayden later that night. He's gotten himself in trouble before for doing the same thing."

"For doing what?" I ask.

Austin looks at me. "I know you're a smart person," he says. "So, I don't know if you actually don't understand what I'm trying to say or if you're just pretending. Or being polite, like always."

"I don't . . . know," I say honestly.

Austin blows out a breath. "Okay," he says. "Here's the thing, Mattie. I try to be friendly to everyone on set. I'm always the good guy, right? But normally, when I go to wardrobe for my fittings or to get dressed, I'm in and out. I don't hang around. I'll be social, but I don't make a habit of inviting female coworkers to music festivals with me. I don't invite them for drinks or for morning walks."

He fixes me with his green-eyed gaze.

"Maybe I've been unprofessional," he continues. "That's what Hayden warned me about. But I didn't even really stop to think. Ever since that first day I met you, I've just . . . wanted to be around you."

I can't figure out if my heart is dancing on the floorboards or stomping. If what I'm feeling is butterflies or something bad.

"Why?" I ask finally, in a small voice.

"Why?" Austin repeats with a laugh. "Why am I so attracted to you? I mean, have you seen yourself?"

His words reverberate in my head. He's attracted to me. The regular, self-doubting part of me wants to be shocked, but that feels disingenuous. I've known this, of course. Despite my denial to Florence, to myself, of course I've known this.

"Though, it's not just physical," Austin continues. "Every time we talk, I want to know more about you. You make me laugh without realizing and you see details in things that other people don't and . . . I mean, I could go on, but I won't, because the whole point is . . . I realize now that maybe you don't feel the same, and I've been trying too hard. So, I wanted to get it out in the open."

Austin takes his hat off and runs his hand through his hair. Even if his voice has sounded cool, his hands look unsteady.

"It's not that I don't feel the same," I say finally.

Austin's eyes glint.

"No?" he says.

"Of course not." I gesture to him, to his whole body. "Have *you* seen *yourself*?"

"I mean, we never really see ourselves. Because we look different in real life than on screen."

They were the first words he spoke to me, the day I met him for his fitting. And I know what he means about how it felt that day. I remember how that fitting felt different from how it normally would and how I chastised myself for it.

"Well," I say. "There's a reason why you can make a career out of people looking at you."

Austin smiles, but it's a little sad.

"You know, it's not just about that," he says. "I didn't get into acting 'cause I'm vain or anything."

"I know that," I reply.

"I love the craft of it. I love the characters and the storytelling . . . and God, I wish I had a script right now, because maybe I wouldn't be fucking this up so badly."

"You're not fucking it up," I say.

"I'm not?"

"No." I shake my head. "You haven't done anything wrong. You haven't come on too strong or misread anything. I'm just . . ." I falter. I look out beyond Austin, to the old stump next to the lookout, where the new tree is growing. I know now that this must be the stump of the original fallen tree, the one that created the bridge. To cross or not to cross. That is the question.

"I just have some things going on right now," I say to Austin.

Austin looks choked for a moment, like someone's fastened a tie too tightly around his throat.

"I'm sorry," I say. "That sounds like *I'm* reading from a script. A bad one."

"No," Austin forces himself to say. "I wanted to hear how you felt. I wanted to talk about this."

"It's a weird time for me right now," I continue. "I don't want to get too deep, but I came into this shoot allowing myself this next month to figure some things out. I was thinking this might even be my last film job for a while."

Austin's brow furrows. "Why? You're so good at it."

I shrug. "It's just a lot sometimes. You know how it is."

"Yeah, of course." Austin leans back against the railing. "I've thought about quitting before too."

"Really?"

"Yep. After every failed audition. Every negative review. Every bad take."

"You don't seem to have any bad takes."

"I straight-up forgot my lines the other day," he laughs.

"I didn't notice."

"That's because you were busy taking your sweater off, on the sidelines. Which was why I forgot my lines."

I flush. "Well then, I've failed at my job. Because I'm not supposed to be a distraction."

"Unfortunately, you have definitely failed at that. At least with me."

We smile at each other, but Austin's doesn't reach his eyes like normal.

"What would you do if you didn't act?" I ask him.

Austin shrugs. "You know, being at the festival the other day, I was thinking more about the whole music thing. Maybe it would have been nice to try a bit harder at that."

I want to tell him so badly. I want to tell him that there's another world out there where he did pursue music. I want to tell him everything. Maybe, instead of pulling away, I should be leaning in. The way I did in that other timeline.

But I think I've already made my choice.

"You'd be good at it," I say instead.

"I don't know. I find songwriting difficult. It's too personal. It's easier to tell other people's stories."

"That's what I've always thought too." I sigh. "But somewhere along the way, I think I've gotten lost telling other people's stories. I'm trying to find my own again."

It's one of the first times I've said it out loud. And I've said it out loud to Austin, of all people. The person I've been trying so hard to keep the truth from.

Austin reaches his hand out to where mine rests on the railing. He places it over mine, but our fingers don't intertwine. It's a reassuring touch, rather than a romantic one.

"I get it, Mattie," he says. "You need some time."

He does get it. He's not affronted by my rejection, the way some guys might be. And he's not pushing it. He's being perfect, as always. Which makes it even more painful.

"Thank you," I say quietly.

I see something then, out of the corner of my eye. It's come from the tree growing out of the old stump. It's a flash of something dark, like a person wearing a black T-shirt. I squint, wondering if we're being watched.

But when I crane my head to look around the tree, there's nothing there. I must have imagined it.

The rain chooses that moment to start up again. It comes down in sparkling sheets, which mingle with the waterfall's cascade.

Austin pulls up the hood of my jacket.

"We should get back," he says.

"That's supposed to be my job," I reply, as I pull up his hood in return and straighten it around his face.

He smiles down at me, and I know how easy it would be for me to rise and bring my lips to his. I know there are other worlds where I've done it.

But I'm in this world. And Austin's right—I need some time.

So we start to walk back down the trail, leaving the crossroads behind us.

THIRTY-THREE

Maybe I've made a terrible mistake.

I had this beautiful guy standing in front of me, wearing his heart on his sleeve like the perfect accessory, telling me how he feels. That he's attracted to me. That he wants to be around me. That he's felt this way since the day we met.

And I turned him down.

On paper, it seems like a mistake. And I have moments throughout the rest of the day where my stomach churns, and I wonder, if I could rewind the clock and do it again, if I'd make the same decision.

I'm almost certain there's a timeline out there where I said something different at that falls. A part of me hopes I'm going to find it the next time I open the wardrobe door.

But another part of me is starting to suspect that obsessing over what-ifs and if-onlys isn't the reason I found my portal. That maybe I need to start owning the decisions I've made that have led me to where I am now.

So even though my mind seesaws and my stomach churns and my heart patters on and off for the rest of the day, I force myself to look forward instead of back.

This afternoon, we're on the eastern side of the regional park. The park here is filled with tall, elegant trees, generously spread apart to allow for good camera setups. When sunlight peeks through the clouds, it hits the moss-covered logs and trails in an artful way that our cinematographer is obsessed with capturing.

Magic Season is set in December, of course, which isn't your typical hiking season. But this scene is a part of a Christmas hiking challenge that Raquel, Grant, and Mitchell are all taking part in. Things get a bit competitive between Mitchell and Grant, and Grant ultimately ends up the winner—revealing that he's not just some precious rich boy; he volunteers as a firefighter, despite being wealthy enough to not have to work. Raquel falls for Grant even harder, Mitchell gets discarded, and we start building up to our big happy ending.

I feel guilty that, after our conversation this morning, Austin has to film a scene where he gets bested. But if any of this is weighing on him, he doesn't show it. He's back to being charming, friendly, focused Austin, and I'm back to being a wardrobe assistant who should be trying to make a good impression, given the promotion that's on the line.

Today does feel like the kind of day where I could love my job again. While everyone's still nervous about the storm, moods are elevated by being out on a different location. Our set looks beautiful. We've taken over one of the wider trails by a clearing, and the art department has sprinkled artificial eco-friendly snow effects over everything, like a dusting of icing sugar. There are battery-powered stake lights by the edge of trail, marking the way. More Christmas lights are strung through the trees, because I'm not sure if we have a single set that *doesn't* feature a plethora of twinkling lights.

Above us, the rain holds. The sky is far from the periwinkle blue we had yesterday, but the feeble blue gray actually works well in the wintery context of the scene we're filming.

Kandace looks great in her burgundy hiking jacket, which is the size I picked out for her—I knew it would be a better fit. And Austin looks at home among the trees, of course. We have him in mustard today, rather than his regular green, which would blend in too much with the forest. It suits him, though. Earthy colors look good on him. So does navy blue. And white. And red.

Thankfully, the rest of the day is too busy for me to entertain any thoughts about what colors look good on Austin and whether I've made the right decision. There's a minor emergency when some press and photographers arrive, tipped off by a couple of local hikers that we're filming here today. Us filming *Magic Season* isn't exactly national news, but a story broke in an entertainment magazine yesterday that Kandace is indeed divorcing her quite-famous husband, so she's in the spotlight at the moment. She doesn't want the photographers anywhere near her, so the locations and security teams have a challenge on their hands trying to keep the press at bay.

Austin and Hayden also get on board. They take turns shielding Kandace from view whenever they can. And when they're resetting for a new shot, I see Austin head over to the photographers and strike up an overly friendly conversation with them. They become flustered then, trying to figure out if Austin is someone tabloid worthy, which gives Kandace time to get her makeup touched up in peace. I feel an ache inside me, watching this. He's so damn nice. What the hell am I doing? As his head turns in my direction, I duck into the video village, not sure that I can handle his direct gaze.

The photographers eventually become uninterested after that—or maybe they secretly get the photos they want—and we keep filming undisturbed. I watch the monitors, keeping an eye out for costume malfunctions or adjustments, and help the locations guys control the public when I'm not needed for wardrobe.

We wrap filming when the good light leaves the forest, midevening. The sky is still clear of rain, but I can feel the air pressure dropping. I head into our wardrobe trailer while the cast members get changed in their trailers. Kandace and Hayden's assistants return their costumes to me, and I sit on a stool in the trailer checking over the clothes to see if there's anything that needs to be repaired before tomorrow.

When someone knocks on the door, I call out for them to come in.

"I hoped I'd find you here."

My stomach seizes at the sound of that voice.

For a moment, I feel like I'm back through the portal again. That's the only way I could possibly be hearing that voice. The only way I could possibly be seeing the face that's appeared in the doorway of the trailer.

Stubble on his chin. Lopsided smirk. Steel gray eyes like knives.

"Jack . . ." I murmur.

"Surprise?" he says in response.

I recover quickly. More quickly than I would have if I hadn't already been through this last night. I stand up from the stool and fold my arms across my chest.

"What are you doing here?" I demand.

"Oh, good to see you too," Jack says in response, leaning against the doorframe. "I just heard that there was filming going on in town, and I knew this was one you were on. Hannah told me the other day. That's all."

The trailer seems to spin around me. "But why are you . . . why are you even in Casey River?"

"I didn't come all the way here to see you—don't worry," Jack says with a sharp laugh. "I'm in town with the boys for a few days. It's Blake's bachelor party."

Blake's bachelor party. Right, of course. Blake and Hannah used to be mutual friends of ours, though I haven't seen either of them much since the breakup. I was invited to the wedding when I was still with Jack but have since declined the invitation. Partly so that I don't have to see the face I'm staring at right now.

"We haven't spoken in months," I say bluntly.

"Believe me, I know that. I've messaged you a couple of times. But you haven't replied."

"I blocked your number."

I feel bold. If I could stand up to Jack in the alternate timeline, I can stand up to him here.

Jack blows out a breath. "That's a bit dramatic, isn't it?"

"No," I reply. "It's a completely appropriate reaction, actually."

"Come on, Mattie." Jack takes a step up, until he's almost in the trailer. I keep my arms folded and my gaze steely. "We were together for a year," he continues. "I know I hurt you, and I'm sorry for that. Really, I am. I've been thinking about it a lot, and it doesn't make sense to me that we go from being something to just . . . being nothing. That's why I've been wanting to talk to you."

"Yes, it does make sense, actually. You made it make sense when you decided to end things with me. For the third time. Anyway, I'm at work now, so I really can't talk about this. I don't want to talk about this."

Jack climbs up the final step and into the trailer. I take a step back.

"I didn't invite you in," I say.

"You're overreacting a bit, don't you think?" asks Jack. "I'm not an axe murderer."

"But who are you, exactly?"

My heart flips at the sound of this new voice. Austin appears in the doorway. He's holding his costume in his hands and frowning at Jack.

Jack turns around to face him. "Who are you?" he challenges.

"I'm part of the cast," Austin replies calmly. "You don't appear to be."

"I'm a friend of Mattie's," Jack replies.

"No, he's not," I say.

"Yeah, I was getting that impression," says Austin. "How about you leave now, man? We've all had a long day, and we need to pack out."

Jack spits out another laugh. "Who *is* this guy?" he says to me.

"He's part of the cast, and he's here to return his costume, because we're both working," I reply calmly.

Jack squints at Austin. "I don't recognize you," he says. "Have you been in anything I'd know?"

"Probably not," Austin replies.

"What, do I not look like someone who watches films?" Jack says.

"No," Austin answers evenly. "I just haven't been in anything that big yet."

"Oh. Well, that's too bad for you."

"*Okay,*" I say. I move around Jack, so that I'm closer to Austin and take the costume Austin's holding out of his arms. "Austin's right—we have packing to do. And I need to sort out our laundry."

"I can wait," says Jack.

I look over and catch Austin's eye. He doesn't say anything out loud, but his expression asks me silently what I need him to do. *Do you need me to get rid of this guy for you? Or do you want me to back up? I'll take your lead.*

I square my shoulders and face Jack.

"I already told you," I say. "I don't want to talk to you. Go enjoy your party. We're done here."

I manage to hide the tremble in my voice, although I know it wants to come out. I feel Austin's arm right by mine, just an inch away.

Jack looks between the two of us and lets out one of his signature laughs that doesn't even come close to reaching his eyes.

"Okay, I get the message here," he says. "I always knew you had a thing for actors."

I can't bring myself to look over at Austin.

"Goodbye, Jack," I say.

"Yeah, last time I try to be nice, I guess," he says.

Austin tenses beside me but stays silent.

"I guess so," I say coldly.

Jack doesn't seem to like that I'm getting the last word. He never did. But then he glances out of the trailer and sees one of our security guys in a high-vis vest walking our way. And he decides to simply shake his head at me and Austin and back down the steps.

I wait until Jack's across the parking lot before I let out a breath. I can feel Austin shift beside me, but then the security guard pokes his head into the trailer.

"Everything okay?" he asks.

"Yeah," I reply. "Yeah, we're fine."

"Who was that? Sorry he got past us—we were helping the locations team."

"No one," I say. "It's fine; he's gone now."

"Not one of those photographers, was it?" the security guard continues.

I shake my head. "No. Just someone I used to know."

The words settle in my chest. *Just someone I used to know.* That's all Jack is. That's all he'll ever be now. I let out another long breath.

"All right. Well, if I see him come back, I'll get rid of him."

"Thanks, man," Austin says.

The security guard gives us a nod and then leaves.

"Are you okay?" Austin asks once we're alone.

He puts a hand on my arm, and I don't even mean to, but I jump a little at his touch. It's like all the nerves I kept from unspooling when Jack was in here suddenly unravel now.

"Sorry," he says, and pulls his hand away.

"It's all right," I say. "I'm all right."

I head over to our laundry sink and turn the faucet on, just for something to do. I rinse my hands under it, then turn it back off.

"I'm guessing ex-boyfriend?" Austin asks.

"Unfortunately, yes."

Austin raises his eyebrows. "Recent?"

"Not really. We haven't been together for . . . I dunno, maybe six months? I stopped keeping track."

"And you didn't know he was coming here."

"No. I haven't spoken to him in however long it's been since we broke up."

"That's not cool, then. Him just showing up like that."

"No, it's not cool at all."

I dry my hands on a nearby towel and then grip the edge of the counter.

"Are you sure you're all right?" Austin asks, taking a step toward me.

"Yeah, I'm just . . . it was a shock, that's all. But it's okay. He's gone now."

Austin looks behind us, out of the trailer, as if making sure.

"It's not true, you know," I say. I don't know why I'm saying this, but somehow, I feel the need to clarify. "That I have a thing for actors. It's not something I make a habit of or anything. He was just saying that to make you feel bad."

Austin frowns. "Is that what he did to you? Make you feel bad?"

I let out a bitter laugh. "Honestly," I say. "It's in the past."

Austin's eyes bore into me. I can see him connecting the dots. I can see him understanding how Jack fits into what I told him this morning. Why I need time.

But he doesn't probe.

"I can give you a ride back, if you need," he says instead. "Make sure you get home all right."

"Oh, you don't have to do that. I'll be at least half an hour, if not more."

"I was gonna go for a run while we're out here, anyway. I can check in when I'm finished and see if you're done then? The offer's there. But I don't want to intrude. I think you've had enough of that."

I look up at Austin. His eyes are still creased with concern, and they suddenly seem like such a stark contrast to Jack's. Summer green versus winter gray.

"Okay," I say. "Thank you. Only if you're going to stick around anyway, though."

"It's no problem. I'll be back in about half an hour, okay?"

I nod and watch Austin as he heads out of the trailer and jogs slowly toward one of the trails.

Once he's gone, I turn back to the sink and wash my hands three times, as if I might be able to rinse the last ten minutes off them.

THIRTY-FOUR

I move through my pack-down tasks robotically. I'm not even thinking about what I'm doing—I keep playing the Jack encounter over and over in my head. Twice now in the last week, I've had to see his face. After six months of none of it. My stomach roils. I keep folding and unfolding clothes to keep my hands steady.

Outside, the air pressure has dropped even lower. The sky has darkened, and fat drops of rain start to fall on the forest. Since I've moved through my tasks on autopilot, I'm finished within half an hour. Shuttles are taking the rest of the crew back to town, and the swing drivers are starting to drive the trucks and trailers back. But I need to wait for Austin now. I watch the rain fall into puddles on the trails and forest undergrowth and try to remember if he was wearing his rain jacket when he set off.

He wasn't. He comes back in a soaking-wet white T-shirt, and I can see everything underneath it. The material clings to his frame, showing off his broad shoulders and his hips. The swirling in my gut speeds up.

"You're soaked," I tell him.

He shrugs and lifts up his T-shirt to wipe his face, exposing the flat of his stomach.

"It's refreshing," he says, as I try not to stare.

"Here," I say. I head into the trailer and find a dry T-shirt for him.

"I can't take that," he says. "Doesn't that belong to the production?"

Now it's my turn to shrug. "We have so many."

"Well, if you're sure . . ."

Austin peels off his wet shirt, and I distract myself by giving the trailer a final once-over and letting one of our drivers know it's all okay to go back to base now.

When I turn back to Austin, he's in the dry T-shirt and shaking his wet hair out of his face.

"Shall we head back?" he says.

"Sure."

Austin's driven his own car to the location. It's a nice, shiny truck, the inside of which seems just as well maintained as the outside.

"Is this new?" I ask, as I hop into one of the shiny leather seats.

"Nah," Austin replies. "I'm just a bit particular about my truck."

"As every good wannabe cowboy should be."

"Oh, is that what I am now? A wannabe cowboy?"

I shrug, smiling. "You said it yourself."

Austin laughs. "You got me. At least I grew up in the country."

"On an apple orchard. Not a ranch."

"Wow, you know how to wound."

I bite my lip. "I'm sorry."

"I'm kidding, obviously."

The rain is coming down heavier now. Austin turns on the windshield wipers and whistles as he looks out the window.

"I don't think we'll be coming back here tomorrow," he says.

"No," I reply. "I think the storm's well and truly here."

"So I won't wrap early. Which means you haven't gotten rid of me yet."

I give a weak smile.

"Sorry, bad joke," Austin says, as he begins to drive out of the parking lot. "Given that you literally just had to get rid of another unwanted guy."

"That's different," I say.

Austin glances at me out of the side of his eye. "Do you wanna talk about it?"

"There's not much to say. We were together for a year. It was a toxic relationship. I got myself out of the cycle. I haven't had to think about him for six months."

That last part isn't strictly true, but I want to keep things simple.

"I'm sorry," says Austin. "That you had to go through that."

I shrug. "I almost feel like it's a rite of passage."

"What, like it's something all women go through?"

"It seems like it."

"Well, that's fucked up." Austin's fingers tighten on the steering wheel. "It shouldn't be like that."

"No. It shouldn't."

Austin's truck is tuned into the country music station, of course. I let myself feel comforted for a moment by the twang of guitars and whiskey-smooth voices.

"Sorry. I can change it if you want," Austin says, noticing that I'm looking at the stereo. "Is it giving you bad memories from the festival?"

"I actually mostly have good memories from the festival," I answer quietly.

Austin bites down a smile. Then he reaches over and turns the music up.

We're both silent for a few moments, listening to the song. The singer's talking about buying land, settlin' down, finding out what life's all about. The rain beats down around us as we drive, thick and impatient.

"Thank you, by the way," I say to Austin.

"For?"

"For helping out, back there. And for the ride."

"I didn't have to do much to help. You stood your ground just fine."

"I only wish I could have done that a year ago."

"Better late than never."

"I guess."

"Am I taking you home, by the way? Or to the office?"

I pull out my phone and have a quick glance over my emails. Everything's in order back at the office, though we were right—filming for tomorrow is on hold until we know exactly how bad this storm is going to be. We've all been advised to head back to our accommodation and wait for further instruction.

"Just home," I say. "If it's not too out of your way."

"Well, I'm not exactly going to make you walk in this, am I?" Austin waves his hand at the sheets of water that are bouncing off the hood.

"You said it was refreshing," I tease.

"That was before it got torrential." He looks at the trees swaying around us. "Man, I used to love storms like this when I was a kid."

"Really?"

"Yeah. We used to get them a lot in summer out this way." Austin smiles wistfully. "I know they were stressful for my parents, but Parker and I would get real hyperactive when one was coming. We'd roll around on the front porch, counting the seconds between lightning and thunder. I think it was just the disruption to the routine that wound us up."

"I get it. Kind of like getting excited about snow days when you're a kid. You don't have to worry about the logistics of how messed up the roads are going to be or whether the pipes might freeze. You can just enjoy the novelty of it."

"Exactly."

As if on cue, the sky lights up around us in a brilliant white flash of lightning. Austin glances at me out of the side of his eye, and, in unison, we both count:

"One . . . two . . . three . . ."

The truck rattles as a deep roar of thunder sounds. Even though I knew it was coming, I still jump a little, and Austin laughs.

"Why does that happen?" I muse. "Why does the lightning always come first?"

"Fun fact," Austin replies. "Lightning and thunder actually happen at the same time. The thunder is the *sound* of the lightning. But light travels faster than sound. So you see the lightning first."

"Woah," I say.

"I know, right?"

I think about that for a moment. Light travels faster than sound. Centuries ago, people wouldn't have known this. Like Florence pointed out the other day, there's so much we're still discovering about the world. I imagine a time in the future when portals to alternate timelines are common knowledge, and someone's sitting in a very clean truck (or spaceship) somewhere, musing that once upon a time, people didn't understand the multiverse. Except for a select few.

As we cross the bridge, we can see that the river is already raging below it. Austin whistles.

"Does the river here flood?" I ask.

"It can," Austin replies. "But let's hope it doesn't."

"Or I'll be cut off from town," I half joke. "Stuck on the wrong side of the tracks."

Austin shoots a stern look at me.

"I won't let that happen," he says.

"Oh, you'll come to my rescue?" I ask.

"Of course."

"How?"

"I'll find a boat."

We both laugh at this. Then we're turning into my street, and Austin's pulling up in front of my apartment complex.

"What I mean is," Austin says, as he puts his truck in park, "I'll find a boat if you want me to. But not if you don't want me to."

"Austin . . ."

"No, I'm sorry. I feel like I'm doing it again. I heard what you said this morning—honestly, I did. I just wanted to make sure you got home all right."

"And I really, really appreciate it."

"I get it even more now. Especially after seeing your ex. That guy would be enough to scare anyone off men for life."

"I'm not scared of you," I say softly.

"Well. That's good."

Behind Austin, through the truck's window, I can see the golden glow of the streetlight. It illuminates the sideways rain and makes it look like falling jewels.

I unbuckle my seatbelt, and I put my hand on the door.

"Wait," Austin says.

I turn, but he's not looking at me. He's leaning over my seat and looking up at the apartments instead.

"I feel like I know this place," he says.

"You met me outside this morning," I reply.

Austin shakes his head. "No. I feel like I know it from before then." He glances behind us, down the street, and back up at the apartment complex. "But that's weird, because I don't ever come down these streets."

My skin prickles. I wonder if somehow Austin's memory is tapping into that other timeline, the one where he lives here. Can you remember something that happened to a different version of you? I wonder if that's part of the explanation behind déjà vu.

"Maybe you came here as a kid," I suggest weakly.

"Yeah," Austin murmurs. "Maybe."

He leans back again, into his seat.

"I better let you get back before the river floods," I joke, as I crack open the door to the truck.

Austin nods and presses his lips together.

"Stay safe," he says. "Make sure your phone's charged and you've got candles and a flashlight handy in case of a blackout."

"I don't know if I've got a flashlight in the apartment."

"Here."

Austin reaches over me for the glove compartment. He riffles around in some papers and pulls out a small battery-powered flashlight.

"Take this."

I let him hand me the light, and our fingers brush briefly, before Austin pulls his back.

"Thank you," I say, holding his gaze.

"Anytime."

He smiles, but it seems like only a half smile compared to his regular eye-crinkling beam. I have a vision of touching my fingers to the corners of his lips and watching his eyes light up.

But I know I can't stay like this any longer. My right leg is hanging out of the door, and it's already soaked.

So, I tuck Austin's flashlight under my jacket and dart across the sidewalk and into the apartment foyer.

Austin waits until I'm safely inside before he leaves. Maybe hoping I'll turn back around.

THIRTY-FIVE

I pour myself a glass of wine and wrap myself in a blanket on the sofa as the storm rages around me. It's here now—really here. The wind is rattling the windows, and I've pulled in the two chairs from the balcony, worried they're going to be snatched up into the angry sky and end up floating down the river. I watch as the lighting illuminates the apartment, and I count the seconds out loud before the thunder hits. In my head, I imagine little Austin and little Parker on the wraparound porch at the apple orchard, chanting their countdown while their parents fret in the background.

I want to message Austin to check that he got back to his hotel all right, but my fingers hover above my phone screen, still hesitating, always fucking hesitating. I thought I'd become bolder over the last couple of weeks—bold enough to stand up to Jack, at least, but obviously not bold enough to lean in to Austin.

Something's still holding me back. There's still this fear in me, still this mistrust.

When a message pops up on my phone, I lunge for it. But it's just Deidre asking me in a matter-of-fact way if I got home all right. Paranoid, I wonder if there's more meaning in that message than it seems. Does she know that I got a ride home with Austin? Did someone see us? What's Deidre going to think of me not heeding her warning . . .

Then a creeping feeling comes over me. And the pounding in my head stops for a moment, replaced by a cold clang of clarity.

This whole time, I've been assuming that Deidre's warning had been about Austin.

Be careful of that young man.

But what if it wasn't?

What if the wardrobe trailer on location wasn't the first place Jack had come looking for me?

What if he'd gone to the production office first, before today? And word had gotten around to Deidre?

"Fuck," I say out loud.

Deidre has never been one to explicitly talk about our personal lives outside of work, but she knows the general story about Jack. I told her wife, Eleanor, about it, one night at an event after having a few too many drinks. And Eleanor probably filled Deidre in. Deidre never said anything directly to comfort me, but she did point out a handsome male model that night and told me, "That style would look better on you." I didn't realize until the next day that she hadn't been talking about clothes.

Fuck. I've been clinging to that warning from Deidre as a justification for why I feel so nervous about Austin. But maybe I've been using it as crutch. An excuse to stop myself from being brave. To stop myself from leaning in.

I've been worried about the wrong guy.

I pick my phone back up and open a message to Austin.

But just as soon as I start typing, I see the icon at the top of the screen that tells me I've lost cell service, thanks to the storm.

I groan and toss my phone onto the blanket.

Of course. I had my chance, and I blew it. I had more than one chance, actually. The festival. The lookout. The goodbye tonight in his truck. How many more chances can the universe give me? How many more chances can Austin give me?

Thinking about the universe giving me things, I drain my glass of wine and head into my bedroom. I hadn't originally planned to go through the portal tonight. It almost feels like I'm overdoing it, being gluttonous. You can have too much of a magical thing.

But with the cell service and internet down, and the claps of thunder making me too jittery to focus on a book or magazine or to try to fall asleep, this seems like the best way to spend my time.

When I cross through the wardrobe, I can still hear the storm raging on the other side. This answers a question I had. When I visit these parallel timelines, they must exist at the exact same physical time and date as each other. I can make as many drastically different decisions that result in different pathways as I want, but still the natural world will turn on around me. My decisions don't influence the weather. It's almost a small comfort that some things stay constant.

What's not a comfort is that when I open the door of the wardrobe, someone's standing in the bedroom. Someone I recognize immediately from her long mane of red hair and the wooden pendant hanging around her neck.

"Florence," I say.

I wait for Florence's eyes to widen at the sight of me standing in the wardrobe.

But instead, she just looks vaguely in my direction with a mildly puzzled expression on her face.

"I'm sorry, I know this is weird," I say, gesturing at the wardrobe, realizing that the Florence in this timeline might not know about the portal, might not know me at all. "I can explain . . ."

I'm thrown back to the time I was in a similar scenario with Austin, caught red handed creeping in his bedroom. But while Austin had a fairly typical reaction to finding a stranger in his room (arming himself with a makeshift weapon), Florence seems to be reacting slowly. She still hasn't said a single word, and her expression is strange. Almost as if she's looking through me, rather than at me.

Then, before I can continue with my sentence, she walks over to the wardrobe.

And she simply shuts the door in my face.

I crouch there in the dark for a moment, stunned.

What the fuck?

I'm still there in the closed wardrobe, shocked into immobility, when I hear Florence mutter to herself on the other side of the door.

"Sage," she murmurs. "We need sage to get rid of this ghost."

I haven't even realized it, but my hands have suddenly become clasped together so tightly that my fingernails are digging into my skin. I relish the feeling. Because it means I'm real.

I'm not a ghost.

I'm not a ghost.

I fling open the door to the wardrobe. Florence stumbles backward, obviously seeing the door moving.

But not seeing me.

"What ghost?" I ask.

When she doesn't answer, I move forward, until I'm standing right in front of her—so close that any normal person would take a step back. Florence takes a deep breath in, as if she can sense something there, but stands her ground.

"*What ghost?*" I repeat.

But she still doesn't answer, because she can't hear me. Just like she can't see me.

I know people have been able to see me in these worlds before. Austin saw me. Jack saw me. The other version of me, on the phone, saw me. I'm not normally invisible.

Which must mean . . .

I'm invisible now because I'm invisible in this timeline.

I turn shakily back to the wardrobe and stand in front of the mirror, where my reflection would normally be.

But there's nothing there.

———

To be honest, I've been expecting this.

It's only natural to wonder. If you suddenly have access to different timelines of your life, where one decision leads you down a different path, it's only natural to wonder if, in any of those timelines, you've died.

And it appears that, in this one, I have. And for some reason, I've been haunting this apartment, if Florence is talking about burning sage to get rid of me.

Florence leaves the bedroom then, and I don't immediately follow her. I give myself a few moments to reconcile with this. I've experienced so many levels of bizarre over the past few weeks that I thought I was past being shocked, but this is something new all over again.

I died. *I died.* Jesus Christ.

How did it happen? When did it happen? What was my funeral like? Who came? What did they say? I think of my parents. I think of Margot. I think of everyone I love—how they must be feeling. Oh God. I can't handle this. I suddenly feel panicked, pinching my skin over and over to remind myself I'm not really a ghost. I head back toward the wardrobe four times, tempted to jump right back to my original timeline and call everyone I know just to have them acknowledge my existence.

But I resist the temptation. If I leave, I might not be able to come back. If I leave, I might never know what decision I made in this timeline that led to my death.

I head out to the living room to find it empty. Florence is gone—likely back to her own apartment. In fact, I'm not sure why she was even here, in number eight, in the first place. Maybe she was sent here by the owner to deal with the ghost. To deal with me.

I decide to try something I haven't yet in other timelines and leave the apartment. It felt like Florence could sense me—maybe I can try to communicate with her somehow and get the answers I need.

But when I try to open the door to the hallway beyond, I find that I can't. It's the strangest sensation. The door is right there, my hand is on the doorknob, and yet, I simply can't turn it. It's like it's a motion my body physically can't perform—like doing a backflip or running at twenty-seven miles per hour. I know it's humanly possible, and yet, there's no way I can do it.

So that answers at least one question I've had. I've wondered before whether I have access to these parallel worlds beyond this apartment. I've been able to look out the window before, but it seems like there's some kind of boundary within the apartment walls that I'm not physically able to cross. So these rooms are all I have to determine how I died.

Unfortunately, the apartment is giving little away. It looks to have had a deep clean recently, maybe in an attempt to make it feel less haunted. It looks ready for new tenants but not like there's anyone currently staying in it. When I open the refrigerator, I find nothing except for a few glass bottles of water and the strong scent of cleaning product.

Then I look at the recycling box next to the refrigerator. And I see a local newspaper tossed in there.

I reach for the newspaper with shaking hands. Then I spread it out on the kitchen counter and meticulously go through every page.

At first, it's just the standard Casey River stories. Locals opposing a new property development. Something about a charity golf tournament. A new café opening.

But then I see it.

A small headline, buried in the middle pages of the paper.

Carrickvale Fatal Crash Driver Charged.

The words swim before my eyes as I read the article. About a recent accident in Carrickvale, where a distracted driver ran a red light and crashed into a vehicle on the highway right by the Carrickvale Mall. About how the collision killed the driver of the other vehicle—a twenty-eight-year-old film industry worker by the name of Matilda Bridges.

I grip the counter with my hands. My name looks both real and not real. Like it belongs to someone else. And it does. The other version of me. Who's no longer here.

Because I died. In a car crash.

In Carrickvale, the week we started filming.

But I didn't go to Carrickvale the week we started filming.

Unless . . .

"Holy shit," I say out loud.

My mind is wrenched back to that day. I remember standing in the production office, watching as Henry flipped a coin to see who'd get to go shopping and who'd stay at the office to do Austin's fitting. I remember the coin landing on heads, meaning Henry went to Carrickvale instead of me. I remember that he spent too long shopping and then got stuck in traffic coming back. Traffic that he said was caused by an accident.

Of course. If I'd gone to Carrickvale instead—if the coin had landed on tails instead of heads—then I would have been there. And I wouldn't have spent too long shopping, because I'd have been too scared of facing Deidre's wrath for being late. So, I would have been on the road before Henry was. I would have been right in the path of the car that ran the red light.

I feel sick all of a sudden, picturing it in my head.

That coin flip saved my life.

As the rain and wind and lightning and thunder continue to churn outside, I stand there in the kitchen, and I wonder how many other moments like this have happened in my current timeline. How many small decisions or coin flips might have saved my life or saved someone else's life—like Austin's had with Parker. Days when I was late to work, or took another route through the city, or decided not to go out for a drink, or decided *to* go out for a drink. I wonder how many different timelines exist out there—out *here*—unspooling like thousands of threads. I wonder in how many of them I've died.

And suddenly, the miracle doesn't seem to be the fact that I've found a magical portal in my wardrobe.

The miracle seems to be that, in all the timelines I could possibly be living in, I'm living in my current one.

Where I'm alive.
Where I have people who love me.
Where I have a dream job that I'm good at.
Is that the real miracle?
Is that the why?
The kitchen lights up then with the most blinding flash of lightning yet. It's brilliant, bright, and silver white, and there doesn't seem to be a single thing it doesn't touch.

But when it disappears, it takes the rest of the lights with it.
And I'm plunged into darkness.

THIRTY-SIX

I've never experienced darkness like this before.

Margot told me once about a spelunking trip she'd been on—caving, for us regular people—where they all turned off their headlamps and became immersed in total, true pitch black, the kind where you can't even see your hand in front of your face.

I feel like this darkness would match that. If I were able to put my hand in front of my face.

But I can't. I can't move. It reminds me of when I tried to open the door to the apartment and found that I simply couldn't do it. I feel like I've forgotten how to exist. Like maybe I never did. I can't tell if my feet are still rooted to the floor of the kitchen. I can't tell if I'm right side up or upside down. All I'm aware of is the darkness—solid and liquid at the same time—and the fact that my heart's still beating, which is all that reminds me that I'm real.

At least, I hope I'm real. Because suddenly, I'm not so sure I am.

Maybe I've messed with things. By coming into a timeline where I'm no longer alive, maybe I've torn the fabric of reality. This parallel universe has realized I shouldn't be here and has spat me out, into this purgatory I'm now floating in.

I start to panic. I can feel something heavy pressing on my chest, like a booted foot, applying increasingly more pressure as the seconds tick on. I can't lift my hands to touch my chest or clutch at my throat, which feels like it's starting to close up. I'm meant to be dead, so now I'm dying. I'm sure of it.

But then, before I let the panic completely consume me, I tell myself to breathe. If I can breathe, I'm still alive. So I take a long, deep breath in, and then a rattling breath out. Then again. Over and over, until the exhale becomes less rattling. Fuller. My lungs are working. My throat is open. The weight on my chest starts to lift.

Then the darkness around me begins to weaken and a soft glow appears somewhere in the distance, like a far-off sunrise on the horizon.

I can move my fingers and toes. I can breathe again. I can open my eyes. I can see again.

I'm back in the kitchen. I'm back in the kitchen, slumped against the counter, as if I've passed out for a moment. The newspaper that details my death isn't there. I look around me with bleary eyes but can't see it anywhere.

That's when I hear a scream.

I scream back. It's my first instinct, and it comes out almost involuntarily.

It takes me a moment to realize the person who's screamed is standing across from the kitchen, in the doorway to the bedroom.

I see red hair again, but it's not Florence this time.

"Mattie, what the hell?" Margot says.

She's wearing pajamas, and her hair is up in a messy bun. She's also clutching her hand to her chest like she's seen a ghost.

But she can't have seen a ghost. Because if I were still a ghost, she wouldn't be able to see me at all. Like Florence couldn't.

"You can see me," I whisper.

Margot blinks at me. "Yeah, I can see you," she says, letting out a shaky exhale. "But fuck, you scared me to death."

I hold on to the edge of the kitchen counter to keep myself steady.

"Why . . . why did I scare you?" I ask.

"Because you said you were staying at the hotel tonight?" Margot replies. "What happened? Is everything okay?"

"The hotel . . ." I repeat slowly, like I'm just learning to speak. Which it feels like I am, after that dark purgatory I was suspended in only moments earlier.

"Yes," Margot replies. "You wanted to stay with . . . wait, are you drunk?"

She comes over to me and places a hand on my back. A tree branch scratches at the window behind us, swaying in the stormy wind. I wince and realize my head is pounding and I feel dizzy.

"Here," Margot says, reading my face. She turns on the faucet and pours me a glass of water. She hands it to me, and I drink it quickly. As I do, I give myself a moment to dwell on this.

I'm alive. Margot can see me. She's talking to me. I'm drinking a glass of water. It's running down my throat, which is a part of my body, which is solid and real and alive.

I finish the glass and immediately reach for another one.

"Okay," Margot says. "You've had too much to drink, haven't you? But how did you even get back here in this weather? Is everything all right with Austin?"

My heart leaps at the sound of the name.

"Austin?" I repeat.

"Yeah. Everything seemed great with you two when I left you at the bar. I thought you wanted to spend your last night here with him."

"With Austin? Austin Farrow?"

"God, how much did you drink?" Margot's eyebrows knit together. "Maybe I shouldn't have left you."

"No," I say. My brain still feels like it's in pieces, but the pieces are slowly starting to meld together, forming a lumpy shape I don't quite recognize. "It's fine. I'm fine. I'm just . . ."

"Do you need something to eat? I'll toast a bagel."

I watch as Margot walks over to the pantry and pulls out a bag of blueberry bagels. I don't typically buy blueberry bagels, but Margot does. I can also see a half-empty bottle of tequila in the cupboard.

And I suddenly have a flashback. To watching through the crack in the bedroom door as Margot and I took tequila shots in the living room, country music blasting from the speakers, glitter glinting on our eyelids.

"The country music festival," I say suddenly.

"Yeah?" Margot replies. "What about it?"

"We came to Casey River for the Valley and Hills Country Music Festival, didn't we?"

Margot's forehead is still creased with concern, but she seems to simply think I'm wasted, rather than losing the plot.

"Yes," she says slowly. "We did come here for the festival. Where you met Austin."

The kitchen begins to fill with the smell of the warm blueberry bagel as it heats inside the toaster. I don't feel as nauseated as I did a few moments ago. I feel like I'm starting to figure out what's going on here.

I've skipped timelines. I have no idea how, because I didn't go back through the wardrobe, but I've somehow skipped timelines. I've managed to sidestep from the timeline where I died in Carrickvale and into the timeline where I became a teacher and traveled to Casey River to unwind at the festival with Margot.

I try to remember what I saw and heard in that timeline a few days ago. Margot got free VIP tickets to the festival through a guy she met hiking, who was playing there. She played one of his songs for me that day, and it was the same song I heard in my real timeline, at the festival with Austin, when we watched his friend play at the River Stage.

Which means that Austin's friend was the guy Margot met hiking.

But there was something else. Margot talked about how the friend she met hiking had another friend who was also playing at the festival, on the Main Stage. Margot showed me a picture and teased that this guy seemed like my type.

I can see it now. This isn't just a timeline where I became a teacher instead of a wardrobe assistant. It's also a timeline where Austin pursued music, instead of acting. Where he ended up playing on the Main Stage at Valley and Hills.

And where, according to what Margot's saying now, I must have met him. And decided he definitely was my type.

"I met Austin at the festival," I say.

"Yes, that's right," says Margot, like she's talking to a small child. She picks the bagel out of the toaster, slathers it in butter, and hands it to me. "Eat this. And tell me . . . what happened? He seemed like a good one. But now you're here. And not at his hotel."

I lift the bagel to my mouth and take a bite. I can smell the sweetness of the berries and the richness of the butter, but I don't taste as much as I should. Like I'm still not quite here.

"He's a good one," I repeat. "Austin really is a good one."

"Damn, you are wasted," Margot says. "You're just repeating things I say. You know what, I'm gonna call Austin, and . . ."

"No, don't! It's not his fault."

I reach out to stop Margot from grabbing her phone, and at the exact moment I do, another flash of lightning pierces the kitchen.

And once again, everything goes dark.

THIRTY-SEVEN

This time, I'm not as terrified of the darkness.

I'm not as terrified of my inability to move.

I hang there, suspended, waiting for the universe to drop me.

And when it does, I'm not surprised to be in the kitchen again.

The nausea and dizziness pass more quickly this time. My head snaps up from the kitchen counter, and I call out around me.

"Hello?"

I wait for movement from the bedroom. For Margot or Florence or someone else to come out. But no one does.

I look around me and see that the apartment is sparkling clean again. I immediately look over at the recycling box for the newspaper, wondering if I'm back in the timeline where I died, but there's nothing there. There are also fresh flowers on the dining table and a bowl of glistening fruit in the kitchen, which weren't there in the other two timelines either. In the living room, the carpet is spotless, and the magazines stacked under the coffee table are neatly aligned.

As I stare at the magazines, the cogs in my brain whir and click into place.

I walk over to the coffee table and slip one of the magazines out of the pile.

Up Close.

Of course. This is the world where I'm a successful journalist.

But the apartment seems unoccupied now. Other than the flowers and fruit, the only remnant of me having been here is the copy of *Up Close* I've obviously left behind. When I wander into the bedroom, I find it similarly empty. No suitcase. No toiletries in the bathroom. No clothes in the wardrobe.

It does make sense. Journalist Mattie was likely only visiting Casey River for an assignment. That was several days ago now. It makes sense that I've left.

"Okay," I say out loud, to no one, to nothing. "I get it. I've been here before. I know what happens in this timeline. You can take me back now."

I close my eyes and wait for the bolt of lightning. But nothing comes.

I blink my eyes open again. I press the panel in the wardrobe, but there's nothing behind there but a wall.

Frowning, I do another circuit around the apartment, wondering if there's something I've missed.

I think back to what I remember about this timeline. I remember finding the notes on the coffee table—the ones that seemed to be preparation notes for my *Up Close* interviews. But they're all gone—there's not even an ink spot on the coffee table to indicate they were ever here.

There is, however, a TV remote lying on the table. I contemplate it for a moment and then pick it up and turn the TV on.

It opens to a streaming service, still logged into my account according to the name on the bottom of the screen. Underneath my name is a list of titles I've recently watched.

The last thing I watched appears to be a western film, released this year. Starring Austin Farrow.

I sink down into the sofa and stare at the screen.

When I first wandered into this timeline, the TV in the living room was frozen on a pane of jumping horses.

With shaking hands, I hit play on the TV. I watch as a scene fills the screen. A one-street western town appears, filled with the usual facades—a saloon, a barber, a blacksmith, a jail. Carriages trundle down a dusty dirt road. An ominous whistle sounds in the distance. I take a moment to admire the costumes: ruffled saloon-girl skirts, cowhide chaps, and the slick waistcoats on men from the city.

Then we cut to the inside of a bar. And a close-up of a man's face. Austin.

He looks the same but different. Smoother skin. More depth in his eyes. A bit more facial hair, but no Sundance Kid mustache. On the bar next to him is a Stetson with a curved brim—the exact kind I said would suit his face.

He looks up from the glass of whiskey he's drinking, and I feel a shot of warmth rush through me, like I've just injected the whiskey straight into my veins.

He made it. Austin made it. He's starring in a western. He finally gets to be a cowboy.

And then I realize. I realize why I was in the middle of watching this movie while I was taking notes for my interview.

I was getting ready to interview Austin for a profile in *Up Close* magazine. Austin was the reason I was in Casey River.

And I'm beginning to realize something else too. Something that wasn't immediately obvious to me the first time I visited these timelines. Something that seems to have decided to spell itself out to me now because I was too foolish to realize it before.

I hear Florence's voice in my head, asking that question several days ago.

Have you noticed if the timelines have anything in common with each other?

I'm not even surprised that the lightning chooses that exact moment to crack into the room, as fast and furious as a gunslinger's shot.

———

I travel through the rest of them as if I were on that CD carousel.

In the timeline where I was supposed to marry Jack, the apartment is also empty. There's a heady smell of disinfectant hanging in the apartment and a large crate of empty beer bottles and crushed silver cans sitting by the doorway, ready to be collected. There's no Margot to talk to. No Florence to haunt. When I turn on the TV, a music channel starts pumping out a heavy beat, and I immediately turn it off again.

I wander into the bedroom, where the sheets have been stripped, the blow-up mattress dismantled, and a window left open to banish the smell of alcohol and sweat. Though now it's spilling heavy rain onto the carpet. I walk over and close it. I can't see anything outside but the dark gray of the storm, and I think about the other version of me. What's she doing right now? Did she listen to my warning and call the engagement off?

Deep in my bones, I feel like she did. And the reason I feel this is the reason I think I've been brought back here.

I sit down on the same bed Jack sat on when he called me. When the other version of me answered, I was having dinner at the winery where I was staying for my bachelorette party. I told Jack that I ran into some friends from the film industry. They were here filming a movie. *Magic Season*, I assume. Just because in this timeline I don't work in the industry anymore—likely because of pressure from Jack—doesn't mean that *Magic Season* didn't go ahead without me.

Jack interrogated me about who exactly I ran into from the film at the winery. I told him Henry and Loren and Val were there. A couple of the stunt guys.

And one of the actors.

———

Next is the timeline where I stayed working as a production runner rather than moving up into wardrobe. As soon as I'm catapulted back here, I realize I have to be careful. This version of the apartment isn't empty. Someone's here. I'm still here. I can see one of my old sweaters draped over the sofa and a water bottle monogrammed with my initials sitting on the kitchen counter. The door to the bedroom is closed, and I imagine the other version of me in there—likely in bed, trying to drown out the roar of the storm as she attempts to sleep. Her day tomorrow will be busy, running around after the producers, trying to fix whatever mess this storm has made.

If I'm a runner in this timeline, then runners interact with actors less than wardrobe crew members do. In this world, I'd certainly rub shoulders with Austin Farrow as we pass each other on set, but it seems like a stretch to believe that he'd pay any attention to me beyond that.

Then I see it. It's sitting on the coffee table, in the same spot I put it in my current timeline.

The flashlight Austin gave me when he dropped me off.

———

In the next timeline, the apartment is dark and quiet. It's so nearly identical to my original timeline that I think I've come full circle and am back where I started again.

But then I look at the coffee table. And unlike what I could see in the previous timeline, there's no flashlight. Even though I know that's where I left it.

My jacket also isn't hanging up on the hook by the front door where I hung it when I walked in. And my shoes aren't there either.

I scan through the timelines I've visited in my mind, and I remember one I've missed. The one I only glimpsed briefly, before I panicked and shut the wardrobe door.

It's the timeline where I invited Austin home with me from the festival. I imagine that's why I'm not here right now. I must be with him instead. Huddled away from the storm in the comfort of his hotel room.

Because I appear to have figured things out more quickly in that timeline than I have in my own.

———

I know there's only one timeline left.

The final timeline is the first timeline.

When I arrive out of the darkness and into the kitchen, I'm greeted with a meow.

I press myself off the counter and look down at my feet. Boots curls his downy body around my ankles and peers up at me with those yellow-moon eyes. The same eyes that greeted me when I first found the portal. He doesn't seem surprised that a stranger has magically appeared in the kitchen out of nowhere. He gives another meow, as if he was expecting me.

"Hey, buddy," I whisper. I crouch down and scratch the cat between his ears. He presses his soft head into my palm and begins to purr.

When I straighten back up, I see a figure standing in the doorway to the bedroom. I open my mouth to explain, but Austin speaks first. And when he speaks, he sounds calm. When he speaks, he almost sounds relieved.

"Finally," he says.

THIRTY-EIGHT

Austin doesn't pour me a drink.

I feel like I need one. I'm not surprised to end up here, in the first timeline. I knew it was coming. But what's throwing me is the fact that Austin isn't shocked to see me here. There's no confusion in his eyes or guitar brandished defensively in his hand. And that's not the only thing that's different.

The Austin who joins me in the kitchen is definitely the darker version of Austin, the one I met on that first night. But even so, he seems different. His facial hair is trimmed. His hair is neater. The shadows under his eyes haven't completely faded, but they're better than they were before. He's like an in-between Austin, standing half in the shadow and half in the sun.

"I'm very confused," I say out loud.

"So was I," Austin replies. "Have a seat."

I take a seat because my legs are shaky. Austin stays standing up in the kitchen.

"I'd offer you a drink," he says. "But I got rid of all the alcohol in this place."

"Oh," I say softly.

"Coffee?" he asks.

"Sure."

I stare at Austin as he turns to prepare the coffee—at the slope of his shoulders beneath his thin T-shirt and the set of his lips.

"You don't seem surprised to see me here," I say eventually.

"I'm not," Austin replies. "Though I somehow didn't see you come through the wardrobe."

"Things have been a bit different tonight. And weren't you going to board up that passageway anyway?"

"I was going to. And then . . ."

He pauses and stirs the coffee. Then he hands one to me and sits down at the dining table.

Boots chooses that moment to jump up into my lap, which I'm grateful for. I stroke the old cat's fur and try to let the rhythm of his purr relax me.

"And then what?" I ask.

"Should you go first, or should I?" Austin asks.

"I vote you. My head is pretty scrambled right now, and I need to know why you're not pointing that guitar at me again."

Austin gives a small smile.

"All right," he says. "I'll go first, then."

He takes a long sip of his coffee and looks down at it, perhaps wishing it were something stronger. Then he begins.

"That night, after I found you in my bedroom, I couldn't stop thinking about it. I woke up in the morning wondering if it was all a dream or a drunken hallucination, and for a while I thought it was. I checked the wardrobe again, and there was a panel in the back, but it didn't lead anywhere. Just to a solid wall. I even went next door and knocked on the door, but an old dude answered who said he was a friend of the owner's and had been staying there by himself. He didn't know anything about a girl."

I nod and press my fingers into Boots's fur.

"The next day, I went into the bookstore in town. And there you were. Working behind the counter, just like I thought. With a name tag that read Mattie. With two *t*'s. I tried to talk to you about the night before, and it only took a few minutes for me to realize you genuinely had no idea what I was talking about. You thought I was a crazy person. Wouldn't be the first time someone's thought that in the last few years."

I want to explain to Austin that it wasn't me, not really, but I have to be patient. I have to let him tell his story. My heart is thudding in my throat, and it's hard to drink—my mouth is dry no matter how many sips I take.

"You might already know this . . ." Austin continues. "But the night you met me, I wasn't doing so well. I've been struggling for a while. I've been trying to use music as an outlet, but liquor seemed easier. I was due to play at a local festival this past weekend, but I decided to cancel. If I was literally starting to see things that weren't there, that was rock bottom. I needed to sort my shit out.

"So I decided to get back into running. I started going for a daily run every morning, out on the trails through the park. My favorite trail is one that leads to the waterfall."

"Fallen Tree Falls," I murmur.

"Fallen Tree Falls," Austin confirms. "There's something about those falls that makes me feel better. I like to take a break there and just listen for a moment."

"I like it there too," I say.

"I know."

I frown. "How do you know?"

Austin leans forward in his seat.

"There was this one morning," he continues. "I was there at the falls, and I could hear something other than the water. It sounded like someone singing, though I couldn't see anyone around. And as ridiculous as it sounds, it seemed like the voice was coming from a tree. You know that tree that's growing from the old stump?"

"That's where the original fallen tree was," I murmur.

Austin nods. "I'd never noticed it before, but there was this hollow in the new tree. It was at an angle, so you had to be standing at a specific spot to see it. I had to crouch down a bit and move sideways to step into it, so I did. Which was a fucking weird thing to do, but I dunno. I could still hear that voice."

A shiver runs through my body. I know I've spent the last few weeks journeying through magical portals and exploring alternate worlds. I just visited a reality where I was *dead*, for heaven's sake. I thought I'd seen it all. But if Austin's saying what I think he's saying, then the hits just keep coming.

"As soon as I stepped into the hollow," Austin continues, "my foot was out the other side again. I was on the other side of the tree. But I could still hear that voice—someone singing. Only, now the sound was coming from the lookout. And when I looked over there, I saw the wildest thing I've ever seen in my life."

I drain the rest of my coffee like it's a shot and place the cup on the table. Boots has gone very still, and I wonder if he's asleep, but he's not. He's just rapt with attention. Waiting for what comes next.

"Any guesses?" Austin asks me.

I take a deep breath in. "You saw yourself."

"Bingo." Austin taps the table with his hand. "I saw *myself*. I saw myself, standing at the lookout. With a different haircut, wearing running clothes I don't own, listening to headphones that are far more expensive than anything I can afford now. It was me, singing along to a song in my headphones. Loudly, as if I thought no one else was around."

"What did you do?" I ask, my voice barely above a whisper.

"Hit myself on the head a couple of times, wondering if I was losing it. But when nothing changed, I had to face the facts. As impossible as they were."

Austin fixes his green-eyed gaze on me.

"You know where this is going, don't you?" he says softly.

I nod silently.

"Because my tree hollow is your wardrobe," Austin continues. "Isn't it?"

THIRTY-NINE

I'm not alone.

This whole time, I've been searching for some kind of kinship in this whole impossible experience. Someone to talk to about this new world—these new *worlds*—that I've discovered. And now here it is. And I oscillate between wonder and relief as Austin's revelation sinks in.

Austin has a portal too.

Austin can travel to different timelines of his life through the hollow at Fallen Tree Falls.

I'm not alone.

I never have been.

The feeling that comes over me then is overwhelming. It feels like a runner's high or a hiker's epiphany, only I'm not on a mountain or a trail; I'm sitting in the kitchen with Austin Farrow in a world I shouldn't be in, holding his cat while a storm rages outside.

"You have one too," I say.

"I have one too," Austin confirms. "And now I want to hear about yours."

I start to talk, and once I start, I find I can't stop. I tell Austin my story, from the beginning—or most of it, at least. As I talk, I find myself dancing around the topic of Parker, unsure how to bring up the fact that, in my world, Austin's brother is alive and well. I'm not sure what reaction this is going to get from Austin. He seems so much more together than when I last saw him. I don't want to rattle him.

But he realizes, eventually. And he tells me it's okay.

"We can talk about Parker," he says. "It was the first thing I had to reconcile with when I started visiting the other timelines."

"If you don't mind me asking," I say, "what exactly happened to him? In this world?"

Austin shrugs, as if the nonchalant movement will make him feel less. But he's not as good an actor in this timeline as he is in mine.

"Parker died when I was twenty-one," he says eventually. "Just after I got my first real acting role. He was traveling on his own and drowned while swimming at a beach in Thailand."

The words rumble through me, like thunder in my chest.

"I'm so sorry, Austin," I say.

"Of all the decisions in my life, that one has haunted me the most. I can't tell you how many times I asked, *What if?* What if I'd been with him instead?"

"Of course you would," I say.

"When I realized what was happening with the tree at the falls," Austin continues, "my first thought was Parker, of course. There was a morning when I could see myself there at the lookout again, talking to someone on the phone. I realized I was talking to Parker. He was still alive. My first instinct was to go over to the lookout, to grab the phone out of my own hands so that I could talk to my brother again."

I look at Austin carefully. That shadow has begun to creep back into his eyes, but it seems like he's keeping it at bay. Barely.

"And did you?"

Austin shakes his head. "I caught myself in time. I thought about what might happen if I confronted myself like that. I'd lose it, probably. Maybe push myself into the water. It was too dangerous. So I just watched from afar instead."

"That must have been tough."

"It was tough, but it also brought me this weird sense of peace. I knew that Parker was still alive somewhere. And that was better than nowhere."

I feel an unexpected sting in my eyes, and I furiously blink it back.

"I saw myself a few times too," I say, in an attempt to change the topic. "Once, I talked to myself on the phone. Maybe I shouldn't have, but I don't regret it."

"Really? How did that go?"

"I freaked out, naturally. But I think I got my message across."

"Which was?"

"To break up with my toxic ex."

Austin's face has softened now, the darkness vanquished.

"You know, I saw you as well," he says. "In the other timelines."

"You did?"

"Yeah. A couple of times, actually. One of them was just this morning. You were there with me—the other version of me. You two were having a really serious conversation."

I think of this morning . . . of the flash of black I saw by the tree while Austin and I talked at the lookout.

"That was you," I say.

"I worried for a moment you might have seen me," Austin continues. "So I came back through right away. But I have been wondering what you were talking about."

I realize that, as we've talked, our chairs have inched closer to each other. Austin's elbow is lying on the table mere inches from mine.

"We were talking about what's going on between us," I say.

Austin's eyes flash.

"Something's going on between us?" he asks.

"Well . . . not *us*," I say. "I mean, it's a different version of us. A different version of you."

Austin stares. Then he lets out a nervous laugh.

"Of course," he says.

"Of course what?" I ask.

"That's the last part. The part I haven't told you yet."

I raise my eyebrows at his pause, urging him to go on.

"After I found my own portal," he says, "I kept thinking back to the night you appeared in my bedroom. I started to suspect that version of you was from a different timeline too. That would explain why the version of you in the bookstore didn't know who I was. I kept hoping you'd turn up here again so that I could ask you, but you never did. So instead, I went back to the bookstore. Where you work. Or where the version of you in this world works."

"I'm curious about this version of me," I admit.

"So was I," Austin replies. "Remember, this version thought I was potentially a bit deranged, given that I'd turned up that day at the store talking about an encounter between us that never happened—at least to her knowledge. I decided to apologize and explain that I'd mistaken you . . . her . . . God, this is getting confusing . . ."

"I get it."

"That I'd mistaken her for someone else," Austin concludes. "She was cool about it, of course. Always so polite. We got talking about books after that. I mentioned Louis L'Amour, and she told me her dad is a fan."

"It's true," I say. "He is."

Austin smiles. "We chatted for a while that day. And then I found myself passing by the store again the next day."

I press my lips together, trying to stay straight faced.

"It didn't take me long to realize that . . . I wanted to be around her," says Austin. "You. All the versions of you. I even had a stupid crush on the versions of you I saw from a distance at the lookout. It's not the world's greatest mystery, seeing as you're beautiful and kind and smart and funny . . . God, it's more than that." He takes a breath in but keeps going. "It's like, in here." He touches his chest. "When I pluck my guitar strings, I feel a vibration in here. That's what I feel when I'm around you. Like it's the universe itself pulling strings."

My cheeks are burning. I press the back of my hand against them to cool them, but my hand is hot too. Every part of me is on fire, flooded with sunlight.

"Well, I'll tell you what," I say, surprised I can find my voice at all. "You're a *little* more poetic than you are in my timeline. It must be all the songwriting."

Austin laughs and it reaches his eyes, reaches his whole body. For a moment, he feels like my version of Austin. Like mine. I dare to press my arm against his, and he presses back. But then the smile slips from his face.

"This feels . . ." he says. He shifts his arm away, until there's a gap between us again. "I'm sorry, but this feels weirdly disloyal. Because you're *you*, but you're also not you, you know? Your hair is different than my Mattie's. Your face . . ."

His eyes rove over my face, and his gaze—combined with the way he says "my Mattie"—makes me flush. But I also know what he's trying to say.

"I know that my Mattie is at her place right now," Austin continues. "In the little garden studio she rents in the backyard of the bookstore owner's house. We've gone on three dates now, and she stayed over the other night, and I've been thinking just today that I don't think I'm going to go back through the portal again. This morning was the last time. I don't feel like I need to anymore."

I take a deep breath in. And a long breath out. I'm still sitting in the kitchen, but for a moment I feel like I'm suspended in air again. Suspended in light this time, rather than in darkness.

"I get it," I eventually murmur. "It's taken me a while, but I think I finally get it."

"Well, what I really need to know," says Austin, "is if the version of me in your timeline has also figured his shit out and told you all this yet."

I let out a sigh.

"He has," I say. "This morning. But I'm the one who's been holding back."

Austin frowns. "Why?"

"I don't really know," I reply. "I think I've been afraid."

"We're all afraid." Austin tosses his hands in the air. "All the time. For so long, I was afraid of making any decisions. I convinced myself that a decision I made led to my brother's death. I thought if I did as little as I possibly could, maybe my decisions wouldn't have as big a consequence again. But it's impossible to be alive without making choices."

I nod. "And I want to be alive," I whisper.

"Me too," says Austin. "I realize that now."

I hadn't even noticed until now that the storm outside has stopped. Since Austin and I have been talking, the rain and wind have calmed down, and no lightning has illuminated the room for a while now.

"I need to get back," I say.

Austin nods.

"But I don't know how," I continue. "Things have been different tonight. It's like the storm has messed with everything. I've been jumping from timeline to timeline without going through the portal. The system's gone haywire."

Austin rubs his bottom lip with his thumb in thought. "It's like a crescendo," he says. "In music. You know that part when everything gets louder and more frantic, right before the end? It seems like chaos, but there's normally some kind of structure to it."

"But what structure? The storm's stopped now. Maybe I'm stuck here."

Austin gives a half smile. "I can think of worse things than having you stuck in my apartment forever."

"Hey," I reply lightly. "Stop that. You're spoken for, remember?"

Austin laughs and shakes his head.

Then suddenly, Boots stands up in my lap. He shakes himself, meows, then jumps off and pads over to the bedroom.

Austin and I look at each other.

"I think he wants us to follow him," Austin says.

We both rise from the table and follow the black-and-white cat with moon-yellow eyes into the bedroom. When I enter the room, I can smell that familiar scent again—the fresh and piney smell of Austin's clothes hanging in the wardrobe. The guitar is lying on the bed next to a sheaf of papers.

"What have you been writing about?" I ask him.

"Epiphanies," Austin replies. "Impossible things. And a girl."

The door to the wardrobe creaks open then. Boots is sitting by it, blinking up at me, just like he did on that first night.

I walk over to the wardrobe and open it. There's the panel, staring back at me. And when I press it, it springs open at my touch.

There's no wall beyond. Instead, there's a passageway. That leads into the world next door.

Austin blows out a breath. "Well," he says. "The universe sure knows the right strings to pull at the right time."

I straighten up and turn to face him. He looks back at me, and his eyes seem even lighter than they did before. As if he's almost completely in the sun now, rather than only half.

He hesitates for a brief moment. Then he reaches out and draws me into him.

I wrap my arms around his neck and press my face into his shoulder. My lips are inches from his collarbone, but I'm not tempted to bring them closer. It seems that we belong to other people.

"All right," I say, eventually pulling myself away. "You look after that girl, okay?"

"Oh, I will," Austin replies. "So long as you look after that guy."

"I will," I promise. "If he hasn't given up on me."

"I have a feeling he hasn't."

I could stand here looking into those eyes all night, but I know I have to go. I reach down to give Boots one last final scratch between the ears, and he gives me a meow in farewell.

It started with a meow, and now it ends with a meow. How fitting.

"Goodbye, Austin," I say, as I step into the wardrobe.

"See you on the other side," he replies.

III: THE ROMANCE

FORTY

On the other side, my regular tangle of clothes greets me.

I run my hands through my shirts and stroke the hems of my hand-made dresses. I'm feeling unmoored, disoriented, even though I'm back where I'm meant to be.

My head is thick and heavy with thoughts of the seven different worlds I just visited, as if jet lag and motion sickness have both hit me at once.

The Death timeline.

The Teacher Mattie timeline.

The Journalist Mattie timeline.

The Marrying Jack timeline.

The Production Runner Mattie timeline.

The Bringing Austin Home timeline.

The Not-So-Dark Austin timeline.

Seven timelines. Seven different pathways I could have walked down if I made a different decision at some past point in my life. Pathways that have all intersected in this one place, Casey River—like a train terminal, a crossroads, the center of a multipointed star.

My eyes fall on the corduroy shirt I would have been wearing on the day I drove to Carrickvale in the other timeline. I pick it up and stare at it. This is the shirt I died in. What happened to this shirt in that other world? Did it end up in a plastic bag of my belongings, along with my cell phone and pomegranate moisturizer and miscellaneous hair ties?

It's then that I become aware of a fervent knocking coming from outside.

Someone is pounding on my door.

I drop the shirt and pull myself up off the floor, where I've ended up. It takes a moment for my legs to start working properly. The air back in my normal world feels thicker, as if I were walking through the ocean or a field of dense grass. My vision is blurred at the edges, and I splash my face with water from the kitchen sink before heading to the apartment door.

Before I open the door, I pause. I consider that it might be Austin on the other side. My heart speeds up. Am I ready for this? I need to be ready for this.

But when I open the door, it's not Austin.

It's Florence. And her normally calm face is creased with concern.

"Mattie," she says, letting out a breath. "Thank God you're all right."

I take a moment to gather myself.

"I am all right," I say, both to myself and Florence. "Why wouldn't I be?"

"I just had a terrible vision," Florence continues. "This happens when it storms; it's like the veil between the worlds is thinner than normal."

I widen the door to let Florence into my apartment.

"What kind of vision?" I ask.

Florence shakes her head. "Never mind. What matters is that you're okay."

"Does the vision involve me dying in a car crash?"

Florence pales and clutches at her wooden pendant. "How did you know?"

I walk over to the kitchen and pour us both glasses of water. Outside, the rain has slowed to a gentle patter. The next rumble of thunder sounds far away.

"It happened in another timeline," I explain to her.

I tell her about it all—the seven different worlds and how I spun through all of them, like a piece of driftwood caught in a storm surge.

"You say that storms make the veil between worlds thinner," I say, once I've finished. "That must be why the portal went wild tonight."

"Probably," Florence replies. "Storms contain terrific energy. It was a storm that felled the tree that led to the founding of Casey River, remember."

"Which created the portal," I add.

Florence nods. "Storms can be the universe's tantrum when it's not getting its way. It needed you to wake up and see what you haven't been seeing."

I drain the rest of my water.

"I see it now," I say.

Florence smiles and opens her mouth to speak. But then she cocks her head to the side.

"What's that sound?" she asks.

"Huh?"

"Did you leave a tap on in the bathroom? I can hear running water."

I frown and make my way to the bathroom with Florence on my heels. When I open the door, it's immediately obvious what's making the sound.

There's a giant leak in the ceiling, gushing water onto the bathroom tiles, like my own private waterfall. I didn't hear it before, but I was in a daze.

"Well, shit," I say.

Florence heaves a sigh. "Yes," she says. "It appears the universe has indeed been quite frustrated with you."

———

The production office has fared even worse than my bathroom ceiling.

A large piece of the roof to the old bed-and-breakfast has been dislodged in the storm and ended up somewhere on the other side of town. This left a hole in the roof above the props room, through which heavy rain fell hard and fast all night, ruining almost everything.

On the bright side, most of our electronics and files were in the main office area, which stayed dry. On the even brighter side, our wardrobe room was also untouched. Though I don't say any of this in front of the props team, who look as mournful as if one of them had died.

No one has died, thankfully. Our production accountant bumped her head when the power went out in her hotel room, and one of our camera guys had a minor car accident getting back from set in the rain, but otherwise, the crew are unscathed.

We planned well enough in advance to take down our set dressing from the Main Street set, but the street itself isn't looking too hot. The cobblestones are strewn with debris, stormwater pools in the gutters like spilled oil, and one of the shop windows has a large spiderweb-esque crack in it from something crashing into it. Locals have already begun to band together to help clean up, and it's quickly decided that the crew will help too. We're split in two, with half helping to take care of the production office mess and the other half dedicated to helping with the town cleanup.

I'm part of the group helping with the latter. I walk alongside Loren, wearing plastic gloves and a high-vis vest, picking up bits of debris and garbage and placing them in the large dumpsters that have been rolled in. As we walk, Loren tells me about how she thinks she might have been struck by lightning.

"Honestly, I swear I felt it," she's saying. "I was in the bathroom washing my hands during the storm, when I felt this sting on my hands, and then these little dots appeared. See?"

She holds out a freckled hand to me, and I examine the two small, round red marks on her skin. They kind of look like bug bites, but I don't say this. Loren is prone to dramatics, and we always just roll with it.

Besides, who am I to think Loren's claim of being struck by lightning is far-fetched? Stranger things have certainly happened.

"You know, I think it's lucky to be struck by lightning," I say. "You should buy a lottery ticket or something."

"Speaking of getting lucky . . ." Loren murmurs. "Look who's here."

I look up from the dumpster to see what Loren's very conspicuously nodding her head toward.

I didn't expect Austin and Hayden to be helping with the cleanup. The producers definitely wouldn't have told them they had to. But regardless, there they are, walking along picking up garbage just like the rest of us. Some of the townspeople have pulled out their phones to snap photos of Hayden, who has more star power than Austin, thanks to his soap opera days.

Austin sees me looking and tips his head back in acknowledgment. He pauses, as if thinking about whether he should come talk to me.

But I save him the decision. He's made his way over to me enough times. He's tried to tell me, over and over.

It's my turn now.

Austin waits for me by a lamppost. As I approach him, I feel like I can see all the different versions of him, leaning against the light.

The cowboy I interviewed for *Up Close* magazine.

The actor I met at the winery.

The musician playing at the festival.

The incredibly attractive guy I kissed on my bed.

The healed man I held for a moment last night.

It's like they're all there on the sidewalk, lined up shoulder to shoulder.

But then the line shrinks, until it's just Austin again.

Just the one.

"Morning," he says to me.

"Morning," I reply.

"You survived the storm," Austin says.

"I did," I reply. "Though my bathroom ceiling wasn't so lucky."

Austin's eyes narrow. "What happened?"

I pull out my phone and show Austin the video I took of the leak in my bathroom. He comes close to look at the screen over my shoulder, and I know people are watching. I can feel Loren's side glances, even though she's trying unconvincingly to look like she's still collecting garbage on the other side of the street. I'm pretty sure she's picked up the same stray coffee cup three times.

"Jeez," Austin murmurs. "You're not hurt at all, are you?"

"No. I was . . . I was safely in my room when it happened."

"Thank God." He looks over at me. "You know, I was worried for some reason. After I left you at your place last night, I just had this bad feeling. I tried to message you."

"The lines were down," I say weakly.

"I know. I just felt like I shouldn't have left you."

"Well, I didn't invite you to stay."

Austin's eyes crease for a moment, before I take a breath in and carry on.

"I should have invited you to stay," I say boldly.

A few weeks ago, I wouldn't have dreamed of saying such a thing. Even last night, I could barely dream of it.

But things are different now. Now, I know.

Austin's lips turn up. I can see the sun glint in his eyes.

"Really?" he asks.

"Really," I reply.

"But I thought you didn't want that."

"I've never not *wanted* it."

"I thought you needed time."

I toss my hands up. "How do I even know if I have time? My ceiling could have caved in last night. I could die in a car crash tomorrow. Time is the last thing I should be relying on right now."

Austin eyes me suspiciously. "Are you sure you didn't hit your head?"

I laugh. "I'm sure."

"You haven't been struck by lightning?"

"No, Austin. I'm perfectly fine."

"So, then . . . what are you saying?"

"I'm saying that . . ." I take a breath in. "I'm saying that I want to be around you too. That I want to get to know you too."

Austin takes a step closer to me. His voice is low.

"In what way?" he asks.

I breathe out. "God," I say. "In a way that makes me wish we weren't surrounded by people right now?"

Austin glances up, as if he's only just remembered that we're in public. It feels, for a moment, like we could pretend that we aren't. I wonder if this is what actors do when they're about to film an intimate scene. There are cameras in their faces, lights and boom mics above them, a band of crew encircling them like an army. But for a moment, they have to forget all that. They have to pretend it's just the two of them.

With Austin in front of me, I imagine it would be easy.

But then Austin clears his throat, and reality falls around us again.

"I have an idea," he says.

"Oh yeah?"

"Yeah. After we're done here, I'm heading out to the orchard to help my family for a bit. They weren't hit too badly, but there are a couple of things to clean up."

"Okay." This seems like a decidedly unsexy turn of conversation, but I'll roll with it. "Do you need help?"

Austin smiles. "I was actually thinking about the guesthouse we have on the property. You'll need somewhere else to stay, won't you?"

He gestures down at the video of the leak on my phone, and my stomach stirs. I've reported the damage to Val already, but she's dealing with a growing list of accommodation crises. I figured if there was nowhere else for me to stay, I'd either just try to sleep with the leak or else bunk with Loren and Heidi or one of the other girls from the crew.

But honestly. How many more times does the universe have to hit me over the head with this before I start listening?

"The guesthouse," I say slowly to Austin.

"It's completely separate from the main house," he says. "My brother rents it out sometimes, and the tourists love it. It's very orchard chic."

"That's a *thing*?"

"I made it up just now, but I think so."

I laugh. "I guess that's nicer than sleeping on someone's floor."

"So, is that a yes?"

Zero more times. The universe has to hit me over the head with this zero more times. I'm finally listening now.

"Yes," I reply. "It's a yes."

FORTY-ONE

The Farrow orchard sits on a pocket of land backdropped by green hills that the sun seems to hit in a special kind of way. The apple trees stand in neat, orderly rows, though the trees themselves have a wonky charm about them, like unruly children forced into a line.

The orchard emits a fresh, sweet smell that I wouldn't have known I recognize until it hits me. The strange thing is, I can't tell if I recognize it from the past—perhaps from one of those trips I made out this way with my parents or my friends. Or from another timeline entirely.

Austin and I have driven to the orchard separately. When I pull up at the end of the driveway and park in front of an apple-red barn, he's waiting for me outside a large brown-and-white farmhouse on the left.

"Welcome to the orchard," he says, stretching out his arms.

I can see that the collar of his denim shirt is tucked under. I walk over to him and untuck it, then smooth my hand across his collarbone. He sucks in a breath, and it feels good to be the one making him nervous for once.

"It's very charming," I say. "The orchard."

I take a step back and look around us, nodding my approval.

"It's not the flashiest," Austin says, clearing his throat. "Some of the other, bigger orchards 'round here have leaned into the whole cute touristy thing. They have apple-picking experiences and fruit stalls and tractor rides and all that. We just have the guesthouse. And even then, Parker only rents it out when he's feeling sociable."

"That's not all the time?"

"Parks is a funny one. You never quite know what you're gonna—ah, and here he is."

I look up to see Parker Farrow walking down the farmhouse stairs toward us.

It takes me a moment to remember that I don't know Parker. I've never met him—not even in another timeline—and so all I have are the stories Austin has told me.

But I feel like I do know him. He's a slightly shorter, darker-haired, bespectacled version of Austin, with a thinner frame and more serious face. And he's alive, obviously. Thank God for that.

"Hello," Parker says, nodding at me politely as he approaches.

"Mattie, Parker. Parker, Mattie," Austin introduces us. "That's Mattie with two *t*'s."

Parker holds out his hand to me, and I shake it.

"Mattie with two *t*'s," Parker says. "That's going to get confusing."

"Because I'm Maddie too!"

A young girl comes bounding down the stairs of the farmhouse. She has dark hair like Parker but green eyes like Austin. She runs straight into Austin's legs, where he catches her and stops her from rocketing straight on into me.

"But mine's spelled with *d*'s," Maddie continues confidently. "Like *d* for 'duck.' It's short for Madeline."

"Mine's short for Matilda," I tell her.

"Maybe we could call you by your full names while you're here," Parker suggests.

"But you only call me Madeline when I'm in trouble," Maddie protests.

"Same as me," I add. "Matilda immediately makes me feel like I've done something wrong."

"We can just both be Maddie," Maddie says.

"But will it be spelled with *t*'s or *d*'s?" I ask.

Maddie grins at me.

"Both!" she says.

"Which will come first?" I ask. "The *t* or the *d*?"

"I'm already confused," says Austin, wincing.

Parker shakes his head. "We'll figure something out."

"Hey, thanks so much for letting me stay," I say.

"It's our pleasure," Parker replies. "I will warn you, though. Our old cat has a bit of a penchant for that guesthouse. You might find him poking around a bit."

"His name is Boots," Maddie declares. "He's ten."

I smile. "That's okay," I say. "I like cats."

———

The guesthouse is on the other side of the orchard. It's an old worker's cottage that has been renovated into a cute studio suite, and if "orchard chic" is indeed a thing, then the cottage has it in spades. There's a crocheted blanket on the bed under cushions cross-stitched with apples. A jug printed with a rooster sits on the kitchen counter, and the coffee table has been hewn out of an old barn door.

When I comment on this, Austin laughs.

"Yeah," he says. "That's all thanks to Janey, my sister-in-law. This was her little project."

"Well, she's done a great job."

I set my bag down on the floor inside the cottage. Austin is standing in the doorway, his hand resting on the frame.

"Do you want a tour around the orchard?" he asks.

"Sure."

"Do you wanna walk, or do you wanna take the tractor?"

"Um, obviously the tractor."

The tractor is actually a little John Deere ATV that's barely big enough for two people. Austin and I are squeezed so close together in the seat that we have no choice but for our arms to overlap. My stomach floods with warmth at the feeling of his forearm pressed against the top of mine.

"Spacious, huh?" Austin says, raising his eyebrows at me as he begins to drive.

"Yeah, you might need an upgrade if you want to offer those tourist tractor rides."

"Well, luckily these are currently reserved for VIP guests only."

My stomach rises and falls as the ATV trundles across the soft ground. But I don't know if it's the clank of the machine that's doing it, or something else.

"So, these are the trees," Austin says, as he drives us down a row of apple trees.

"Really?" I say. "I was wondering what those were."

Austin nudges my side with his elbow. "To be specific," he says. "They're Ambrosia apple trees. Which is the best kind of apple."

"Ambrosia was said to be the food of the gods," I reply.

"Exactly."

"They're not ready to eat yet though, are they?" I gaze at the fruit as we pass, which still has large patches of pale green showing through the soft yellow red.

"Not until September, probably."

"Is that your busiest time?"

"Yep. Parks and Janey will start recruiting for pickers now. It was always my favorite time of year as a kid—the harvest. I loved how buzzy things would get."

"You seem like you had the best childhood."

Austin smiles and shrugs. "I can't complain."

"I'm an only child. On days when that was hard, I would have loved to have lived somewhere like this."

Austin frowns. "Was it lonely?"

"Sometimes. Though my parents did a good job of trying to surround me with other kids. I have a lot of cousins, and my mom's very social, so we were always hanging out with her friends' families. We had this big group vacation we'd do in the late summer every year, before school started again. We actually came out here once."

"Really?"

"Yeah. I can't remember exactly where, but it was a big farm stay. I loved it."

"This place suits you."

"Does it?"

"Yeah. Wanna drive?"

Of course I want to drive. I shuffle over into the driver's seat, sitting temporarily on Austin's lap as we switch, where I could happily stay. He gives me a short tutorial, and then I drive down one of the rows for a short distance until I somehow manage to stall it.

"That's okay," Austins says, laughing. "We're at the end, anyway."

He offers me his hand to get down from the ATV, and I take it. He doesn't let go as he finishes off the tour of the property. He shows me the vegetable gardens, the sheds, and the chicken coop. We end up at the back of the property, where the land slopes up into the hills.

"Where are we going now?" I ask.

"You like to hike, right?"

I follow Austin's gaze up the hill in front of us. And without another word, we both start to climb.

This is a hill, not a mountain, so we're at the top of the slope in less than ten minutes. It's only then that I turn to look behind us and realize exactly why Austin's led me here.

The view is stunning. From up here, not only can I see the whole orchard spread out below us, but I can also see almost the whole valley. There are other orchards dotted in the distance as well as vineyards stretching out in slanted rows. I can see the campgrounds where they held Valley and Hills Country Music Festival, and the straight streets of Carrickvale. If there weren't more hills blocking the view, we'd be able to see all the way through to the cobblestoned Main Street of Casey River.

Austin settles himself on a flat patch of grass and pats the ground next to him. I sit beside him, my hip pressed into his.

"This was one of my favorite spots as a kid," he says. "I loved coming up here at golden hour to look at the view."

"See? The best childhood."

Austin's legs are bent up in front of him, his arms resting on his knees. We're quiet for a few moments as we both look at the view. As I pull my legs up in front of me too, my elbow comes to rest in the crook of Austin's arm, and I don't shift. Neither does he.

"You want to know the truth, actually?" he says quietly.

"About what?" I ask.

"It wasn't always the best childhood," Austin says. "I was very lucky, I know. But sometimes, I'd come up here to look at the view, and I'd wish I was somewhere else."

"Somewhere like where?"

"I don't know. Somewhere other than the orchard." Austin shakes his head. "I know what you mean about this seeming like the best place to grow up. I guess it was just that . . . when you live somewhere like this, home and work have no clear boundaries. So, it just kind of felt like work, all the time. My parents were always busy. A lot of the time they were stressed too. They talked about the orchard at dinner and at breakfast. Sometimes, they'd argue."

I press my elbow more firmly into the crook of his arm.

"I think I liked harvest so much because new people came along," Austin continues. "And I got to talk to them about other things and other places."

I nod slowly. "And is that why you ended up getting into theater?"

Austin looks at me.

"You're right," he says. "I don't know if I realized it at the time, but yeah, theater school gave me something else to do. It was an escape. And it was also . . ."

Austin hesitates. I press my arm gently into his again, urging him to go on.

"I guess I liked people looking at me," he says. "Maybe that does make me sound vain and self-centered. Maybe I am a stereotype. But I just . . . liked people paying attention to me for once."

"It's okay to want people to look at you sometimes."

Austin turns his head toward me. The sun is beginning to set, making the view more golden and beautiful by the minute, but neither of us is facing it anymore.

"I like looking at *you*," Austin says softly.

I flush, but I don't look away.

"I like looking at you too."

Austin gives a shy smile I haven't seen before. It makes it easier for me to press even closer to him and dare to rest my chin on his shoulder.

Austin tilts his face down so that his forehead is touching mine.

"And right now," he murmurs, "I sure as hell don't want to be anywhere else."

He places his hand gently on my chin and tilts my face up. We pause for a moment, our lips half an inch from each other. Then I make the final move and lean in.

I can feel Austin smiling as I kiss him. I move my hand to his shirt collar and pull him in tighter. And as sunlight floods my body, I marvel at how this doesn't feel like the first time we've kissed. Because maybe, in a way, it isn't.

FORTY-TWO

As I try to fall asleep in the guesthouse that night, I run through the scenes of the day in my mind. I think about sitting with Austin at the top of the hill for an indiscernible amount of time. I think about his body pressed against mine and the warmth in my core. I think about our foreheads touching, my eyes so close to his that their green was temporarily my whole view. I think about how it felt like learning something brand new and recalling a favorite memory at the same time.

I think about dinner with the Farrows earlier that evening. The table was laden with roast chicken, salad, and pitchers of apple cider. I'd been seized by boldness the whole day, but I became suddenly shy in my seat at the Farrow table. Meeting the family is meant to be something you do several weeks into a new relationship. And what Austin and I have can't even exactly be called that yet, by normal standards.

But this isn't normal standards. I'm not following the regular road map of a relationship here. In a sense, I feel like I'm cheating. Like someone's opened a secret detour just for me that bypasses all the wrong turns and missed exits and dead ends. I know this is the right way, because I've seen it happen multiple times, in multiple worlds.

But Austin doesn't know this. This is what I have to remind myself. This is what causes me to jolt back a little, when the warmth in my stomach becomes almost too searing to handle. This is what made me hesitant to invite Austin to stay with me in the guesthouse tonight, rather than in his childhood bedroom in the farmhouse where he normally sleeps.

Austin doesn't have the same secret knowledge that I do.

Austin doesn't know that we've met each other in at least seven different lives.

Unless he does?

This is the thought that catches me and keeps me from sleep.

I know that my wardrobe is Austin's tree hollow. I know that, in the Dark Austin timeline, he found his own portal and gained the same road map that I did.

So, it's not impossible to think that this Austin, my Austin, could have also found the portal too. I know he goes running to Fallen Tree Falls. Maybe he also heard voices through the tree one day. Maybe he stepped into the hollow.

Maybe that's why he's been so up front about this connection between us. Maybe he knew even before I did.

On the old barn stool next to the bed that serves as a nightstand, I see my phone light up.

It's Austin, asking me if I'm managing to sleep well.

I stare at the screen. It's a redundant question, of course. If I'm sleeping well, then I won't be awake to answer.

It's almost as if he wants me to still be awake. My heart rate increases as I think about the message I want to send in response.

I hesitate.

I type it.

I hesitate again.

Then I hit send on the words: Not really. Could use some company.

———

The door to the cottage creaks open such a short amount of time later, I wonder if Austin ran here.

He stands in the doorway, silhouetted by the moonlight. He's wearing sweatpants and a light pullover, and his hair is tousled, as if he's been tossing and turning as much as I have.

"Hey," he whispers to me.

"Hey," I whisper back.

I'm sitting on the edge of the bed, shivering against the cool night air in my linen pajamas. Austin closes the door and walks over to the bed. He leans over and grabs the crocheted blanket, then drapes it around my shoulders.

"You're cold," he says, as he lowers himself onto the bed beside me.

"Only a little," I reply.

He moves to pull the blanket tighter around me. But instead, I open it up and tug his body toward mine, wrapping the blanket around both of us.

Austin presses against me, and his mouth meets my collarbone. I feel his lips open in a kiss. I breathe in sharply as he moves his mouth to my neck, then to my cheek, then to my lips.

The blanket doesn't stay wrapped around us for long. Soon, it's slid to the floor, and Austin's covering me with the warmth of his body instead. I lean back into the multitude of cushions and hook my leg around him, pulling him closer. My hands follow the slope of his shoulders under his pullover, then run down to the small of his back, where I push up the wool to find bare, hot skin.

Austin's breathing grows heavier, and his kisses grow deeper. He reaches up under my linen shirt with one hand, and his thumb traces my hip bone. He moves his fingers higher, past my ribs, brushing my chest so lightly it's like a whisper, before coming to rest close to my heart.

"Is this all okay?" he murmurs.

"Yes," I reply. "Yes."

Every piece of clothing that comes off is like something being gained. First, it's Austin's sweater, revealing broad shoulders with a dusting of freckles over them that I press my mouth to. Then it's my shirt, followed quickly by my shorts. It's bare skin moving on bare skin, and it still doesn't seem like enough. Why have I put so much effort into putting clothes *on* Austin when this is so, so much better?

We take our time. Austin seems to find parts of my body fascinating that I've never given much thought to before—my navel, the palm of my hand, the space between my breasts, the inside of my thigh. It's like he wants to feel it all, and every part of me is on fire in response. I can't imagine that I felt cold earlier. I can't imagine ever feeling cold in my life when I'm currently flooded with this much heat.

Eventually, waiting any longer is too much to bear. I wrap my legs around him and grip him tightly, telling him without words exactly what I want.

As he moves into me, he steadies his eyes on mine. Green fades to black as I involuntarily shut mine in pleasure.

For a moment, I'm suspended in darkness again. But this is a place way above purgatory. And I sure as hell don't want to be anywhere else.

FORTY-THREE

The orchard wakes up early. Birds start trilling in the hills, and I can hear the sound of car tires crunching on the driveway as either Parker or Janey heads off somewhere just before dawn.

Austin has stayed the night. He lies beside me, still sleeping, his lightly freckled shoulders rising and falling slowly as he breathes. I watch them for a moment, feeling dozy and dreamy and warm and like I never want to leave. We could stay here in the cottage for days if we needed to. We could survive on the chocolates and local honey Janey has kindly placed in the kitchen. There are plenty of books and copies of the Farmers' Almanac on the small bookshelf in the corner. Though I don't think we'd be short of other ways to entertain ourselves.

But it's not long before the work emails start arriving on my phone. I read them with bleary eyes, and the real world begins to settle around me again.

From the emails, I deduce that we plan to start filming again in a few days' time. We're going to start by filming interior scenes, to give the art department more time to reinstall the Main Street set and replace the damaged props. Some teams will come back a day early to prep, including mine. Given that the production company is still having to pay for everyone's accommodation and per diems while we're here, they're eager to get things back up and running as soon as possible.

This means I only have two more days to spend unencumbered at the Farrow orchard. I place my phone beside me and roll over to Austin, wrapping my arm around him. He makes a satisfied sound and raises my hand to his mouth.

"Is it wake-up time?" he murmurs.

"The sun's beginning to rise," I say.

"Oh, that's late on the orchard clock."

He rolls onto his back and runs his hand through my hair. I begin to lean down to him, but the sound of the cottage door creaking causes both of us to jump.

The door slowly opens, but no one walks through.

At least, no human.

I start to laugh as I see the slinking body of a black-and-white cat moving through the cottage.

"Ah, here he is," says Austin.

Boots walks confidently over to the bed and jumps onto it like he owns it. He trots straight up to me and looks at me with those moon-yellow eyes.

"Hey, buddy," I whisper. I scratch him between his ears and feel the vibration of his purr under my hands.

"Hmm, he likes you," says Austin. "Sometimes he can take a minute to warm to people when he first meets them."

As I look into Boots's eyes, I know that this isn't actually the first time we've met. And I know that the old cat knows it too. Though I can't tell Austin that, of course.

At least, not yet. Not here. Not when the young morning sun is so perfect and the haze of last night still envelops us like a crocheted blanket.

"Okay," says Austin, reaching over to give Boots a scratch of his own. "I need coffee."

Over breakfast with the Farrows, I insist to Parker that I be put to work for the day. Parker resists until I become almost annoying; then he finally relents and allows me to help with one of the day's tasks.

"I warn you, it's not glamorous," he tells me.

"I honestly don't mind."

Parker goes on to explain that a key element of orchard management is protecting the trees from pests. One of their defenses is hanging ball traps on the trees to catch pests like apple maggot flies, which can lay eggs in the apples and destroy them.

The morning's job is to go around hanging these sticky little spheres from the tree branches, almost like Christmas ornaments. Parker's right—it's not glamorous at all to think about something called apple maggots. But even still, I kind of enjoy walking among the trees, tying the traps and sneaking glances at Austin down the row, where I always find him already looking at me. You'd think that fly trapping wouldn't be conducive to steamy thoughts, but the memory of last night is so heady, I can't help it. The scenes roll on repeat in my mind, like a film projector that's glitching.

After we're done for the morning, Austin tells me he wants to take me out for lunch. We hop into his immaculate truck and drive a short way down a back road, past fields and fruit trees, the truck's wheels lifting whirls of dust around us.

"Thanks for helping out," Austin tells me.

"It's the least I can do," I say. "For letting me stay."

"You know now, right, that the invitation was mostly for *my* benefit?"

"Mutual benefit, I'd argue."

Austin grins. "Parker knew right away, you know. Sure, I was just being charitable, inviting a poor stranded girl from the crew—who just so happens to be hot as hell—to come stay in the guesthouse."

"Well, you are super nice. I'd believe it."

"I try my best. But trust me, Mattie. I don't just go around inviting anyone to come stay at my family's house."

"No. Not anyone. Just the hot ones."

Austin shoots a glance at me out of the corner of his eye.

"So, just you then," he says.

I roll my eyes, but I can't stop smiling.

Austin's smiling too, as he shifts his free hand off the steering wheel and onto my knee, where I place my hand on top of his.

Our lunch spot turns out to be at another orchard down the road—the kind that most definitely has leaned in to the whole "orchard chic" thing. There's an animal petting area when we pull in, a meeting spot for tractor rides, a large, open lawn dotted with picnic tables, and two food trucks parked under some trees.

One of the food trucks has a bright pink-and-white-striped awning. Inside, a woman with long gray hair swept up behind a kerchief is scooping ice cream into cones and passing them to eager children.

"Is that the famous Virginia?" I ask Austin. "Of Virginia's ice creams?"

"The one and only," Austin replies.

Virginia is so delighted to see Austin that she rushes out of the truck to give him a hug and a kiss on the cheek. Then she looks at me with sparkle-eyed interest.

"This is Mattie," Austin explains. "She tried your ice cream at Valley and Hills the other day."

"It single-handedly helped me recover from a fainting spell," I explain.

"Oh yes, it does that," Virginia says. "I'm glad you liked it. And how do you two know each other?"

"Work," I reply.

"Ah, are you an actor as well?"

"Oh, no. No, I work behind the scenes."

"Well, I just thought seeing as you two look so good together, you might be an actor too," Virginia quips.

She raises her eyebrows at Austin, and for a moment, she reminds me of Florence. I muse that maybe Cupid shouldn't be a plump male cherub but a keen-eyed, silver-haired woman.

Austin just laughs and places his hand on the small of my back. Virginia has to tend to the long line of kids clamoring for ice cream, so she hands us each a small tub of the apple pie flavor for free and returns to her customers. We also get burgers from the other food truck and then sit down at one of the picnic tables to eat.

Our knees knock against each other under the table, and neither of us shies away from the contact. As I look at Austin sitting opposite me, the sun illuminates his face in a way our film lights aren't able to—every freckle, line, and angle is a perfect design. I suddenly want to touch more than just his knee, but I'm conscious we're in public.

Plus, there's a faint murmuring inside my head that's preventing me from fully settling into this beautiful day. It's telling me that there's something I need to do—something risky and uncomfortable that feels at odds with this soft, warm feeling I have right now. But I just don't think I can let myself fall completely until I get it over and done with.

FORTY-FOUR

After lunch, we take a walk around a nearby lake. It's a wide, silvery lake with a trail looping all the way around its perimeter. Cyclists wheel by, boats drift in the calm water, and vacationers set up picnics by the lakeshore. We walk until we find a quiet spot to rest, where there's a bench set back a small distance from the trail, away from the cyclists and walkers, the picnickers and boats.

"I'm so full," Austin declares as we settle into the bench.

"Me too," I say.

"I probably didn't need that second ice cream."

"It's just so good, though."

Austin raises his arm up, draping it over the back of the bench and around my shoulders. A slight press of his hand against my shoulder pulls me closer to him.

"This is nice," I murmur against him. "Why do we even have to work?"

"Maybe we should just give it up. Live a life of leisure."

"Sure. With all the money I have."

Austin looks down at me.

"What are your plans, by the way?" he asks.

"You mean like . . . in life?"

"I mean, after *Magic Season* wraps."

"Oh." I bite my lip. "Well, like I told you, I'd kind of been thinking of taking a break after this job. A break from film work, anyway. But then Deidre told me she has a supervisor role available on her next project."

"Really? Wow, Mattie, congratulations."

"Well, she didn't exactly offer it to me. She told Henry about it as well."

"She'd give it to you over Henry, for sure."

I frown. "How do you know that?"

"Because you're great at your job. And I've heard people talk about you. You're really well respected in the industry. You don't know that?"

My first instinct is to shake my head. But I stop halfway.

"I mean," I say, "I do think I'm good at my job."

"Of course you are."

"But so's Henry."

"I like Henry—don't get me wrong. But he hasn't been doing this for as long as you have, and he still seems a little green. If you told Deidre you wanted that job, it would be yours, Mattie."

Austin pulls away for a moment to look me square in the face.

"Do you want it?" he asks.

I think back to how I felt when I first arrived in Casey River. I felt like my life had become the same as the sets I work on. Not the interesting parts on screen, but the drudgery behind the scenes. Someone else was always the director, the writer, the producer, the lead, the designer. I was just playing my small assistant role, letting someone else call the shots. I was floating. I was numb. I knew I needed a big change if I was ever going to feel different. And I thought that change would involve walking away.

Walking away *is* sometimes the answer. Like getting out of a relationship that's no longer serving you, for example.

But that's not always the case. Sometimes it's not a matter of walking away.

Sometimes it's a matter of leaning in.

"I do want it," I say.

It's the first time I've spoken the words out loud. It makes me feel lighter. If Austin's arm weren't around me, I feel like I might float up into the air.

"I wasn't sure, for a while," I continue. "For a long while. The industry was making me tired. I thought there were so many other things I could be doing instead. And that maybe they'd make me happier. But the problem wasn't with my job. I realize that now. The problem was with me."

"What problem?" Austin asks.

"I guess I felt like I didn't have ownership over my own life," I say. "Or like I wasn't living the *right* life. But I've realized that changing careers or industries or lives isn't going to magically fix that. It's one of those things that has to start from the inside. As corny as that sounds."

Austin nods and pulls me closer again.

"It doesn't sound corny," he murmurs.

"It's kind of exciting," I continue, feeling my cheeks flush. "I could really own that supervisor role. I think I'd be good at it."

"I *know* you'd be good at it," Austin replies.

I can feel my heart rate rising and the lightness bubbling up into my chest. This is the right moment. I feel it.

"There's something I have to tell you," I say to Austin.

His brows crease.

"Oh yeah?" he asks.

"Yeah." I swallow. "It's a bit . . . crazy, though."

"Like crazy good or crazy bad?"

"Crazy like you might not even believe me."

Austin leans back into the bench.

"Try me," he says.

———

I can vividly remember the look on Austin's face when he found me standing in his bedroom that first dark night. His forehead was furrowed, his green eyes faded. He clutched at that guitar so tightly, likely to hide the fact that his hands were shaking against the wood.

He looked dark and disturbed, and I know a big part of that was because a stranger had turned up uninvited in his bedroom.

But I also remember the way he gritted his teeth and insisted to me *I'm not mixed up* when I told him I wasn't the girl from the bookstore.

He wasn't just scared of me. He was scared of himself. Scared that he might be losing his mind. Scared that he'd finally found the bottom.

That version of Austin seemed so distant from the version I know now. Moonlight compared to sunlight.

But I've always known that one decision, one incident, can't turn you into a completely different person. A different version of yourself, yes. But not an entirely new thing. Every version of ourselves must exist inside us concurrently, like nesting dolls—some hidden, some overt, some hovering in the in-between.

I guess, given all that, I should have known exactly how this was going to turn out. And I decided to do it anyway.

———

Austin stares at me. His arm slips from my shoulders, dangling over the back of the bench instead. He doesn't say anything for a moment. I feel his leg shift away from mine, and my heart falls into my stomach.

"Mattie," he says eventually, in a quiet voice. "You know that's impossible. Right?"

"I know it *seems* impossible," I reply. "But is it really? Scientists have never disproven the theory of parallel universes."

"That doesn't prove they're real."

"Well, no, it doesn't. But what does prove they're real is the fact that I've seen them. I'm not making this up." My voice shakes a little at the end, and I remember for a moment how this felt with Jack. Pleading my case. Insisting I'm right.

"I'm not . . ." Austin pauses and runs a hand over his face. "I don't think you're making it up. I think you *think* you've experienced this. But are you . . . ?"

Austin hesitates again.

"Am I what?" I ask.

"Have you ever taken drugs?"

I sit back, startled, creating even more distance between us.

"Drugs?" I repeat. "Are you serious?"

"Well, it's not the most ridiculous question. Half the people in the industry are on them. And this . . ."

"Well, I'm not," I say, trying to keep my voice steady. "I drink sometimes. Normally responsibly, despite what you might think after the festival. But that's it. This has nothing to do with drugs."

"What about prescription medication? That can have side effects."

"This doesn't have anything to do with drugs or medication. This is real."

I stand up suddenly, feeling hot.

"You don't believe me," I say.

Austin is still and calm on the bench. "Like I said," he replies. "I believe that you believe it."

"That's something a therapist says to a patient."

Austin doesn't answer for a moment.

"Do you go to therapy?" he asks gently.

I suddenly feel like I want to cry, which I hate myself for. I turn away from Austin for a moment, looking at the lake, which shimmers and shifts in front of me.

I hear Austin get up from the bench and come to stand beside me.

"Mattie, I'm sorry," he murmurs. "I'm not trying to offend you. I've just seen this kind of thing before."

"What kind of thing?" I ask.

Austin blows out a breath. "Well, there was Parker, for one. Remember how I told you that he had a bit of a breakdown a few years ago and I took some time off to go traveling with him? He got into drinking and dope for a bit, and it was a rough time, but he got out of it toward the middle of the trip. Just before he met Janey."

I look at Austin hard, swallowing the lump in my throat. When I told Austin my story, I was light on the specific details of his presence in my timelines. I figured that would be something I'd tell him fully later, once he came to terms with the whole thing. So, I didn't tell him about Parker dying. And now I'm glad I didn't.

"Oh," I say quietly.

"And it runs in the family," Austin continues. "My dad also struggled with alcohol. We had a couple of really bad years on the orchard when I was a teenager, and my parents lost a bunch of money. Dad started drinking. Like, a lot. Sometimes he'd talk about things that hadn't happened and people who weren't there."

I think of Dark Austin throwing out all the whiskey bottles in his apartment. The lump in my throat isn't dissolving, and I find it hard to speak.

"Well," I force out. "I'm sorry that happened."

"And I'm sorry for being touchy about all this, but do you get it now? It makes me nervous when people aren't completely with it. It's not because I don't care. I do care. I just never know exactly how to help."

"I wasn't asking for your help." It comes out sharper than I intend, and Austin takes yet another step away.

"I was just trying to . . . tell you," I finish weakly. "The truth."

Austin runs a hand through his hair. "Okay," he says. "Okay, I get that. But I honestly don't know what to do with all this, Mattie."

Believe me, I want to plead. Just believe that I'm telling the truth.

But when I allow myself to take a deep breath in, I put myself in Austin's shoes for a moment.

Would I believe him, if he were standing there telling me the same thing? If I never found the wardrobe, but he found the tree hollow, would I believe his outrageous story? Probably not, in all honesty. No matter how attractive he is or how nice and normal he seems, I imagine I'd feel that stone dropping into the pit of my stomach, telling me that, yet again, I'd ended up with a dud.

Then something stirs inside me.

The tree hollow.

Of course.

"Okay," I say, steadying my voice. "Okay, I get it. It sounds crazy. It sounds impossible. Maybe it is."

Austin nods slowly.

"I'm going to walk back to the house and pack my things," I continue. "I can find somewhere else to stay tonight."

"You don't have to do that . . ."

"Do you want me to stay?"

When Austin doesn't reply right away, I have my answer. I nod and swallow, hard. A part of me wants to beg. But I know better now.

"It's fine," I say softly. "I'll talk to Val about staying somewhere else."

"I don't want you to go," Austin says. "Not after we . . ." He sighs. "I think I just need a moment to think about this all, okay? And maybe it would be good for you to talk to someone else too. Maybe Val or Henry?"

"Okay," I say in a small voice. "I will. I'm sorry for dropping this on you so soon. And I know I'm not in a position to be asking any more of you, but . . . if you want to understand what I'm trying to say, could you do something for me?"

"Of course. What do you need?"

"Fallen Tree Falls," I say. "The tree that's growing out of the old stump. There's a hollow in it, big enough for a person to fit in. You have to stand at a specific angle to see it."

I know I'm not helping convince Austin that I'm not crazy. His Adam's apple bobs up and down as he swallows and tries to take in my words. I force myself not to think about my lips on his throat last night. It's too painful now.

"Okay . . ." he says slowly.

"Maybe, if you go in there, you'll understand what I'm talking about."

Austin fixes his gaze on me. For a moment, I can see all the different versions of him again, overlapping in his river-green eyes, and I want to keep imploring. But I told myself I'd never plead again.

So, I leave him with those last words and turn and walk away.

FORTY-FIVE

The next few days are agony.

There's a slightly cursed feeling to the production now. Like a staging of *Macbeth*, it's like everyone's waiting for something heavy to fall from the ceiling or someone to collapse to the ground. One of the props guys has quit, and the bump on our production accountant's head turned out to be a mild concussion, so she's out for a few days now too. We haven't been able to completely replace all the items that were damaged in the storm, so compromises need to be made, and more money is spent than anyone planned. The show will go on, but the atmosphere is tense, to say the least.

It suits my mood. I haven't heard from Austin since I left the orchard. I walked back from the lake, and of course, halfway down the road I heard the sound of his truck tires crunching in the gravel behind me. My confession apparently didn't override his desire for me to get back to the orchard safely. But I insisted on walking. I didn't want to sit beside him in his clean truck and palpably feel what might be lost between us.

Back at the orchard, I thanked Parker and Janey and told them production had sorted out some other accommodation for me. Parker told me he was sorry to see me go, and his shrewd eyes indicated that he suspected I might have a different reason for leaving.

When I tried to pack my things, Boots crawled into my bag. I'm still finding black-and-white cat hairs on my clothes.

I wasn't totally lying. Val actually did manage to sort out alternate accommodation for me. It's a room in a motel on the edge of Casey River, where a few of the other crew are staying. The room is small, clean, and devoid of personality. There's no leak in the bathroom, and there's no portal in the back of the wardrobe, which is just a standard sliding-door closet. As I stare at the empty closet, a lump forms in my throat.

There's a chance I might never go back to that apartment. And that should be fine. I knew this part of the story was ending. I knew I'd seen and heard and learned almost all that I could from the worlds beyond that wardrobe.

But I thought it was ending because another one was beginning.

Now I'm not sure. Austin's name stays absent from my phone screen. The lump stays present in my throat. The motel room and the world around me stay remarkably unmagical. And the memories of that kiss on the hill and our night together start to take on a warped quality, like pictures that have become overexposed.

On the night before we're due to start filming again, I decide to fulfil my promise to Austin and talk to someone. I call Margot.

The sofa of my motel room is stiff and squeaky and not half as comfortable as the one back in the apartment. I struggle to settle as Margot's face fills my phone screen. She has a scratch on her cheek from some adventure, and I remember the times I saw her in my other lives, the constant she's always been.

I start to cry before she's even finished saying hello.

"Mattie, what the hell?" she asks. "Who do I have to hurt?"

Only a fool would tell the same impossible story twice in one week. Only a fool would tell it all again after seeing the reaction it got me with Austin.

But I've never had to worry about Margot believing me. I've never had to worry about Margot thinking I'm crazy. Most of the time, Margot considers my main flaw to be that I'm not crazy enough.

She already knows part of the story, of course—about the passage-way and the version of Austin I saw through there. But she's been off hiking, and I've been so caught up in my other timelines that I haven't had a chance to tell her the rest yet. Until now.

Unlike Florence and Austin, Margot doesn't wait until I'm finished to react. She interjects throughout my story, punctuating the tale with insistent questions and requests for clarification. She's fascinated by the timeline that she appeared in, eagerly digging for more information about her alternate life, which I regret now that I don't know more about. But the important part is that I don't even need to get to the end to understand what she thinks.

"You believe me," I say shakily.

"Of course I fucking believe you." Margot is standing up, pacing her bedroom, the phone shaking in her hand. "This isn't the first time I've heard this kind of thing. There was this podcast episode . . ."

"Of course there was," I say it in jest, but my laugh is one of delir-ious relief.

"I'll find it for you," Margot continues. "It was the same scenario, only it wasn't a wardrobe. It was like, this crawl space under some-one's house."

"And there was a portal there?"

"It sounded like it. Of course, everyone tried to tell the person that they must have just hit their head in the crawl space and hallucinated the whole thing. Despite them having no other signs of having a TBI. People just don't want to believe this kind of thing. I swear to God, aliens could be walking among us, and we wouldn't notice for years."

"That's why I didn't want to tell anyone."

"And now we've arrived at the most important question. Why the hell did it take you this long to tell *me*?"

I bite my lip. "I wanted to. But you've been away, and I guess . . . it felt like my thing to figure out. I worried that maybe if I told you, it might all disappear."

"You told that old neighbor lady who you barely know! Quite frankly, I'm offended."

"Yeah, and the day I told her, the portal closed up."

"All right." Margot clicks her tongue. "Fair enough. And now you've told Austin."

"And that went great."

I wait for Margot to berate Austin. I wait for her to say that he's being a real jerk about this whole thing—not believing me, insinuating I'm on drugs, asking if I'm seeing a therapist. I wait for the fire I've always needed from Margot.

But surprisingly, it doesn't come.

"I mean, I get where he's coming from," Margot says. "He has a history of alcoholism in his family, and he hangs out with actors all the time. That crowd seems sober like, zero percent of the time."

"But I'm not like that," I insist.

"*We* know that. But despite the fact that Austin's obviously your soulmate, he doesn't know that yet."

"What did you just say?"

"What part?"

"The part about . . ." The words stick in my mouth. "The part about Austin being my soulmate."

"I said exactly that. That he's obviously your soulmate."

"Since when do you believe in all that?"

"Oh, I believe in soulmates. I know my relationship history doesn't exactly demonstrate it, and I'm starting to doubt whether my time will ever come, but from an observer's perspective, I definitely believe in soulmates. You've seen me at weddings. I'm a mess."

"I thought that was the free wine."

"The wine doesn't help, no."

"But you're so independent."

"Yeah, I am. That's why my past relationships haven't worked. But they obviously haven't been my soulmate."

I smile, a little sadly. "But you think he's out there? The perfect guy for you? Who'll love your independence and your conspiracy theories and keep up with you on your crazy hikes."

"No, fuck dating a guy who hikes. They're all so annoying. I think my soulmate is a man who has dinner and a hot bath waiting for me when I get home from a hike."

I laugh. "I hope you find him."

"Me too. But this isn't about me. This is about you and the fact that you've already found him. Multiple times."

I sigh. "But I screwed it up," I say. "I told him too soon. Maybe I shouldn't have told him at all."

"It would have eaten away at you. You're a bad liar."

"Thanks."

"Okay, I'm going to give you some advice that is extremely hypocritical and definitely not something that I'd ever be able to do myself."

"Which is?"

"I think you just need to wait it out. Give him some time."

"So . . . do nothing?"

"Exactly. Do you think the universe brought you together so many times only for it to end like this?"

"I don't know. I have no idea how the universe works anymore."

"Just be patient. You're good at being patient."

"You hate that about me."

"I know."

We both laugh.

"I have something that might occupy you in the meantime," says Margot.

"Oh yeah?"

"Yeah. We should get you on a podcast."

—

I love Margot, but I refuse to be on a podcast. Despite having now shared my story with three people, I think it needs to end here. I don't want to become some online sensation, or a cult oddity, or, even worse, a laughingstock. Even though Margot says I could do it anonymously, it just doesn't feel right.

Instead, I decide to go back to the old apartment early the next morning. I know they're in the middle of repairing the storm damage and I have no business being there anymore, but I make up some excuse about thinking I've left something behind, and Val says the owner's happy for me to stop by.

When I get there, there are two contractors inside number eight working on the leak. It's strange to see people I don't know inside this apartment that has held multiple worlds for me. It makes it seem incredibly mundane, and a few weeks ago, that might have been enough to cause me to question everything I've seen. But I'm done doubting my mind, doubting myself.

"Hey," I greet the contractors. "I'm the previous tenant. Just stopping by to pick some things up—the owner knows."

One of them shrugs. "Help yourself," he says.

I hesitate in the doorway to the bathroom, glancing at the wardrobe. I can't just climb in there with the contractors standing on the other side of the wall.

There's a buzz from a phone then, and one of the contractors, reading a message, says, "Ah. Ms. Casey wants us to put this on hold and go look at the roof now."

"But we're almost done," the other protests.

"She's the boss."

I watch as they gather their things and exit the apartment. I'm struck by both the incredible timing and what he'd just said—he referenced a Ms. Casey. Casey? As in the family that founded the town? I haven't come across any Caseys in my time here, but there must still be descendants of the family living nearby. Whoever Ms. Casey is, I'm grateful to her for pulling the contractors away right when I needed one final moment by myself with the wardrobe.

As I open the door, I don't even really know what I'm looking for.

And when I find the portal open, I feel a little surprised.

A part of me thought that the spinning cluster of timelines I experienced during the storm might have represented the end of my story with the portal. Like Dark Austin said, it was a crescendo, right before the song quieted to an end.

But it's still there. It's still open for me.

It isn't over yet.

I check behind me, but the contractors are definitely gone. And so, for what feels like the final time, I step through the wardrobe.

When I get to the other side, I think I've been here before.

The wardrobe is hung with clothes of a minimalist, masculine style—a couple of T-shirts, several button-up shirts, a leather jacket, and a coat. I can smell crisp laundry soap and the lingering scent of a sweet, piney cologne that's all too familiar.

I frown as I push open the door and see a bed neatly made with basic navy-and-cream linen. Leaning up against the wall is an empty guitar case. A book lies open on the nightstand. There's no glass of whiskey next to it.

I appear to be back in the first timeline. Which was also the last timeline. The world of Dark Austin, who ended up not being so dark after all.

I can hear the shower running in the en suite bathroom. My heart speeds up, thinking of Austin standing there under the hot water. I know it's a different version of him, but my mind leaps to the night we spent together at the orchard—my hands running over his bare shoulders, my lips on his collarbone. He slept next to me without putting his T-shirt back on, and his chest stayed warm against my cheek even when the cottage cooled down.

I miss him, I realize. It's only been a few days, but I miss talking to him. I miss the way he calls me "Mattie with two *t*'s" and the easygoing lilt of his voice. I miss how he always listens so carefully to what everyone's saying, even when they're talking complete shit like Henry does. I miss his self-deprecating jokes and his overly clean truck. I miss the way his eyes seem to change when he sees me, like a cat's when they look at bright light.

I didn't realize that the pain I've been feeling these last few days is a kind of grief. To be perfectly honest, I've never lost something I really care about before. Jack doesn't count. That was painful, but it was dulled by a subconscious understanding that it was never really real, anyway. And my other breakups before then were all mostly mutual or expected or overdue.

I've never experienced the acutely unique agony of finding what might be my soulmate over and over again in multiple worlds. Only to lose him as soon as I finally had him in the real one.

The shower in the bathroom stops. I can hear the shower door sliding open and the rustle of a towel being pulled off the rack. I brace myself, emotion making my face hot and my chest tight. I don't know what I'm going to say to Dark Austin when I see him. *Help me?* I contemplate. *Help me fix this.*

But when the bathroom door opens, it's not Austin standing on the threshold.

FORTY-SIX

Standing in front of me is a girl. A girl who's slightly taller than average, with light-brown bangs and denim-blue eyes.

I watch as those blue eyes widen when she sees me.

She clutches her towel to her chest and backs into the doorframe.

"What the fuck," she says.

It's me. It's another version of me, standing there in a towel, gaping as if she's seen a ghost. Which would make more sense than this.

"It's you," I say thickly. "I mean, it's me."

The other version of me slams the bathroom door shut, which I'm not entirely surprised or offended by. I hear the shower running again, and I imagine that this time it's freezing cold. She's trying to shock some sense back into herself. I know, because it's exactly what I would do.

I take these few moments to gather myself. I've had a couple of close calls running into myself in these alternate worlds—the closest being when I literally talked to myself on the phone in the Jack time-line—but I haven't yet interacted with myself in the flesh. I've always been afraid that it's going to break a rule of some kind. But the time of worrying about broken rules is over. I was called back here for a reason. And I don't run away anymore.

"I'm still here," I call out from the other side of the door, when the water stops running again. "I'm real. I know it's impossible to believe, but if you come back out, I can try to explain."

The door to the bathroom opens a crack, and the other version of me peeks out. I'm holding out her dress to her, which I've found bundled in the chair in the corner.

"I've always loved this one," I say, shaking the floral material. "I made it second year of college, for an assignment."

Her face is pale.

"Or I guess, *we* made it?" I say. "I don't really know what the right terminology is."

She takes the dress from me and closes the door again. I think I can hear her swearing to herself. She coughs once or twice over the sink, as if she might be sick.

When the door opens again, she looks slightly more put together. She squares her shoulders and lifts her chin to face me.

There are some subtle differences between the two of us, I notice. Her hair is longer and thicker than mine, as if she hasn't had it cut in a while. She's slightly thinner. Her nails are painted with burgundy polish, which I've given up on because polish chips too easily when I'm working.

"Hi," I say quietly.

"Is this all some kind of prank?" she asks. She looks around the room. "Am I being filmed right now?"

I shake my head. "I know it seems that way. It took me a while to believe it too."

"You're not, like, some actor wearing a mask or something?"

"Believe me, even the most experienced prosthetic artists wouldn't be able to achieve something this realistic."

She glances past me, and I realize she's looking at the wardrobe. At the mirror in the door and the bizarre reflection in it.

There we are, the two of us. Almost identical save for tiny discrepancies, like twins or body doubles in a film.

Of all the wild things I've seen through the portal, this is the moment where the impossibility of it all hits me like a truck.

And I'm relieved when she lets out a shaky, delirious laugh so that I don't have to be the first to do it.

"Impossible," she repeats.

"And yet, somehow not," I say.

She walks over to the edge of the bed and sinks down onto it.

"He tried to tell me," she says. "But I didn't believe him."

"Austin did?" I ask.

She nods. There's enough room on the bed for me to sit down too, so I join her—both of us perched there like book ends.

"You work in the bookstore, don't you?" I ask. "That's how you and Austin met."

"That's right." She swallows unevenly. "It's been a couple of weeks now. And everything has felt so good between the two of us, but last night . . ."

She hesitates, remembering.

"He told you something that made you think he was crazy?" I guessed.

"Not crazy." She shakes her head. "I wouldn't ever call him crazy. I know what he's been through. But come on, what would you think if he told you all that out of the blue? Magical portals and alternate timelines and . . ."

She looks at me, blinking, still trying to convince herself that I'm real.

I don't have to wonder what it would feel like to have this story dropped on you. My chest twinges as I remember Austin's face when I made my own confession to him, on that bench by the lake.

"I'd find it very hard to believe," I admit. "I'd probably worry he'd started drinking again."

"Exactly." The other me plays with the hem of the floral dress we made in college. "I decided to give it until morning, to see if maybe he'd be better after a good night's sleep and admit it was some kind of temporary break in logic or something. But this morning, he was still adamant that he was telling the truth."

"Where is he now?" I ask gently.

"He went to work. He's doing some work on a nearby farm in between playing gigs; he has to be there pretty early."

"Were you getting ready to leave?" I nod at the shower.

"I'd been in there for about half an hour," the other version of me says. "Replaying it all in my head. Trying to decide what to do. And resisting the temptation to look through all his cupboards for hidden liquor, or maybe even something worse. I didn't want to betray his privacy like that, but I . . . I guess I felt kind of scared. Not *of* him, but *for* him."

I nod, understanding.

"But he was telling the truth," she says, in barely more than a whisper.

"He was," I confirm.

She turns, bending one leg up onto the bed so that she's facing me.

"Can you tell me your side of the story?" she asks.

"Of course. But I have some questions for you too."

"Okay, deal."

So we sit there, these two different versions of Matilda Bridges, telling our stories. We have to go way back, I realize, beyond just the discovery of the wardrobe. We have to begin in our third year of college, which was when our worlds split into two different paths.

It all led back to my first film job as a production runner on that local TV show. In this second world, I turned the job down. Something about it was making me anxious, though I couldn't put my finger on why. I knew I was potentially making a foolish mistake—declining an opportunity to break into the film industry—but at the time, it seemed like the right choice.

Though I regretted it for a while. I spent my final year of college somewhat adrift instead and ended up taking on a camp counselor job for the summer after graduation. The camp was on the outskirts of Casey River, and I developed an affinity for the cozy little town, especially visiting the small bookstore on my rare days off. It reminded me of that bookstore I'd visited on the beach trip during college break. A cloister from the world. A second home.

I moved back to the city when summer ended, but something kept calling me back to Casey River. I kept following the bookstore on social media, and when a job advertisement was posted, I applied.

"And here I am," the other version of me says with a modest shrug, once we've both swapped stories. "Living the simple life."

Something about her story is sticking in my mind.

"You were a camp counselor for a while?" I say.

"Yeah." She smiles. "At the time, it was just something to do while I figured out the rest of my life. But I ended up enjoying it more than I thought, and I loved working with those kids—getting out in nature, making friendship bracelets, hearing their ridiculous ghost stories . . . If things hadn't worked out with the bookstore, I was thinking of getting my teaching credential so that I could teach elementary or middle school."

I can almost hear the satisfying click in my brain as the pieces lock into place.

"Let me guess," she continues, reading my expression. "There's a timeline where I did that."

"Yep." I nod. "I was surprised by it, when I first visited, but it kind of makes sense. We like helping people. And kids do often have the best stories."

"Oh, they're hilarious. I've started running this children's story time at the bookstore, and it's manic, but also normally the highlight of my week."

"You know," I admit, "sometimes I'd daydream of this alternate life. A quiet, small-town existence working in a bookstore. I wondered if I'd be happier here."

"I am happy most days," she says quietly. "But I spend so much time reading; I'm constantly dreaming of other lives as well. Sometimes I go on weekend trips to the city, and I watch all the people rushing in and out of stores and cafés, and I wonder if maybe life would be more interesting there. And whenever I see something filming in the streets, I think about that runner job I turned down and what that kind of life would have been like."

"This." I gesture to myself, to my whole being. "This is what that kind of life is like."

"But are you unhappy?" She frowns. "Is that why you found a portal but I didn't?"

I pause. "I wouldn't say I was terribly *un*happy before all this. It's not like I had a real reason to be, like Austin does with his grief. 'Jaded' is maybe a better description."

"A quarter-life crisis," the other me says.

"I think that's exactly it."

"Some days, I felt like that too. Maybe I would have found my own portal if I kept on going that way. But lately, with Austin . . . I haven't been thinking so much about other lives."

She can't hold back her smile.

"It sounds like you found each other at exactly the right time," I say.

"I've been thinking about that." She toys with the bedspread. "It feels wrong, to think that I could save Austin, or the other way around. Like that's an outdated idea of love. The way I see it, love isn't about being rescued. It's about being rewarded. It's not the thing that saves you from the war—it's the feast after the battle, or the castle you come home to."

I stare at her, reminded of the way the Austin in this timeline also had a way with words that stunned me.

"Wow," I say. "You're a lot smarter than I am."

She flushes. "I just read a lot. I sound too much like a book sometimes."

"No, it's beautiful." My voice cracks a little on this last word.

"What is it?" she asks, noticing. "What's wrong?"

I haven't told her yet about the final part of the story. My own failed confession. The fact that I haven't spoken to my version of Austin in days. That I got my reward after the battle, and yet somehow, I let it escape me.

"No," she says, once I've finished. She shakes her head. "He was there, in every timeline. The universe gave him to us, in every timeline. He's our common thread. This can't be the end of it—he has to come around."

"Would you have come around?" I ask. "Would you have decided to believe him, if I hadn't turned up here?"

She stands and begins to pace the room.

"I wanted to believe," she says. "There was a small part of me that *did* believe. I sell fantasy worlds for a living. I want to believe in the impossible. But I will admit, proof is really helpful."

She pauses and turns to me.

"Proof," she repeats. "We just need to get him proof."

"Like what?" I ask. "I can't bring him through the wardrobe. I told him to go to the tree at the falls, but maybe that won't work either. Because he seems happy . . . I don't think he needs a portal."

"There has to be something else. Something here." Her eyes widen. "We should take a picture together."

"My phone doesn't work in here," I say.

"But what about mine?"

"And how would you send it to me in another world?"

She sighs, thwarted. Then her eyes light up again.

"What about this?"

She goes over to Austin's nightstand and picks up the Louis L'Amour book. She slides something out of it that he's been using as a bookmark and passes it to me.

I look down at the piece of card in my hand.

It's a strip of three photos, the kind taken at an arcade. In each one of them are Austin and me. Bookstore Mattie and Not-So-Dark Austin. Smiling at the camera. Laughing at something. In the last one, he's kissing her cheek.

I run my thumb over the photos.

"This was just the other night," the other version of me says. "We went out for dinner in Carrickvale and there was one of those old photobooths at the mall. But you didn't do that, did you? These photos don't exist in your timeline?"

"No." I shake my head. "They don't."

"That's it, then! That's the proof."

I look up at her, at me.

"What if he thinks I've edited them or something? It could make things worse."

She closes my hand over the photo strip.

"If he's anything like me," she says, "he'll want a reason to believe. Trust me. Trust *us*."

I sigh and then nod. I felt like there was something tugging me back to the wardrobe, and maybe this is it. Maybe three small, grainy photos are all it's going to take.

"Well," I say. "Honestly, I want to sit here and talk to you all day. But I do need to go to set soon."

"See, *go to set*, that sounds so exciting."

I laugh. "It can be exciting," I admit. "It's not the worst life."

"Far from it, by the sounds of it."

"And anyway, I'm not the only one who has somewhere to be."

She tilts her head at me.

"You know," I continue, "your Austin's probably in agony right now, at whatever farm he's working at, thinking you still don't believe him. You need to go and put him out of his misery."

She laughs. "You have a good point."

We stand up. And then we both reach simultaneously for each other and pull each other into a tight hug.

"I'm glad I met you," I murmur over her shoulder. "In fact, I think you might be the best person I've ever met."

"Stop it," she says, laughing. But when she pulls away, I can see the wet shine in her eyes.

This timeline is the hardest to leave. As I step through the wardrobe, I'm more certain than ever that I won't be back.

But I know that's a good thing. Because I don't need to explore all these what-ifs anymore. I have my answers.

FORTY-SEVEN

Of course, I can't leave the apartment for the last time without visiting Florence.

When I knock on her door, she shouts at me to come inside. She's out on the balcony when I enter, leaning on the railing and talking to the contractors on the roof.

"Yes, you can bill for overtime," she's saying to them. She glances back at me, standing in the kitchen. "And you can finish up in number eight whenever you're ready now."

I stare at her, listening to the thud of the contractors' footsteps on the roof.

"Ms. Casey," I say eventually, as the dots fuse in my mind.

Florence smiles, looking a little guilty.

"Yes?" she says.

"Do you . . . own these apartments?" I ask.

Florence breezes into the kitchen. "Did I never mention that?"

"No. You absolutely never mentioned it."

"Oh well, it mustn't have been important."

She busies herself filling a teapot with boiling water.

"Is it just the apartments you own, or like, the whole town?"

She laughs. "No one owns the whole *town*," she says. "A bit of land here and there has stayed in the family, but that's it."

"And by 'the family,' you mean the Caseys," I continue. "Your family, who founded the town. Another detail you forgot to mention."

"Well, I told you that story, didn't I?"

"Yeah, but like it was a folktale or something. Not family history."

Florence sighs. "Look," she says. "I don't typically tell people that I own this complex or that I'm a Casey, because I don't want them acting all funny and careful around me. If you'd known I was your landlady, would you have told me everything you did?"

I chew my lip. "Probably not."

"Exactly."

I click my fingers. "That explains why you were in number eight in the timeline where I died," I say. "You were talking about trying to clear the energy with sage."

"Sage often does the trick," Florence says, as she stirs the cups of tea.

"Is that something you have to deal with often around here? Hauntings and portals to other worlds?"

Florence hands me my tea and heads into the living room, where she settles down in the maroon armchair.

"I wouldn't say *often*," she replies.

"But I'm not the first."

"Certainly the first in a long time."

"Okay, the time for vagueness is over," I say. "I've visited a world where I was dead. I've apparently met my soulmate in multiple timelines. I've just come back from speaking *to myself* for over half an hour. I don't think there's anything too fucking strange in this world for me to handle anymore."

Florence's eyes widen before she lets out a laugh.

"My, you've gotten a bit feisty. I like it."

She places her teacup on the table.

"My daughter," she says. "When she was younger, she found her own portal in the wardrobe. It's a family heirloom."

"I didn't know you had a daughter either."

"Just the one. Claudia. She reminds me a bit of you, actually. She likes fashion and she apologizes too much."

"How did she find the portal?"

Florence takes a deep breath in. "She was thirteen at the time—a quiet, precocious child, who I left alone too much back then, because she was never one to complain about anything. The first night it happened, her father and I had just had an argument because Claudia wanted to get a cat and he wouldn't allow it. Never mind that I owned our home, and it should have been up to me. I . . . I didn't know my own power back then."

"What did he have against cats?"

"Oh, he didn't like animals in general."

I frown. "Always a bad sign."

"Mm-hmm," Florence says, pressing her lips together. "He stormed out after the argument, like he was prone to do, and Claudia retreated to her room. She didn't tell me until a few days later what had happened that night."

"She found the portal?"

"Eerily similar to your story," Florence continues. "She heard a cat meowing, so she followed it through. And there, in the world next door, she discovered a version of our home and our life where it was just the two of us and a ginger kitten. Her father was nowhere to be seen. We were laughing and playing, and she said that everything seemed brighter."

"Another timeline," I say.

"It was hurting her," Florence says, speaking slowly, as if trying to control a tremor in her voice. "The way her father and I always fought. Seeing me so unhappy. In the real timeline, she'd never spoken up about it until then. But there must have been a world out there where she'd said something earlier. Where I'd listened. And gotten her the kitten she deserved."

"So, you believed her right away, when she told you about the portal?"

"I should have," Florence says. "I wish I had. But Claudia had always had a vivid imagination, so I simply humored her and tried to put it to the side. It can be so easy to lie to ourselves sometimes."

I swallow. "I know."

"But the universe was determined," Florence says.

Her gaze is resting on the old, ornate wooden chest by the television—the one I'd noticed when I first visited her apartment.

"Wait," I say. "Is that—?"

"Another family heirloom," Florence says. "A twin of the wardrobe. Created by the same craftsman."

"And it's a portal too?"

"Well, for many years, it was simply a wooden chest where I kept our family board games and my tarot cards. But he didn't like me reading tarot and he didn't play games—at least not that kind—so I hadn't opened it for far too long. Then I did, one afternoon during a spring clean, and I was puzzled to find, under the stacks of dusty old boxes, a trapdoor concealing a staircase."

"A trapdoor? Okay, that's actually kind of cooler than a passageway in the back of a wardrobe."

"Naturally, I followed the staircase down into the floor, and yet somehow, in the middle of the stairs, I found myself walking up again, like the world had been flipped on its head. And I emerged back inside the chest, surrounded by board game boxes again. But these weren't dusty. They were well used. We must have played more in that timeline."

She smiles softly here.

"And is that when you decided to leave?" I ask quietly.

"It took me a few more trips through my own portal," Florence replies. "I kept wanting to find a world where I'd stayed with Claudia's father and was happy. I became almost obsessive. But that world didn't exist. There was no timeline where I was happy with him. So finally, I listened."

She exhales and runs a finger over the wooden pendant she always wears around her neck.

"I've wondered, from time to time, if it was negligent of me to move the wardrobe into one of our rental apartments, knowing the power it holds. But I've always seen it as a gift. Claudia agreed. So I decided to put it somewhere where it could be found by someone who really needed it. I just had a feeling that that was where it was supposed to be."

She fixes me with her gaze.

"Will you forgive me?" she asks. "For all the things I didn't tell you?"

I shake my head. "There's nothing to forgive," I say.

Florence exhales. "Good. I'm glad."

My eyes fall to the pendant between her fingers. For the first time, I notice that the color and grain of the wood are familiar.

"Is that also a family heirloom?" I ask, nodding at it.

Florence smiles down at the necklace. "It is. The wardrobe, the chest, and this pendant all have a common ancestor. The wood of a tree that once fell across a river during a storm."

I can feel everything settling into place around me, like seeing the full story on screen for the first time after only glimpsing disordered fragments of the script.

"The fallen tree," I say.

Florence nods. "That tree created a crossroads. It held a kind of transitional energy. And so, it created portals. The wardrobe. The chest. Austin's hollow. I wear this pendant to remind me. Not of the other worlds, but of the one I have now."

She stands up then and walks over to a nearby set of drawers, her long skirt swaying around her ankles, and retrieves something from the top drawer.

"This is another one," she says, handing me a smaller version of the round wooden pendant she wears. "You have it. To remind yourself."

I take it and run my thumb over the smooth surface.

"You know," I say, "you asked me a while ago what all my timelines had in common. I originally thought that the answer was that, in all of them, I ended up in Casey River. I know now that Austin was another common thread running through all of them." I swallow. "But in a way, so were you."

Florence blinks at me.

"If I ended up in apartment number eight—which you own—in every timeline, I must have met you in all of them as well," I say. "So, the universe must have known that I needed someone like you too."

Florence sniffs. "Oh, stop it. I get terrible headaches when I cry."

I laugh. "I'm sorry. I just have a lot of feelings at the moment."

"Well then," Florence says, looking at me pointedly. "As much as I appreciate them, isn't there someone else you should be sharing them with?"

FORTY-EIGHT

Everything seems concurrently clearer and murkier after I leave Florence's. Like the morning after a storm, the sky appears the bluest it's ever been, but there's debris in places it shouldn't be.

I understand the why behind the portal now. And in a sense, I think I understand the how.

There seem to be three factors that need to occur for the portals to reveal themselves.

1. You need to have a crossroads: a place where multiple time-lines of your life intersect.
2. This crossroads needs to be activated by a powerful token of some kind, like the wood from the fallen tree.
3. You need to need it.

It's that last point I find myself dwelling on as I walk down the river path toward town for the final time.

You need to need it. I needed my portal because I felt adrift, sub-missive, unsatisfied with my life, wanting something more. I don't think these are uncommon things to feel in your late twenties—I'm nothing but basic, after all—but still. You need to be searching for something *more* in order to stumble on your portal.

Florence's daughter needed it to give her the confidence to tell her mother how unhappy she was with their family life. And Florence needed it herself to see that there was no universe where she would be happy with her husband.

Dark Austin needed it. He was spiraling to the bottom, unable to rid himself of guilt and grief. He needed to see that, yes, there were other timelines where the tragedy of his brother's death hadn't happened. But those worlds didn't belong to him. He could drive himself crazy thinking *What if?* Or he could shrug off the heavy coat of his past and move forward.

It's for this reason that I'm starting to doubt whether my Austin would find anything in that tree hollow, even if he went to look. Like I told my other self, I don't think my version of Austin needs a portal. He's not flawless, of course. I can see now that he has things that agitate him and bring a shadow to his eyes. And the way he keeps his truck so impeccably clean hints at some kind of fixation that might get annoying after a while. Plus, sometimes when he messages me, he doesn't use punctuation at the end of his sentences and fails to capitalize the *I* when he's referring to himself.

But still. The Austin Farrow I know seems happy and satisfied with his life. And so maybe, if he were to step into that tree hollow at the falls, he'd find nothing there. And he'd wonder how the blue-eyed wardrobe assistant who almost captured his heart managed to pretend to be normal for so long.

Florence told me I've gotten feisty, and in a way, she's right. I have a confidence in my step that intensifies the closer I get to the center of town. I feel like I know more now than I did all those weeks ago when I first made this walk, from the apartment to the production office.

But that confidence doesn't come without concern. I'm still worried that I might mess everything up. That I might make a bad decision. That, maybe, I've gotten everything wrong.

But sometimes, you need to feel the fear and do it anyway.

When I arrive at the production office, things are still quiet. We're working late tonight, so most of us have a midmorning call time. At first, I think I might be the only one there. Which is good. It gives me more time to pump myself up.

But then I see that I'm not alone. Deidre's also here already. She's in her alcove, which was also luckily undamaged by the storm, sipping a latte and looking relaxed.

"Morning, Matilda," she says.

"Morning," I say, stopping in front of the alcove. "You're here early."

"So are you."

"I had a few errands to run in town."

I imagine trying to explain to Deidre what those errands were. Visiting myself in another timeline. Musing about magical portals with my old neighbor. A morning of impossibilities and epiphanies.

"The early bird gets the worm," says Deidre distractedly, still looking at her laptop.

My heart rate is beginning to rise. I know this is the right moment. Deidre and I are here together, alone. Henry's never been early in his life, so he won't be here anytime soon. I know what I have to do, and I know I can do it. But my mouth feels dry, and my hands feel clammy.

Deidre raises an eyebrow at me.

"Everything all right?" she asks.

I swallow in an attempt to wet my throat. I think of the other version of me, marveling at the life I live now, and she makes me braver. I make *myself* braver.

"I've been thinking," I say. "About that opportunity you talked about. The supervisor position."

Deidre appraises me over her latte.

"Oh?" she says.

"Yes," I confirm. "I know you still need time to make your decision, but I wanted to let you know that I'd really like the opportunity. I think I'd be good for it. And I think it would be good for me."

Deidre presses her lips together in what could almost be a smile.

"Well, I agree," she says.

"I know you can't decide yet, and there's also Henry to think of, and he'd also be great, but—"

Deidre holds up a hand.

"You can stop there," she says. "You have the job, Matilda."

I stare at her.

"But . . . Henry . . . ?"

"Henry and I already discussed it, and we both agreed. He's not ready yet. He's going to come on as our assistant, and I'd like for him to shadow you. He has a lot to learn from you."

"So, I'd be in charge of him?"

Here, Deidre's smile is unmistakable.

"Yes, you'd be in charge of him. As much as anyone can be in charge of Henry."

I smile back.

"Thank you, Deidre," I say.

"You're welcome. You've earned it. I was just waiting for you to say so yourself."

I can feel pride blossoming through me. I kind of wish I was standing opposite myself now so that I could give myself a high five.

And maybe it's the adrenaline of this that makes me say what I do next.

"Thank you also for . . . the warning," I say. "About my ex-boyfriend."

Deidre narrows her eyes.

"I don't like that young man," she says. "He was never good enough for you."

The shock of this almost maternal comment just about blows me over.

"No," I say, once I've recovered. "He wasn't."

"He didn't end up bothering you, did he?" she asks. "When he came by?"

"I handled it," I reply.

Deidre takes a sip of her latte.

"Good," she says. "I knew you could."

———

The cameras are finally rolling again this evening. The Main Street set has been restored to its former glory. Everything has been cleaned and mended, the artificial snow is back, and the Christmas garlands once again bedeck the lampposts and shop fronts. If anything, the street looks cleaner than it did originally, which the continuity folks are stressed about, but the show must go on.

We won't be able to film in the park again for a while, due to the storm damage, so the decision has been made to rewrite some of the park scenes with Raquel, Mitchell, and Grant and set them in the town square instead. Yet another script change by the director, but this one we can all forgive. We'll do anything at this point to salvage the production. It's all hands on deck.

The one downside to me accepting Deidre's job offer is that she sticks to me on set like a barnacle. At first I think she's scrutinizing me, wondering if she's made the right decision. But eventually I realize she's mentoring me, as much as Deidre Dotto can mentor someone. Her clipped advice might sound like scolding, but really, she's generously sharing trade secrets with me. She's passing along her wisdom. And for someone who acts like she doesn't like people very much, Deidre is surprisingly perceptive about human nature and character development.

"You can tell that Raquel's aunt knows, before she dies, exactly how Raquel's story is going to play out," Deidre says to me, after Kandace has finished a teary scene in which Raquel speaks about her late aunt. "She was slightly clairvoyant. That's why we gave her that necklace that looked like a third eye."

"I just thought the necklace matched the color of her dress," I say.

"It's never just one thing," Deidre tells me. "Every costume choice has layers to it, Mattie. I have a good book on symbolism I should lend you, by the way. Remind me when we get back to the office."

It's only once Deidre has turned away to talk to one of the producers about something that I realize she's called me Mattie, rather than Matilda, for the first time. And I feel like another extraordinary threshold has been crossed.

I've been trying my hardest to pay attention to Deidre's advice. I've been trying to show her that she's made the right choice. That *I'm* the right choice. But this whole time, I've also been checking my watch, waiting for Austin to turn up.

And then he does.

I see him standing on the edge of the town square, wearing the clothes that Henry has dressed him in. He's facing sideways, and I note the strong silhouette of his jaw and the tight line of his shoulders. He's smiling at something his stand-in is saying, and for a moment, I imagine that it really is two Austins standing there, smiling at each other.

Then Austin turns, as if he feels my gaze on him. When our eyes lock, we both seem to freeze.

Austin recovers first. He raises a hand and gives me a small wave, but the smile on his face has tightened. My heart seems to drop from my throat into the pit of my stomach.

But then he starts to walk over to me.

"Hey," he says, when he's in speaking distance.

"Hi," I reply.

I wonder if Deidre is watching us. But in this moment, I don't feel afraid of that. All I can see is Austin's eyes. And the slight shadow of gray under them that reminds me of another version of him. As if he hasn't been sleeping well. As if something's haunting him.

"I've been meaning to call you," Austin murmurs.

My heart flip-flops, revived.

"You have?" I ask.

"I . . . I know we need to talk. But things at the orchard have been a bit manic. Boots went missing the other day."

My chest clenches. "Is he all right?"

"Yeah, we found him." Austin swallows. "He ended up—"

But we're interrupted then by one of the assistant directors rushing over to grab Austin and usher him over to the director. Austin looks over his shoulder at me as he leaves, like he wants to say more. I think about the strip of photos I have in my wallet. I think of the other version of me saying, *Trust me. Trust us.*

"Meet me at the falls," I say to Austin suddenly. "Tomorrow morning."

He turns back to me. The assistant director frowns, but I don't care.

Austin nods. For a moment I think his eyes change slightly, like a cat looking at the light.

"See you there," he says.

FORTY-NINE

I dare myself to hope as I head for the trail the following morning. I dare myself to hope that Austin agreeing to meet me means that maybe he believes me. That at least maybe he *wants* to believe me. That the photos will be enough.

But now that I'm so close to everything I want, it frightens me. I think of the way, when Deidre told me I had the job, I immediately tried to question it. It couldn't be so easy. Living the life of your forgotten dreams couldn't be so easy as simply asking for it, could it?

But I didn't just ask for it. Like Deidre said, I earned it. And not just by doing one thing, but by a million little decisions I've made along the way.

I deserve this.

I let myself relax into the familiar rhythm of my footsteps along the trail. I listen to the birdsong and look up at the trees. It feels like the sun is breaking over more than just another morning, somehow. Like it's the dawn of a new era.

Soon, the sound of the rushing water drowns out my footsteps and the rest of my thoughts. And then I see him at the lookout.

White T-shirt—the same one he was wearing the day I first met him. Dark-blue shorts. No hat today and no headphones. Just dark-honey hair and amber-green eyes, with only the merest hint of shadow beneath them today.

"Hey," we both say in unison, as I join him on the platform.

I notice he's brought a backpack along with him, and I wonder what's inside it. But before I can ask him for answers, I need to give him some of my own.

"Thank you for meeting me," I say. "You didn't have to. After the other day. But there's something I . . ."

"Mattie, wait," Austin interrupts. "You don't need to thank me. And don't you even think about apologizing. I should be thanking you and apologizing to you. I messed up the other day."

I blink at him.

"I shouldn't have made those accusations," he continues. "I shouldn't have jumped to those conclusions. I was letting my own hang-ups get in the way of what you were trying to tell me."

I rest my body against the railing to keep myself steady.

"I get it," I say. "What I was saying seemed impossible. I shouldn't have just launched into it like that. I should have waited until I had some kind of proof. And now I think I do."

I reach a shaky hand into my pocket and start to pull out the photos.

But Austin steps forward and puts a hand on my arm.

"You don't need to show me any more proof," he says.

I pause and look up at him.

"You mean . . . you mean you believe me?"

Austin smiles gently, and the small amount of hope I've carried along with me starts to unfurl, like spring buds on a tree branch.

"Did you come back here?" I ask. "To the tree?"

"I should have come sooner," Austin says in a low voice. "I know it's what you told me to do. But I kind of . . . froze up after our conversation. I was so confused by what you told me and angry at myself for clamming up about it. I was floating around the orchard like a loser, trying to figure out my next move. And then Boots went missing."

"You mentioned that yesterday. But he's okay now?"

"He is now, but it was pretty stressful. Maddie was inconsolable; she couldn't sleep. We looked everywhere—up every tree, of course—and especially around your cottage, but we couldn't find him. Then the other morning, I just had this weird feeling. I can't really explain what it was. But I decided to take a walk up the hill. To the spot I took you the other day."

The spot where I kissed you, I wanted to say. The spot that looked and felt like heaven for a moment.

"And there he was," Austin continues. "That old cat was sitting up there, in the exact spot where you and I sat that day. Just staring at me with his big eyes. And the thing is, I *don't* believe in impossible stuff. I've always been more into cowboys than wizards. But I just knew, somehow, that Boots was trying to tell me that you were right."

The hope continues to unfurl, to flower now, to grow toward the light.

"Cats," I say softly. "They always know."

"They always do," Austin agrees. "So, yesterday, before I went to work, I came here, like you said. Looking for the hollow in the tree."

"And?" I urge.

Austin glances over at the tree behind us, growing out of the old stump. "I found a hollow," he says. "But it wasn't big enough for a person to fit in, like you told me it would be. Believe me, I tried. After looking at it for way too long, and almost getting my arm stuck inside, I came here to the lookout and tried to work through it all in my head. I knew I wanted to believe you. I knew *Boots* wanted me to believe you, even though he's a goddamn cat and I didn't think he wanted anything other than food and Maddie's constant attention. But I just needed, like, an undeniable sign. And that's when I looked back over at the tree. And I saw someone there."

I follow Austin's gaze back to the tree. And I know exactly what he's talking about.

"You saw yourself," I murmur.

"I saw myself." Austin runs a hand through his hair and gives a shaky laugh. "I fucking saw *myself.*"

"You saw a version of you visiting from a different timeline," I say. "But which one?"

"The one where his girlfriend told him he should pay the portal one last visit. So that he could help me believe you, the way you helped her believe him."

We both screw our faces up in unison, fathoming the mechanics of it all, and then start laughing at the same time. My brain hurts, but I understand. I understand what they've done. Bookstore Mattie said she wasn't sure she'd have been able to believe Austin's story if she hadn't had proof. I was the proof. So, she decided to give me more than just a strip of photos. She decided to send *her* Austin back through the portal to prove to *my* Austin what I proved to her.

That it's real. That it's all real.

I take a moment to process this, watching the water churn beneath us. I feel a fierce flare of affection for Bookstore Mattie and her Austin, stepping onto the carousel one final time to play Cupid.

"How did you feel?" I ask eventually, turning back to face Austin. "Seeing yourself? Talking to yourself?"

"I wanted to run away at first," Austin admits. "Then I felt like throwing up. Then I tried to convince myself that I was drunk or on drugs or having some kind of episode. The same things I accused you of. It took me a while to accept it. But eventually I couldn't deny that he was right. And that you were right. About all of it."

He moves closer to me, sliding his arm across the railing.

"I still don't know how it can be possible," he says. "But the important part is, I owe you an apology. I'm so sorry for not believing you right away."

"Honestly, I don't think I would have believed me either. I mean, I *know* I wouldn't have. Because I've seen that timeline."

"How have you been keeping this to yourself for all these weeks?" Austin asks. "How have you turned up to work and acted like a normal person? How have you managed to talk to *me* like a normal person?"

"I didn't feel like I was pulling it off," I admit. "Sometimes when I'd see you, I'd freeze up."

"See, that's why I thought I was coming on too strong."

"It was never that."

"I really hoped it wasn't."

He moves even closer to me, so that his arm rests on top of mine on the railing. He draws a pattern absentmindedly on my skin with his finger, like the number eight, or an infinity symbol.

"I swear I didn't know about the portals until now," Austin says. "But even still. The day I met you, I felt like it wasn't the first time we'd met. You said we hadn't worked together before, but I went back to my hotel room that night and pored over past call sheets anyway, trying to figure it out. Then I looked you up on social media to see if we had mutual friends. I was sure I knew you from somewhere."

"It's a small world," I say.

"Maybe. Or maybe I was remembering times we'd met in other worlds entirely."

I nod. "I've had that feeling too."

"You know . . ." He steps forward, so that his body is flush with mine. "I've been sleeping in the cottage since you left."

"Have you?"

He nods. "It reminds me of you. Of being close to you."

"How close?"

He snakes his arm around me and pulls me into him.

"As close as humanly possible," he murmurs.

He lifts my chin and brings my lips to his. I wrap my arms around his neck as he links his around my waist. I'm unsure of how long we're locked together, until his hands find a sliver of bare skin between my T-shirt and shorts, sending an anticipatory shudder through me.

I break away before we can get closer than is publicly decent.

"Okay," I say, catching my breath. "Let's save some for later."

"But we've wasted so much time already," Austin says, tugging on the edge of my shirt.

"We'll make it up," I say. "Besides, I have one more question."

"Mmm?" he asks.

"I really want to know what's in that backpack."

"Ah, yeah. About that."

I watch as Austin reluctantly pulls away from me to kneel in front of the backpack. As he starts to pull things out, I realize that what's in the bag seems to be a collection of all my favorite things.

There are canned iced coffees, expensive olives and cheeses, and cinnamon pretzels. As the bespoke gourmet picnic grows, I become even more puzzled and suspicious.

"But I don't think I've even told you I like half these things," I say, as I kneel next to Austin, staring in amazement. "How did you know?"

"He told me," Austin replies.

"Ah," I say.

"Good thing your tastes aren't that different in the other timeline," Austin continues. "And given that my man has been wining and dining that other version of you for a bit longer than I have, he helped me plan the perfect date."

I can't help but glance back over at the tree, thinking maybe Dark Austin might have come back for one last look. But there's no one there, of course. He's done what he needed to do.

"Okay, so maybe it's kind of cheating," Austin continues. "However, given the amount you knew about us before *I* did, I think I get this pass."

"You *absolutely* get this pass."

I run my hand over his shoulder, down the length of his arm, relishing the way my heart is beating in that elevated yet comfortable rhythm—like dancing on floorboards.

"This last thing, however, I picked myself."

Austin reaches deep into the backpack and pulls out a small tub of something.

"The best ice cream in the world," I say.

Austin smiles and places the apple pie ice cream with the rest of the collection. His favorite thing next to my favorite things.

"I think this is the sweetest thing anyone's ever done for me," I say.

"Like Val said, I'm as sweet as my apples." Austin rolls his eyes. "Almost certain she was being condescending when she said that, but still, I try. And I felt like this was the least I could do to make it up to you. For not believing you and implying you should go see a therapist."

"For the record, I have seen a therapist before. Everyone can benefit from a bit of a therapy."

"I know." Austin reaches for a cinnamon pretzel. "I go, sometimes."

"Really?"

"Yeah. It's more preventative than anything. Like I told you, there are some things that run in my family. I'd like to stay on top of it."

"That's admirable."

"Ah well, it's what we good guys do."

"You know, you're always saying you're a good guy like it's a bad thing."

"It's not that it's *bad*. It's just not that interesting. In terms of characters, anyway."

"You'll get your chance at playing the morally gray cowboy one day. I know it."

"I hope so. But for now . . . I'm pretty damn happy just to be here."

"Me too."

I rest my back against the lookout railing, and Austin hands me a cinnamon pretzel topped with apple pie ice cream before placing his arm around me. As I nestle into him, I let myself be fully present in this single moment, in this single universe, which feels like the only one I need.

FIFTY

On Austin's last day of filming, he invites everyone to join him for drinks at Three Pines Brewing Co. And pretty much everyone comes. I don't know if it's more of a testament to how much everyone likes Austin or how much we all need a drink after the chaos of the storm, but almost all the cast and crew are here at the bar. It feels like a wrap party, even though we still have over a week until we're completely done.

There was gossip about Austin and me being a thing before we even were a thing, but funnily enough, that gossip has died down over the last week. Austin and I haven't needed to find sly excuses to talk to each other on set or for me to fix his collar when there's nothing there to fix. We've kept things strictly—impressively—professional whenever we've been on the clock this week.

And that's because we've had late nights together instead. Val probably shouldn't have gone to all that trouble to find that motel room for me, because for the most part, I've spent my nights in Austin's hotel room. We're normally too tired to watch a full movie, so we've watched comedy sketches and sitcoms instead, as we pick at leftovers from craft services. Austin likes to lament over not being a better comedic actor, and I like to gush over the '90s fashion in the old sitcoms.

We've talked, a lot. Some of it's been normal, getting-to-know-you-more conversation. But a large chunk of it has been wild-theories-about-the-multiverse conversation. We've listened to the podcast Margot sent me and compared our story to others. One night, we set up an anonymous email account to contact one of the people who was interviewed for the podcast. We didn't get an immediate response, and I don't know how I'll feel if I do hear back. Do I want to keep this story going? Do I want to dig deeper and find out more? Or do I want to just accept it for what it is and what it's given me and leave it at that?

After we've done way more than just talk, I normally take longer to fall asleep than Austin does. I lie with my cheek pressed against his bare chest, watching the moonlight filter through the heavy curtains, listening to Austin's steady breathing. And it is always steady. I always feel safe.

In those moments, I feel reassured that I don't have to keep searching for more.

Tonight, at Three Pines Brewing Co., I'm sticking to the sidelines and letting Austin be the center of attention. He has plenty of people to talk to, plus, Deidre is here, and I'm still trying to maintain a good professional impression. I'm sitting with Val and Henry out in the twinkling garden, in the same spot we sat weeks ago, sipping our pilsners and talking.

I've been noticing things lately. All the little things about the world around me I didn't notice or appreciate before. The patterns in the pines and the blades of grass on the lawn. The maternal way Val always wants to make sure I'm comfortable, whether it's in a motel room or at a music festival or sitting on an Adirondack chair. The way Henry makes me laugh. The fact that this crew around me might drive me crazy sometimes, and the hours are brutal, but I'm starting to think we could be making something special with *Magic Season*. It's still a straight-to-streamer Christmas rom-com, but it might end up being the best straight-to-streamer Christmas rom-com this year, and I know for sure it's going to make people smile.

I'd like to think that, in every timeline, I've managed to find this peace. To not be searching for more, but to make the most of what I've been given.

I'm thinking of this with such a dreamy smile on my face that Henry asks me if I'm okay.

"Oh yeah, I'm fine," I say. "Just thinking."

"Well, Val is telling us she has news," says Henry.

"What news?" I ask.

Val takes a calm sip of beer. "Remember when we were talking about my dilemma—about whether to go traveling with my boyfriend or stay here at home, where I've always been?"

I nod encouragingly.

"Well, we did it. We booked our tickets."

I raise my eyebrows. "You're finally leaving Casey River?"

"Just for three months," she says. "I kept agonizing over whether to do it or not. And eventually I decided to just flip a coin."

"And it landed on the traveling side?" Henry asks.

Val shakes her head. "No, actually. It landed on the staying-home side. But as soon as it did, I felt disappointed. So I knew what I really wanted."

I smile. "That's the way it works sometimes."

"Maybe he is your soulmate after all," Henry says.

"I thought you didn't believe in singular soulmates," Val argues.

"Who knows? Maybe working on this corny-as-hell movie has turned me into a romantic."

We laugh, and I can't help but look up at Austin at this moment. He's over by the covered patio, talking to one of the producers. And it's like he senses me looking, because he catches my eye and gives me a brief, stealthy raise of his eyebrows, like there's a secret shared between us. Which, of course, there is. In more ways than one.

"What about you, Mattie?" says Henry loudly. "What about your big news?"

I try not to look too alarmed.

"What big news?"

I should have known. Nothing gets past Henry. He can read an entire story in a glance or a slight touch.

He rolls his eyes at me and turns to Val.

"Mattie and I are already signed up for our next job," he explains. "Only, Mattie's going to be my boss."

I feel my shoulders relax. Of course. Henry's talking about the supervisor role.

"I wouldn't say I'm your *boss*, exactly. Deidre's the real boss."

"Mattie, hon, this is your first mistake," says Val. "If Henry's calling you his boss, then you need to own that."

"Fine," I say. "I'm going to be Henry's boss."

"I'd be furious if I weren't so proud," says Henry.

"Well, congratulations to all of us," says Val. She raises her glass, and we clink our pints together. "What's the project, by the way?"

"I haven't seen the script yet," I answer. "But it sounds like it's another romance."

Val scoffs. "Of course it is."

We stay at Three Pines until late. I'm so overtired from long days and late nights with Austin that I've almost pushed through the barrier into invincibility. When we finally leave, Austin and I walk back to the hotel together, and he doesn't even wait until we're completely in the clear before he slings his arm around my waist.

"Hey!" I say, laughing and grabbing his hand. "People might see."

"So?"

"So, just because you're wrapped doesn't mean I am. I have a reputation to uphold."

"You know, cast and crew relationships are not strictly *not* allowed. Just frowned upon, maybe."

"I know. And I hate being frowned upon."

"I know you do. It's cute as hell."

When we're back in the hotel room, my reluctance goes out the window. I let Austin put his hands on my waist, my stomach, my upper thighs. Anywhere he wants.

After, he doesn't fall asleep right away, and neither do I. We lie there together, his chin resting on the top of my head, neither of us saying anything for a while.

We've talked about this night. We know it's our last night together here in Casey River, and there is an undeniable weight in the room—the weight of the future and the what-ifs that we can't escape from, even if right now is temporarily more than enough. Austin's next job is in the city and so is mine, but I know that won't be the case forever. I know that, as both of us step up in our careers and keep chasing our dreams, we'll be tugged to different places at different times. Austin might end up riding a horse and slinging a gun in a desert somewhere, while I'm dressing a princess in the ballroom of a castle in another country.

But I'm not too worried. After all, we've managed to find each other in multiple worlds already. And I've read enough scripts to know how this kind of story normally ends.

Author's Note

This story is set against the backdrop of the film industry. While I work closely with the industry in my day job, I confess I've never been a wardrobe assistant myself like Mattie. To bring her story to life, I used insights gleaned from many set visits and coffee chats with the fantastic local film crew where I live in Queenstown, New Zealand. I also conducted desk-based research, lurked on industry forums, and absorbed behind-the-scenes content like the brilliant Ruth Carter installment of Netflix's *Abstract: The Art of Design* and Shondaland's BTS series (highly recommend both).

But this is fiction, not a documentary, so some creative liberties have been taken for the sake of the story. For example, I know the "wardrobe" department can often be called the "costume" department instead, but the former felt more satisfying as a parallel with the portal in the wardrobe.

What I hope is accurate is the general depiction of the hard work that happens behind the scenes to bring stories to our screens. I'm sure Mattie's not the only one who second guesses her life choices after a twelve-hour day on set, but without film crews, we wouldn't have movies. And what would Christmas be without a festive rom-com? So to all the showbiz workers out there, thank you.

Acknowledgments

I always thought that writing a book was a solitary experience compared to the collaborative circus that is making movies. While the drafting stage might be a bit lonesome, I've learned that getting the final product out into the world very much needs a crew, and I'm so grateful for mine.

My agent, Adria: I understand why your clients call you their fairy godmother. If it weren't for you believing in me from the start, and your fervent love for stories full of heart and magic, I might still only be daydreaming about a timeline where this book is getting published. Thank you! And thanks also to the wider KT Literary team for all the work you do to make your clients' dreams come true.

Thank you to the team at Little A / Amazon Publishing: Laura, who understood all the threads of this story from that first phone call; Faith, who asked all the right questions during the developmental edit; Ali, who tied it all together in the end; and Karah, Katie, Jenna, Darci and everyone in the wider team who helped tighten and brighten the book and bring it to the world.

My family: You have always been my biggest supporters, and I know if I confessed that I found a magical portal in my wardrobe, you'd all at least pretend to believe me. Tessa: Thank you for loving this story before anyone else and always being my first reader. Jorden: Thank you for always being a safe space and sounding board, and for having a bespoke cocktail for every situation. Mum: Thank you for cultivating a childhood of wonder and creativity, for buying me thesauruses and typewriters, and for helping me enter all those kids writing competitions (Roberta's Pumpkins!). Dad, whom I miss every day: Your love and support are summed up by that time you took me to the awards ceremony for one of those competitions, where I won a big box of books that we had to get mailed home because we rode there on your motorbike. Bill: Thank you for continuing to let me use the garage and spare bedroom as my library. And a special mention goes to my aunties who buy me notebooks for every birthday—I hope I put them to good use!

My friends and colleagues: Thank you for showing an interest in this weird hobby I have outside of my work and social life. While I kind of dreaded the question, I also appreciate all the times you asked, "How's the writing going?" Here's the answer!

And finally, Joel: Thank you for brainstorming terrible titles with me (sorry we didn't go with *Love in the Wardrobe* in the end) and for never complaining when my 5:00 a.m. alarms wake you up too. I know I would have met you in every timeline, but I'm so happy to be living in this one with you.

About the Author

Kahli Scott was born in the freezing north of Canada and raised on the subtropical east coast of Australia, where she completed her BFA in creative writing at Queensland University of Technology. She now lives in Queenstown on New Zealand's South Island (Te Waipounamu), working as the manager of the regional film office and writing as the sun rises over the mountains. *Our Common Thread* is Kahli's first novel.